Praise for *Follow Me Down*

'a beautifully crafted, spine-tingling story'
Daily Telegraph

'a corker of a novel, original and rambunctious.'
Observer

' . . . here's a new, wild, free voice'
Books for Keeps

'A debut novel which deserves our attention . . . an extraordinary story'
The Bookseller

'This book is gripping, gentle, funny and downright scary at times.'
The Guardian

'One of the best children's books this year.'
Sainsbury's Magazine

'[a] roller-coaster read that's full of drama.'
Mizz

'A gripping debut'
Yorkshire Post

'this immensely accomplished novel is spiked with humour.'
Sunday Telegraph

'[a] richly textured first novel.'
Times Educational Supplement

'although written for younger readers, adults, too, will find it hard to put down.'
Choice Magazine

'[a] breathtaking story'
Sunday Morning Post

'The terms ''gripping'' and ''atmospheric'' could have been coined to describe this breathtakingly accomplished first novel.'
The Glasgow Herald

'A debut that sparkles with drama, emotion and humour.'
The Bookseller

'[a] startlingly original and provocative book'
Yorkshire Post

'A novel to reflect on in its handling of bravery and honesty in testing situations.'
The Bookseller

Follow Me Down

Follow Me Down

Julie Hearn

OXFORD
UNIVERSITY PRESS

OXFORD
UNIVERSITY PRESS

Great Clarendon Street, Oxford OX2 6DP

Oxford University Press is a department of the University of Oxford.
It furthers the University's objective of excellence in research, scholarship,
and education by publishing worldwide in

Oxford New York

Auckland Bangkok Buenos Aires
Cape Town Chennai Dar es Salaam Delhi Hong Kong Istanbul
Karachi Kolkata Kuala Lumpur Madrid Melbourne Mexico City Mumbai
Nairobi São Paulo Shanghai Taipei Tokyo Toronto

Oxford is a registered trade mark of Oxford University Press
in the UK and in certain other countries

British Library Cataloguing in Publication Data available

ISBN 0 19 275341 X

1 3 5 7 9 10 8 6 4 2

Typeset by AFS Image Setters Ltd, Glasgow

Printed in Great Britain by
Cox & Wyman Ltd, Reading, Berkshire

For my daughter, Tilly

A Changeling Child

NOTICE: To be seen next door to the Black
Raven in West Smithfield, during the time of
Bartholomew Fair: a Living Skeleton taken
by a Venetian Galley from a Turkish vessel in
the Archipelago. This is a Fairy Child,
supposed to be born of Hungarian Parents,
but chang'd in the Nursing. Aged Nine Years
or more; not exceeding a Foot and a-half
high. The Legs Thighs and Arms so very small
that they scarce exceed the bigness of a
Man's Thumb, and the face no bigger than
the Palm of one's hand; and seems so grave
and solid as if it were Threescore Years old.
You may see the whole Anatomy of its Body
by setting it against the Sun. It never speaks.
It has no teeth but is the most voracious and
hungry creature in the World, devouring
more Victuals than the stoutest Man in
England. Gives great satisfaction to all that
ever did, or shall, behold it.

1

It was the stench seeping in through the car windows that bothered Tom the most. Rank and beefy, it reminded him of the way dogs smell after a walk in the rain. Smelly dogs made him think of Goldie, left behind in Dorset, and for a moment the page of the London *A to Z* he was supposed to be reading blurred and swam in front of his eyes.

Quickly, he knuckled the wet from his face. Had his mother noticed? If she had, he would say it was sweat. And that he felt sick. It was late morning, the middle of August, and hot enough for even a skinny twelve year old to be melting like a lolly. Add the stink of Smithfield meat market, leaching through traffic fumes, and anyone with nostrils and a stomach in working order was bound to feel bad.

His mother, in profile, looked surprisingly fit considering she was driving in circles, unable to remember where her own mother lived, and had more reason than most people to feel like throwing up, with or without a pong in the air.

'You all right, Mum?' His voice was gruff. A 'yes' or 'no' answer would do him.

'Tired. Just tired. I'll be glad to stop.'

They came to a roundabout. It was somewhere Tom recognized. 'We've done this one,' he said. 'Twice.' His mother circled it three times more, looking for signs.

Go round again, thought Tom, and I really will chuck. The smell was getting worse. He tried breathing through his mouth. Tasted offal on his tongue. Liver without the

3

onions. His mother, he knew, had a brilliant sense of smell; could recognize anything from gas to a bunch of flowers through several closed doors. How come she wasn't complaining?

'Can't stand much more of this stink,' he muttered.

'What stink?' She seemed genuinely surprised. 'I can't smell anything. Oh! Hang in there, Tom-bola. This is it, I think.'

She took a sudden left, sending a training shoe, a tangle of wire coat-hangers, and the book *Living With Cancer: A Family Guide* slithering from a badly-packed wodge of their stuff on the back seat.

'MU-um!'

The book had whacked against the back of Tom's head. He turned and shoved it, hard, out of sight beneath a pile of brightly-coloured towels. The coat-hangers jangled on his lap.

'What's the point of bringing these?' he grumbled. 'Gran'll have loads.'

His mother wasn't listening. She had pulled over, stopped the car, and flung off her seatbelt.

'Give me that *A to Z*,' she said. 'This isn't right.'

They were in a wide cobbled street. One way. No exit. There were no houses, and no other cars; just the flank of the meat market, rearing to their left, and a large white van parked up ahead, its engine thrumming. Two men were trundling what looked like a clothes rack across the bumpy road. Pig carcasses hung upside down from its hooks, their trotters clicking like castanets, their snouts grazing on air. Tom watched the whole contraption go jouncing and clattering along. The smell was so thick here that he feared for his lungs.

One of the meat men, catching sight of the boy's face, pale as a cheese through the car windscreen, winked at him.

4

Tom flinched. 'Hurry up, Mum,' he snapped. 'This is gross.'

His mother looked up. There were dark smudges under her eyes and the bright yellow hat she had put on that morning, to cover the stubble of her hair, no longer looked fresh as a daisy.

'All right, love? Need any 'elp?' The man who had winked at Tom came swaggering across to the car, wiping his hands on his belly. There were smears of red all down his aproned front, as if he had just performed open-heart surgery or painted a field of poppies. The rack of pigs was in the back of the white van now. Refrigerated.

Tom wanted a drink very badly. Something ice cold, sharp, and clear like a Seven Up or mineral water with lime. His gran, when they finally found her, would probably offer him Ribena from the same bottle she had got in for his last visit.

It was hard for him to picture his gran, or her house. How long had it been? Ten years, at least. Almost his whole lifetime. Let's see. Railings. He remembered those. Wrought-iron railings, tall and sharp as spears. He had wanted one to play knights of old with; hadn't understood that you couldn't just pull one up and put it back after slaying a few imaginary dragons. He remembered lots of steps and stairs, a hug that had too many bones in it, and a lunch with too much cheese. He remembered a room, dark as a goblin's yawn; a room where someone . . .

'That's great. Brilliant. Can't think how I missed it.' Tom's mother tossed the *A to Z* on to the dashboard, eased her seatbelt across her chest, and turned the key in the ignition. 'Thank you,' she said through the window to the meat man. Her voice had an edge to it. She was off men. All men. Even helpful ones.

'No problem. You take care, darlin'. Nice old pub next door to yer mum's place. Not too rowdy. Get yerself in there for a bottle of stout and a nice beef sarnie. That'll put the colour back in yer cheeks.' He straightened up, slapped the side of the car, and sauntered back to his van.

'Knucklehead,' muttered Tom. 'Cack for brains. Bilge-artist.'

'At least we know where we're going,' said his mother. 'At least we'll be there in a minute.'

The car kangaroo-hopped as it joined the main road. The animal smell appeared to be fading. Good job, thought Tom. *Good job.*

'A nice beef sarnie indeed,' his mother sighed. 'If only it was that simple, eh?'

Tom had no answer to that. No answer at all. He let his head fall back against the passenger seat; closing his eyes against the traffic, the heat, and the brave yellow hat. Let his mother look out for the right landmarks—the railings, the tall house, the pub sign with the bird on it. This was her journey. Her thing. He hadn't wanted to come.

He felt the car slow then stop, heard the click of his mother's seatbelt coming off, sensed exhaustion and discomfort in the slow exhalation of her breath. 'We're here,' she said. 'Pile out, Tom Thumb.'

It was a relief to get out of the car, to stretch his legs after the long journey. The railings in front of the house looked shabbier than he remembered. Not at all like the spears of a valiant knight. The pub next door looked pretty dingy too. The Black Raven.

'Hello, darlings! Did you have to fight your way through traffic? It's so appalling here now, with those beastly great lorries. I was just beginning to worry . . . '

Tom's grandmother stood in her doorway, several steps up from the street. Tall and slim, her white hair cut in a geometric bob, she wore a pale trouser suit and enough silver chains to anchor a ship. Her smile was a sickle of lipstick; her eyes a mystery behind a pair of shades. There was a glass in her left hand with something fizzy and a slice of lemon in it.

His mother took hold of his arm. He wanted to comfort her and shake her off about equally. Why hadn't his grandmother come down the steps to greet them properly? They were family, weren't they? The only family she had left? And one of them was lucky to be standing here at all! OK, so the old bat had gone ballistic when his mum and dad split up. But that was ancient history now. It was stupid to carry on minding about your precious daughter being a single parent—particularly when your precious daughter had a lot more to worry about, nowadays, than being minus a husband.

As for his mother, she wasn't usually lost for words, however sick, or tired, she was feeling. Why didn't she say something to make this easier?

His mother's voice, when it finally came, was croaky but calm. 'Hello, Mummy,' she said. 'Fab hairdo. Smarter than mine.'

Nice one, thought Tom, and laughed. His grandmother's smile slipped, but only for a second. 'Get yourself in out of the sun, Catherine,' she said. 'Tom will bring the luggage up. Such a tall chap now. I'll make a pot of coffee. You must be gasping.'

Tom tightened his grip on his mother's elbow. She shook him away. 'I'm fine,' she said. 'You go and get our stuff in.'

Tom will bring the luggage. Such a tall chap now . . . Part of Tom wanted to run ahead; to catch his grandmother before she reached the kitchen. She needed telling that his mother didn't drink coffee any more. That, actually, quite a lot of people who had cancer wouldn't touch caffeine with a ten foot bargepole, and wasn't she a stupid old bag for not *thinking* about that?

7

He stood beside the car, wishing he could drive. You wouldn't see him for dust. He would be back in Dorset so fast the tyres would smoke. His mates would be hanging out by the war memorial this afternoon, with nothing to worry about except keeping an eye on their mountain bikes and being home in time for tea. He hoped Matthew's family would remember that Goldie loved chips and was allowed one or two, as a treat.

'Are you coming in, Tom darling? I've poured you some Ribena.'

His grandmother was beckoning from a first-floor window. Sunlight flashed on her rings. She was still wearing her shades. Wearily, Tom grabbed a big armful of clothes from the back seat of the car, nudged the door shut with his hip, and went towards the house.

The railings closed ranks on him immediately, the second he set foot on the first step. Fleetingly, irrationally, he saw them as the spears he had once wished them to be. Only they were leaning rather than pointing. Leaning his way and quivering, like vipers about to strike. And the smell. The smell was back. As putrid as before. Worse.

Tom sank to his knees, trying not to gag. Socks, jeans, and T-shirts fell from his grasp, as lightly and naturally as leaves. It's the heat, he told himself. That, and pelting up the steps too quickly after sitting for hours in a car. Even as he thought it, he knew it wasn't true. He could run for miles, or sit around all day, without feeling anything less than normal.

The railings leaned closer . . . closer still . . . and then stopped. Tom waited a second or two, his heart pounding. No. It was all right. They hadn't touched him. He was safe. He just needed to get his act together. Fast.

And what an act, sir, what an act! Is it not the most wonderful phenomenon of nature ever seen? And you may see the whole anatomy of its body, sir, by setting it against the sun . . .

8

The voice—a man's voice—was coming from the basement. His grandmother must have left a radio playing. That was it. And yet . . .

It never speaks, sir, never a word . . .

Tom peered, tentatively, through the skewed railings towards the basement window. A ray of sunshine, reflected in glass, made him wince.

The man's voice had faded away. But someone else was calling now. A child. A girl. Her cry was as high and thin as birdsong and it touched Tom like a wand.

Help us, it said.

Tom shook his head. 'No,' he replied, the word forming and spilling somewhere deep in his mind. 'Leave me alone. I don't understand.'

He groped for something solid; touched the fallen clothes and began scooping them up in his arms. The railings were straightening, like stalks after rain. Tom bent his face towards the familiar scent of washing powder, and the reassurance of denim and Lycra against his skin.

'Tom! Thomas! Really, darling, there's no need to carry everything in at once. For Heaven's sake, it's like a Turkish bazaar out there. Pick everything up, there's a good chap, and come along in. Your Ribena's getting warm.'

A window slammed.

Tom felt, with relief, the rigidity of the railings as he hauled himself to his feet. The rotting-entrail smell had gone. Completely. And there was nothing unfamiliar now about the sounds in his ears. Just the rasping of pigeons somewhere on the roof, and the distant purr of traffic.

The sooner he did something normal, he told himself, like gulp a glass of tepid squash, the better. He snatched up the rest of the scattered clothes and jumped the remaining steps in a single bound. His grandmother's house smelt of lavender and garlic and he entered it meek

9

as a lamb, determined to make the best of this visit, and to be gentler towards his mother.

Outside, the sun's rays continued to prod the basement window while, a stone's throw away, above the entrance to the Black Raven, the sign with the dark brooding bird painted on it began to swing violently to and fro, to and fro, without so much as a breath of wind to stir it.

2

Breakfast, that first morning in London, was not the cheeriest of meals. Tom, still half-asleep, had nothing to say. He stretched his bare feet along the cold, tiled floor, missing the feel of Goldie's pelt beneath his toes. He was trying not to think about the dizziness, or the voices in the basement.

'It would be so nice,' said his mother, 'if, in future, we could all start the day together. You know, up at a reasonable hour, sitting round the table and *talking*.'

Tom grunted. 'What table?' he said, scraping the last traces of Marmite from a jar. 'Gran's kitchen hasn't got a table. Only this thingo.'

'Breakfast bar.'

'This breakfast-bar-thingo. And you can't sit round it, only along.' He jabbed, peevishly, at his toast. 'And only two at a time.'

It felt good, having a whinge. Comforting. He had slept late, cocooned in a sleeping bag and pestered by dreams. His attic bedroom was under the eaves, full of stale air and boxes of old books.

'Your grandfather's,' his gran had said, kicking some of the smaller boxes out of the way so that Tom could reach the bed. 'Fusty old things. No good to me, darling, although they might be worth a bob or two.' She had swept unsteadily from the room without kissing him goodnight, for which he was truly grateful.

'Is Gran up?'

Tom's mother was chopping vegetables—spinach,

cucumber, and cabbage—on a marble slab beside the sink. Tom recognized the blender from their own kitchen, plugged in next to the microwave.

'Up and out.' She slapped a lid down on her jugful of leaves and chunks. 'She helps out at Oxfam three days a week, sorting through the bric-a-brac people bring in. Putting prices on, that kind of thing.'

Tom frowned. 'I can't imagine Gran doing that.'

'Hang on a sec.' Tom watched as the blender whizzed the contents of the jug to a swampy green pulp. His mother poured some into a tall glass. 'Cheers,' she said. She took a sip and pulled a face. 'Yeuch! That's vile.'

She joined Tom at the breakfast bar, wincing as she eased herself up onto a high-legged stool. 'Your gran,' she said, 'works at a posh Oxfam in the West End. No tat there.'

Tom grunted. He didn't care where his gran worked. He couldn't have cared less if she sold frilly knickers to the queen.

'It's boring here,' he grumbled. 'How long do we have to stay?'

His mother wasn't listening. She was striking her supermodel pose—one hand on her hip, the other against the raw patches of bristle on her scalp. Her hair was beginning to grow back, but not prettily or well. Right now her head looked like a small, scruffy lawn that someone had made a bad job of scattering grass seed on.

'I've told your gran to watch out for headscarves with designer labels,' she said. 'Hair by radiotherapy, headgear by Calvin Klein. Designer stubble, Tomahawk, get it?'

'Cut the crap, Mum. It's not funny.'

Tom slid from his stool, shoved his plate in the sink, and made a big thing of putting the butter and milk away. The fridge, empty of just about everything yesterday, except tonic water and lemons, was chock-full of organic

12

vegetables and cans of his favourite soft drinks. His mother must have been to a supermarket already. He felt annoyed and somehow trapped. Did she have to be a martyr? Was she trying to make him feel guilty for having a lie-in, instead of helping her to push a trolley and choose lettuce?

He shot her a look. She was still sitting at the breakfast bar, hunched over the green drink like a child told not to get down until it has swallowed every last drop. Her eyes were closed; her face as lonely as the moon.

Tom sighed. Pity for her always got the better of him. He hoped she hadn't had to trail all round the East End to find organic food. He hoped the checkout girl at Sainsbury's, or wherever, had put the change straight into her hand—not off to one side as if fearful of catching something. He hoped the green drink was doing whatever it was bloody well meant to do and that his mother would live to be a hundred.

'Thanks, Mum.'

'What for?'

'For the Seven Up and stuff.'

'My pleasure.'

She smiled at him, but there was sadness in her, still, and some other emotion that Tom couldn't quite place.

'What. *What?*'

'Nothing. At least . . . nothing much. I was thinking about your grandfather. You have his eyes—as blue as sparrows' eggs—although not his temperament, thank God.'

Tom thought of the books upstairs, their spines as brittle as sticks. *No good to me, darling.*

'You didn't get on with Grandpa, did you?'

'No. Not really.'

Tom frowned. His mother's childhood had been cack—sort of loveless, and dull. If it wasn't for the cancer

13

they wouldn't be here now, making up with his gran. Tom wondered whether his mother had told his dad about her illness, and whether she might try making up with him. Probably not. He was somewhere in Australia now, anyway, with a second wife, another kid, and a job in computer graphics. He wrote to Tom sometimes, on the back of postcards showing koala bears up gum trees, or in aerogrammes with a restricted amount of writing space made even titchier by borders of Aboriginal art.

One day, if he felt like it, Tom would visit Australia, meet his half-brother, surf a few big waves. Maybe. He wasn't really that fussed. He and his mum were OK alone. They had friends. What did the fob on his mother's keyring say? (The one she had tactfully swapped for a plastic four-leafed clover before coming here to visit Gran): *Friends are the relatives we choose for ourselves.* He was curious now, though, about the man with his eyes.

'What did he die of, Grandpa?' he asked. 'He can't've been all that old.'

His mother made a big deal of scraping the dregs of her drink with a teaspoon. The sound of metal on glass put Tom's teeth on edge.

'Oh . . . some blood thing,' she said. 'And no, he wasn't old . . .'

She lowered herself from the stool, glanced at the clock, and gave an exaggerated tut of surprise. 'I've got my appointment in just over an hour. Chuck us my hat, a-Tomic.'

Tom looked around for the hat. It was a bright yellow beanie, with rhinestones stuck on it, and the worst thing his mother had ever worn. Worse than her rainbow-striped trousers that flapped when she walked. Worse, even, than the T-shirt that said *All Stressed Out And No One To Choke*. It was a hat to die for. Of embarrassment. Still, anything that covered his mother's head at the moment was better than nothing. Tom would have liked her to wear it indoors as well as out.

'Over there. Quick. I'm going to be late!'

The hat was lying, like a jewel-encrusted omelette, beside the cooker. Tom plucked it up and passed it across. 'There you go.'

'Thanks, love.'

'Well. Good luck, then.' He shifted awkwardly, willing her away. She went quickly, blowing him a kiss from the doorway. He was getting good, he thought, at avoiding hugs.

Alone, Tom lingered in the kitchen, prodding dots in a bit of spilt green drink. Usually, he enjoyed being by himself. Not today though. Not here. Everything around him, from the humming fridge to the ticking clock, seemed to be waiting for him to make a move. He couldn't help thinking about the day before. The smell. The voices. The way the railings had shifted, like snakes.

Get real, he told himself. *Get a grip.*

His mother had left him a twenty-pound note and directions to the Museum of London. He stashed the money away, in the back pocket of his jeans. It was going to be another boiling afternoon. Maybe he would just amble down to the nearest video store, to rent a film.

His grandmother had an excellent wide-screen telly in her sitting room, up on the first floor. He didn't like the scent in there, rising from a bowl of pot pourri on the coffee table. Nor would he be able to lounge comfortably in case one of his big feet went crashing into something. Still, it would be a good place to chill out for a while, with the telly on.

He went upstairs to fetch his trainers. The attic bedroom was already like an oven. Yesterday's cruddy socks and underpants remained draped where he had thrown them, over one of his grandfather's boxes. In the harsh light of

15

day, this seemed disrespectful. He picked them off. His mother hadn't told him, yet, what to do with dirty laundry, so he shoved it all under the mattress.

On his way back down, he heard someone chuckle. A woman.

'Hello?' he said. 'Gran? Is that you?'

He pushed open the sitting room door. Nobody there. Just some ladies on the television laughing about their hormones. The video recorder winked at him from its cabinet. He found the remote and switched everything off.

The sudden silence had a peculiar ring to it, but the room was nice and cool, with the shutters closed and the wall lights down low. Tom sat on the settee, and looked around.

No photos. That was strange. Most people's grans had photos everywhere—wedding photos, baby photos, school photos, holiday photos . . . Most people's grans had so many framed photos on display there was nowhere to put a cup of tea down. His, it seemed, had only a golden clock, a bowl of dried rose petals, and more bottles of booze than an off-licence.

He let his head sink back against a cushion. The room's flower-scented dimness reminded him of church. He put his feet up. Defiantly.

Come along down, sir. Step this way. Only a shilling, sir, to view the Changeling Child. Only a shilling to behold the strangest work of nature that ever was. Come, sir. Follow me down . . .

He had slept. He must have slept. But he was awake now, bolt upright on the settee, with an echo of the man's voice swirling in his head. *Not again*, he thought. *I can't handle this again.* Carefully, quietly, he went out on to the first floor landing, placed a tentative hand on the banister and listened. Hard.

Silence.

He licked his lips and swallowed. It *had* to have been a radio. A clock radio. That was it. Set to go on and off at the same time every day. Maybe his gran, when she wasn't working for Oxfam, took naps down in the basement after lunch. Maybe he hadn't heard her come in and she was down there now, enjoying a quick burst of Radio Four and a whacking great gin and tonic.

He crept down the remaining few stairs, past the front door, and along a corridor with the kitchen off to his right. He could hear the fridge working hard to keep his cans of Seven Up chilled. His mother would be home soon. In a minute he would whizz up some raspberries and soya milk, and a few drops of her Rescue Remedy in the blender. A pink drink. His mother had pink drinks in the afternoon now, instead of coffee. A treat, she said. Pure nectar after the earlier dose of green.

The short flight of steps leading down to the basement was uncarpeted and deep in shadow. Tom felt against the wall for a light switch; touched a cobwebby nub and flicked it.

Nothing.

Cold. It 'as always been cold down 'ere. Even in late summer when 'tis 'ot enough to roast the clot of crows a-swingin' and a-feastin' on the gibbet outside Newgate Prison; when the hawkers of ribbons an' gingerbread an' plum pudding are fit to melt upon the cobbles, and the amazin' learned pig at Bartholomew Fair refuses to tell a man 'is fortune, for want of a breath of air. Even then, 'tis as cold as a blessed crypt down 'ere . . .

The girl's voice drew Tom on although he fought against it with every fibre of his being.

Stop pulling at me. Who are you? Leave me alone.

His protests crackled in his head. The girl's tone grew more insistent:

I ain't stoppin'. Not till ye crosses the gap. Only, don't do it now. NOT NOW. Later. Come back later and jump the gap.

What gap? What are you on about?

The gap, you little ninny. Ye surely ain't forgot . . .

A memory pinged, somewhere among the static, and Tom paused for a second, one hand against the blistered surface of the basement door. That voice. He remembered it. It had sung to him. A lullaby about cradles and kittens. A long, long time ago.

Go back . . . Go, I said.

Too intrigued, now, to turn away, Tom pushed open the door. Not that he needed to. Not that there were any surprises waiting. For he knew, he just *knew*, that the basement would be as dank and dark as it had been ten years ago; that the packing crates would still be there, wrapped in the grey lace of ancient cobwebs and that, as he walked in, a hairline crack would spread across the floor like a varicose vein, slowly widening and lengthening to form the gap.

He knew that a boy could spend eternity gazing into that gap, watching people's faces collide, merge, and slide away in a never-ending stream. He knew he was going to jump over those images, for the second time in his life, and that, having done so, nothing would ever be the same.

'Hello. Anyone home? Tom, are you there, son? Can you hear me?'

Tom felt the interruption as a counter force, pulling him away from the basement and back up the steps into the light. It happened in seconds; so speedily that he wondered whether he had been outside the kitchen all along, half asleep, still, and dreaming.

There was a man; a dumpy man, at the foot of the stairs. He had hair like a ginger toilet brush, and was no one Tom recognized.

'Ah,' the man said, turning heavily. 'There you are. You'd better come quickly, Tom. It's your mother.'

18

3

The mid-afternoon heat hit Tom, hard. He was trembling as he pelted down the steps and only vaguely aware of a smell of roast meat and bad drains lingering in the air.

'I'm Declan,' said the man puffing along behind him. 'I run the pub.'

The paving slabs felt tacky under the thwack of Tom's trainers. There was sweat in his hair and his stomach was curdling. Above him, the blue of the sky had a dense coppery tinge. There would be thunderstorms later.

He veered left and pushed open the door to the Black Raven. Disoriented by the change in the light, he peered anxiously around a room made gloomy by panelled wood and dark fittings. What little natural brightness there was in there came filtering through windows so thick and heavily etched that both the glass and the light had the congealed quality of syrup.

Half a dozen men turned uninterested faces briefly in his direction. A barmaid with a halo of curls smiled sympathetically through the steam of a pie she was carrying to a corner table.

'This way,' said Declan. Tom followed him through a cloud of cigarette smoke to a door behind the bar, marked 'Private'.

'Everything all right, Dec?' The barmaid was hovering behind them now, wiping her hands on the rump of her jeans. 'Would a tot of brandy help her?'

'No, no. Everything's grand.' Declan held the door open

and motioned for Tom to squeeze past his beer belly. 'This is Tom, Catherine's son. Everything's grand now.'

Tom's mother was lying on a settee in a small cluttered den—part bedsit, part office; total mess. Her eyes were closed, her body a narrow ridge under somebody's patchwork quilt. She was very still, except for one finger which was stroking a blue velvet square, slowly, over and over. Her face was pale but calm. She looked, thought Tom, like a bald saint. What she didn't look was grand.

'Mum,' he said. 'It's me.' He was aware of Declan hovering behind him and of the embarrassment and irritation he felt in the man's presence. He was embarrassed for his mother, lying there without the hat on. She looked horrible without it, like a person in a concentration camp. The irritation was with himself, for caring more about how his mother looked nowadays than about how she might be feeling.

His mother opened her eyes and smiled, weakly. 'Hello, love,' she said. 'Don't panic. Just a bit of a dizzy turn outside the pub, that's all. Nothing serious . . . ' She groped around for the glass of iced water that somebody had placed on a low table next to the settee.

Declan hurried to her side. He placed one arm around her shoulders, one hand under the bony point of her left elbow and slid her gently up into a sitting position. Tom flinched, then watched in a growing state of disapproval as his mother, smiling gratefully, allowed the quilt to be rearranged into a smooth spill of shapes across her lap, and the glass of water to be held to her lips.

This man was a stranger, Tom raged to himself. A knuckle-head. His mother ought to tell him to keep his grubby mitts to himself. He could hear ice cubes clinking against her teeth and soft gulpings in her throat as she drank. Such little sounds, but they made him want to run amok.

'I hope that's bottled, not tap,' he snapped. 'My mother has to be careful about things like that.'

Declan didn't even turn around. 'Don't worry your head, Tom,' he said, placing the empty glass on the floor. 'Now, Catherine. Are you sure you won't be wanting the doctor?'

Tom's mum had rallied and was peering round the room. Her hat was on a table beside the door. Tom snatched it up and threw it onto the settee, a little harder than absolutely necessary. Without a word, his mother crammed it onto her head, and got shakily to her feet. 'I'm fine, Dec,' she said. 'Really. It was just the heat and all the rushing around. Plus the excitement of having had my . . .'

'*Mum!*'

' . . . of . . . of having had a busy day in town.'

'Well, if you're sure now.'

'I'm sure.' She made a small adjustment to the front of her dress. 'Come on, Tom Thumb,' she said. 'Gran'll be back soon.'

Tom offered her his left arm. She hesitated.

'Please yourself,' he said. 'I was only thinking of the steps. In case you get dizzy again.'

She linked arms with him then, but was careful not to lean too heavily against him as they walked back through the pub. Tom tried to hurry her past the bar. He could feel his face growing hot as the men there swivelled round for a good gawp.

'Steady on,' laughed his mother. 'I'm not running the marathon. Not this year anyway.'

Declan followed them out, dodging around like an anxious referee. Tom's mother stopped to catch her breath under the pub's signpost. 'Caw, caw,' she said, squinting upwards. 'That's always been an evil-looking bird.'

21

Tom, following her gaze, could have sworn that the black raven shifted, just a flicker, the better to fix him in its sights. A trick of the light, no doubt; the light having an eerie quality of its own now beneath a sky slowly turning all the shades of a kicked shin bone.

In the distance the first faint rumblings of thunder.

'Ah, now, if that auld bird could talk,' said Declan, 'it would tell tales to make your heart stop.'

'What do you mean?' Tom turned to look at Declan— to really look at him, for the first time. 'What kind of tales?'

His mother tugged at his arm. 'Come on,' she said. 'Let's get indoors before the heavens open. Dec can give you the freak-show spiel another day.'

Tom stood his ground. 'What freak shows?' he persisted. Declan returned his gaze, quizzically. He doesn't think much of me, thought Tom. He reckons I'm the kind of kid who's obsessed with blood and guts. 'I only wondered . . .' he murmured, looking away. 'It sounds interesting. You know. For school. For history.'

He helped his mother up the steps to his grandmother's front door. She was still a bit shaky. Pink drink, Tom told himself. That's what she needs. Pink drink and some peace and quiet.

'Hey, Tom!' Declan had stationed himself on the bottom step; solid as a pot on a shelf. 'They used to stick traitors' heads on spikes around here. Did you know that? Up on London Bridge they'd be, rotting like turnips.'

'Gross,' said Tom, obligingly.

'And so . . . once in a while, one of these heads would fall off. And where would it land, nine times out of ten, but in the lap of a fine lady being rowed along the Thames.'

'Declan—please!' Tom's mother gave a cross between a groan and a laugh.

22

'But what about here,' said Tom. 'What about the things that happened at the Black Raven and . . . and in my gran's basement.'

Declan raised his eyebrows. 'Well now,' he said. 'Your gran's basement, is it? Well now . . . '

A black taxi swerved into the street from the main road, slowed, and shivered to a halt.

'Talk of the devil,' said Tom's mother.

'I'll be off,' announced Declan, as Tom's grandmother unfurled herself from the passenger seat. 'Will you have your meal at the pub tomorrow night, Catherine, if you're up to it? Tom as well. All on the house, mind. You'll be my guests. How about that?'

'That would be lovely,' said Tom's mother. 'Wouldn't it, Tom?'

'Yes,' said Tom. 'Grand.'

The storm took its time arriving over Smithfield. For more than an hour it remained stubbornly south of the river, leaving the East End to stew under darkening skies.

'Phew, I wish it would break.' Tom's mother fanned herself with the *Radio Times*. 'I'm sweating like a pig here.'

Tom's gran was trying to find a soap opera on the telly. She stabbed the remote control and tutted. A plate of pasta was cooling beside her, while her second drink of the evening bubbled like a spell in a glass big enough to keep a goldfish in. 'We ladies don't sweat, darling,' she said. 'We glow. Have a tepid bath, if you're hot. A nice bath and an early night.'

They were in the sitting room, eating supper from trays. Tom, uncomfortably perched on a footstool, foraged with his fork beneath a crust of parmesan cheese. He had

23

missed out on lunch and was ravenous, but this pasta Gran had given him was inedible. He hated parmesan. It smelt of sick.

'I don't want an early night,' his mother said. 'I'm not six years old.' She passed Tom a basket of bread rolls. He took two.

On the television screen, a woman with big hair and startled eyes began reading a letter aloud. Tom's grandmother put down the remote control and took a sip of her drink.

'Tom,' she said, 'eat some fruit if you don't like your pasta. You'll have shocking constipation tomorrow with only bread inside you.'

'He's fine with bread,' Tom's mother said. 'Let him eat what he wants.' She bent forward to put her own plate down on the coffee table. 'Oops,' she said, leaning back again. 'Nearly lost it then.' She eased the front of her dress away from her chest. Tom shot her a warning look.

'What?' she said, in mock innocence and surprise. *'What?'*

The soap opera woman had begun to weep. 'Oh, Brad,' she whimpered. 'How can you do this to me? To us. Why are you running away?'

Tom's mother pretended to gag.

'Oh, mother,' she wailed, in an exaggerated Australian drawl. 'How can you do this to me? To us. Why are you watching this crap?'

Tom turned a giggle into a cough and waited for his gran to blow her stack. He hated arguments, as a rule, but a big bust-up might mean that he and his mother would have to go home. They could pack their stuff and be back in Dorset by midnight; away from all this . . . this *tension*. And well shot of whatever had been spooking him out downstairs.

But his gran didn't blow her stack. Instead, she turned

24

the TV volume up. Just a fraction. Just enough to make a point. Then she reached across the space between the settee and the armchair and half patted, half squeezed her daughter's hand. 'I do understand, Catherine,' she said. 'You've been through a terrible time. I do understand . . . '

Oh, bloody hell, thought Tom. Not pity. We don't do pity. It's up there with toxic lettuces and people who smoke, at the very top of Mum's hate list. His mother, however, simply stared at the older woman's fingers as if she had never seen them before. Then she grabbed them, quickly, before they could escape.

'Thanks, Mum,' she said. Her voice had gone all high, like a little girl's. She adjusted her dress again. Deliberately. Obviously.

Stop it, thought Tom. *Stop it before Gran asks* . . .

'Whatever is it, darling? Has something bitten you?'

The wall lights flickered. Off they went, then on again behind glass shades the colour of apricots. The storm was almost overhead.

Tom's mother smiled, beatifically. 'Nope,' she said. 'It's my new boob. It keeps slipping. Honestly . . . I thought it was going to shoot out of my bra earlier, and go bouncing round the pub like a tennis ball. I nearly—'

'More bread, Tom?' The older woman grabbed the bread basket and waved it so hard under Tom's nose that crumbs sprinkled his clothes like dandruff. Tom helped himself, his face scarlet. 'Thank you, Gran,' he said. 'You know, I've been meaning to ask. Why don't you use your basement? People do, don't they? As dining rooms and so on?'

His voice was light but his heart was racing. His mother hated being interrupted. She would go ape. Any second now, she would go totally ape . . .

His gran was at the drinks trolley, fussing with cocktail sticks and bits of lemon. 'Well, darling, funny you should ask,' she said. 'I did think, years ago, about doing that room up. I suppose I just never got around to it.'

An almighty crack of thunder exploded over the roof. 'Well,' snarled Tom's mother. 'That's just how I feel. Like a big black cloud that nobody takes any notice of until it makes a lot of noise.' She was sitting cross-legged in her armchair, her spine rigid, her face tight.

Tom swallowed a mouthful of bread. Swallowed it clumsily, as if it had suddenly become something else.

'I think,' said his gran, 'that you had better go and have that bath, Catherine. It might relax you.' She was back on the settee, swallowing her drink and flicking through the *Radio Times*. The soap opera had finished. She put down her glass, aimed the remote control, and killed the sound.

Tom stood up. 'Um . . . Just going to get a Seven Up,' he said.

'Don't you move,' his mother ordered. 'You stay right where you are.' She ran a trembling hand over the stubble of her hair. 'I don't know what's the matter with you two,' she said. 'Anyone would think I'd committed a crime. Anyone would think I had an unexploded bomb in my bra.'

She was talking too fast. She was losing the plot.

Oh no, thought Tom. *I know what's coming. I know what she's going to do.*

He glared at the ceiling . . . at a gin bottle, glinting on the trolley . . . at the sitting room window, lashed now by ribbons of rain. Yet he couldn't help but look back, mesmerized, as his mother fished inside the neck of her dress, pulled out her new prosthesis, and offered it to his gran, like a child playing pass the parcel.

'Here!' she said. 'It's just a piece of squishy plastic. Nothing repulsive. Nothing weird.'

26

Put it away, Tom begged, silently. *Please. Put it. Away.*

His gran didn't move. She was lost for words. She looked as if she might never budge, or speak, again.

'Tom-ahawk?'

It was like the time when, as a very little boy, he had gone to a friend's Hallowe'en party, and all the kids had been made to sit blindfolded in a circle. 'Here comes the dead man's finger!' his friend's dad had shouted, and Tom's own fingers had been forced around a chicken bone, with shreds of greasy meat still attached. 'And here comes the dead man's scalp!' He had tried to get up, but adult arms had pinned him down, while something wet and stringy went flailing across his knees. 'And here's the dead man's eyeball!' He had screamed, then, as someone prised open his right hand and jabbed his index finger into the flesh of an orange.

'Tom?'

His mother's voice was faint and pleading. If she cried now it would be his fault and he would hate himself forever, and her for even longer.

He took the prosthesis from her; felt the warm weight of it in his hands and almost laughed. What was he supposed to *say*? A few seconds more, and he went to give it back; daring to hope that she would expect no more of him.

'Go on,' he said, harshly. 'Take it!'

And the prosthesis slipped from his sweaty fingers, hit the coffee table with a dull squelch, and flipped, jauntily, into the bowl of pot pourri. Appalled, Tom stared at the flesh-coloured shape—a ridiculous blancmange now, with its speckling of dried rose petals—then turned and ran for the door. His mother tried to grab him, her face stricken. He shook her off and stumbled on.

'Let him go, Catherine.' His grandmother's voice was like hail. 'You've gone too far. Let him go.'

27

Down the stairs he ran; past the kitchen and down. Windows rattled as the storm gave the house a final trouncing, and it seemed to him as if his arrival in the basement was heralded by the biggest lightning flash the world had ever seen.

Get yerself over. C'mon.

The gap formed easily.

gap *n.* **1.** An unfilled space or interval; a blank; a break in continuity. **2.** A breach in a hedge, fence, or wall. **3.** A wide (usu. undesirable) divergence in views, sympathies, development, etc. (*generation gap*). **4.** A gorge or pass. **fill** (or **close** etc.) **a gap** make up a deficiency. **gapped** *adj.* **gappy** *adj.*

Concise Oxford Dictionary

No definition, in any book ever written, could adequately describe the break or opening that appeared in the floor of Tom's grandmother's basement. To call it a gap is for want of a better word. To explain it properly would require a whole new language.

Slicing across the concrete it went, to leave less than a metre of recognizable space on Tom's side, and a black void beyond. It looked like a gutter, but the stuff that came gushing along it was nothing like water. Blobs, platelets, and crystals, that's what appeared. Blobs, platelets, and crystals moving in a thick, turbulent stream. When they hit the far wall they went back again, in the opposite direction, slightly bigger, or brighter, or sharper round the edges. When they hit the place they had started from, they repeated the process, growing and altering all the while.

Tom crouched low on his heels. It came as no surprise, this churning up of the basement floor; this teeming of shapes right under his nose. It had happened before. When he was little. In a minute, he would be able to jump.

But he couldn't go yet. He remembered that much at least. He had to wait for the right time. Her time. The girl's.

One of the shapes, growing faster than the rest, came to a sudden halt. Its edges were stuck to the sides of the gap. Its centre bulged, and pulsed, as if something inside were trying to hatch. Slowly, slowly, the outer casing of the shape peeled away, to reveal the miniature, three-dimensional form of a man—a bald-headed man, scribbling so furiously with a quill pen that a splutter of ink hit Tom's left wrist. The man was murmuring to himself as he wrote:

'To sleep: perchance to dream; ay, there's the rub . . . '

Shakespeare. Too early.

A neighbouring blob became a young boy clutching a gas mask and a small, battered, suitcase. He looked up from the gap, with intense blue eyes, said something urgent to Tom which went unheard against the wail of an air raid siren. The Blitz. Much too late.

The shapes were changing, thick and fast now; jostling for space as recognizable human beings before dissolving, like aspirins, in the flow. Guy Fawkes shrugged his shoulders on his way to the Tower. Lady Diana Spencer lifted her wedding veil and blushed like a rose. Nell Gwynne threw an orange.

Then Tom saw her. The fairy girl. The Changeling Child. So tiny and translucent that he could see time rushing through her as she hovered in the gap. She was beckoning furiously with daisy-stalk fingers, and giving him hell.

Now, I tells yer. Now.

And he jumped.

4

It was still his grandmother's basement and yet it wasn't. The commotion out on the street was all wrong for a start: a clattering—wheels, hooves, clogs, Tom couldn't tell—and the kind of raucous shouting and carrying on that, ordinarily, would have lost the Black Raven its licence. The basement window had been blocked up with planks and old sacking so that not a chink or a spyhole remained. As for the smell, it was worse than parmesan; worse, even, than the meat market.

'Bugger. You've grow'd.'

What?

Tom, nervous of making any impression at all upon the thick, foul-smelling darkness around him, kept his feet together, his arms folded, and his hands clamped protectively under his armpits as he turned towards the voice.

'You've grow'd. You ain't a little chit no more. Come nearer.'

Tom hesitated. Crossing the gap had seemed as natural as jumping a ditch but what, really, had he let himself in for? Ten years ago he had felt safe here, swaddled in straw and soothed by the croonings of a mysterious being. But what would the average two year old know? He swallowed hard and took a small step backwards, steeling himself to leap away should this mysterious being turn out to be very bad news indeed.

There was a rustling in the far corner, then a small sigh. An exquisite little face appeared in the glow of a newly-lit candle and regarded Tom, forlornly. He went forward then, just a little way, blinking back the tears that threatened, suddenly, to embarrass him.

'*Hello, Astra.*' Should he hug her or shake her tiny hand? Both gestures, he realized, might easily snap her bones; yet the moment demanded something more than words, so overwhelmed was he to have found, once again, this being who had always been with him, he realized that now, hovering lightly on the edges of his dreams.

'Astra?' Her voice was shrill, her face mewling, like a kitten's. 'Is that who I am then? Is that what I told yer last time? Well. Astra . . . Fairyspawn . . . the Princess of blessed Kolozsvar—it don't matter no more. You can push off. Go on. You're a grow'd man now and grow'd men ain't never done me no kindness.'

She jammed her candle into a rusty sconce, jutting from the wall, threw herself face down onto a nasty-looking pile of rags and straw, and burst into sobs as acute as the flailing of windchimes. 'You was such a dear little mannikin,' she hiccupped. 'Now look at yer.'

Tom stepped closer. '*But I'm only twelve,*' he said. '*I'm tall for my age, that's all. Look at me properly, in a better light. I'm not a man. Not yet, anyway.*'

He was so near to her now that he could see bits of muck caught in the thistledown of her hair. Her spine was juddering like a clothes line beneath the filthy shift she wore. The soles of her feet looked too small to walk on. But for the trembling, and the crying, she could have been a doll; an unwanted doll tossed on a rubbish heap.

Tom reached out a hand, intending only to touch the poor little fingers; to reassure this creature just as she had once calmed and reassured him. In a trice she was up, reeling away against the wall and spitting fury. Tom snatched back his hand, his own fingers scalded by the briefest contact with hers.

'If 'tis touching ye want,' she hissed, 'come back at the proper time, an' pay 'Is Nibs for the pleasure, like all the other fine gentlemen.'

Tom nursed his throbbing fingers against his chest. *What are you on about?'* he snapped, shocked and scared by the burning in his fingertips. *'Stop being so melodramatic. And don't do that to me again.'*

'Do what? I ain't done nothin'. Nothin' 'cept tell yer to cut and run.' She was sitting up now; wishbone legs dangling, dejectedly, over her nest of scraps and straw.

'Nothing? You call this nothing? My fingers are coming out in blisters. Look!'

He knelt and thrust out his hands, palms up. The sudden movement made the candle flame writhe. Astra cast a quick glance at his hands. 'You're foolin' me,' she said. 'Ye know I can't see what's what with thee, no more'n I can tell what's where.'

Confused, Tom spun round on his heels towards the only piece of furniture in the room—an ornate mirror propped directly opposite the blocked-up window and as out of place in this dank hovel as a ruby in a rat hole. It was too far away for him to see his reflection in it, and Astra's candle, wedged in its sconce, was on its last flicker.

'I need more light,' he said. *'I don't understand what's happening to me. Astra? I need to see . . . '*

She tilted her head to one side. Her ears came to points, like a picture-book elf's. For a second or two she remained quite still, weighing him up, taking stock. Then she gave a little shiver and began to ferret around in the straw.

'I bin saving these,' she said, producing the nub-ends of half a dozen candles and dropping them into her lap. 'For a worthy occasion.'

Carefully, she slid down from her perch and tiptoed across the floor, her collection of candle stubs clutched like family heirlooms against the cup of her pelvis. She was no more than . . . what . . . two feet tall? And so frail that Tom hardly dared breathe, as she passed him, for fear of knocking her over. How old was she? he wondered. Seven? Fifteen? It was hard to tell.

He watched, in silence, as she placed the stunted bits of wax in a semi-circle in front of the mirror, then lit them, ceremoniously, with the candle from the sconce. Only then did he step forward to see his reflection—or, at least, his lack of one. His clothes were there—his trainers, jeans, and T-shirt clearly mirrored in the thick, spotted glass. The body that moulded them, however, was invisible. He did a little dance, shuffling on the spot. His clothes moved obligingly. He rolled up the left leg of his jeans. Looking down, he could see his shin quite clearly but, in the mirror, the jeans peeled up over empty space.

Astra was standing beside him, a strange little fossil glimmering in the semi-circle of light. The top of her head barely reaching above the place where his knees would normally be. He considered their two images and managed a faint invisible smile. As trick-or-treaters, they would make a cool team.

'Was I like this last time?' he said. *'Invisible, I mean?'*

Astra looked surprised.

'Course,' she said.

'But you said I was cute back then. A cute little mannikin, you said.'

She shrugged. Her shoulder blades clicked, like a cricket's wings. 'Well, so ye was. Your trousies and shoes was smaller, and ye was all curled up like an 'edge'og, cryin' fit ter break.' She paused. 'Ain't you always bin this way?'

Tom frowned at the blank space above his T-shirt. Then he raised an invisible hand and felt, with relief, the familiar contours of forehead, cheeks, and chin. *'No,'* he said. *'I haven't. Feel my face, if you want to. It's what blind people do . . .'*

She shrank away from him then, and went scuttling back to her pile of straw. Tom double-checked the mirror. No. He still wasn't there. What if he was stuck like it? The very thought sent waves of panic into where he assumed his stomach still was. Get a grip, he told himself. She couldn't see you last time either, and you got back OK; all in one piece and perfectly recognizable.

He took a few deep breaths and tried to think practically.

'What year is it?' he said, at last.

'Dunno. I loses track.'

'What year is it roughly then? Who's on the throne?'

Silence. Tom waited, snapping his fingers and drumming his toes to reassure himself of his own presence. Earlier, peering into the gap, he had known instinctively when it was time to jump. Now time, like Astra's mood, the din on the street, even the nose on his own face, seemed to him a threatful unreliable thing. If he could only pin it down he might feel less deranged. Less . . . absent.

Astra sighed. 'I'm 'ungry,' she said. 'I'm 'alf starved. I can't talk to you no more.'

'Next time I come,' coaxed Tom. *'I'll bring you some food. I'll bring anything you want. Only, just tell me about . . . about . . . what's happening in the world. Just so I know where I am.'*

Another pause, as the Changeling Child trawled her memory for a snippet of something that had nothing to do with her own hunger, pain, or cold; some fact or piece of prattle that she could toss Tom's way in the hope that, having digested it, he might yet be of help or would otherwise just . . . go away.

'I do 'ear tell,' she said at last, 'that the maypole in

34

the Strand 'as been taken down and is to be used by Sir Isaac Newton as a support for 'is new telescope.' She stopped, cleared her throat, and yawned.

No teeth, Tom noted. She has no teeth in her head; not a single one. *'Go on,'* he said.

'I also 'ear tell that dried tongue can be had at 2*s* 6*d* a piece at the oil and pickle shop . . . an' that . . . an' that King George is a prating ninny who can speak not a single word of English.' She sank back against the basement wall, exhausted. ''Tain't fiddle-faddle,' she murmured, closing her eyes and slumping lower. ''Tis what I do 'ear tell when gentlemen enterin' or leavin' this place do stop to converse with 'Is Nibs.'

Tom took a moment to weigh up these bits of information. Newton had been a scientist. He knew that much. But in which century? Eighteenth or nineteenth? As for King George—which one did she mean? There had been three or four Georges, hadn't there, one after the other? Declan would know. Back in his own time he would sit down with Declan in the Black Raven and get the facts straight. Then he would come back and help Astra. Rescue her, if possible, from this Iznibs person, or whoever else was making her live down here in the dark.

'Astra,' he said, *'I have to go now. But I'll come again tomorrow. Will you be all right?'*

No answer. She was lying on her side, eyes closed, fingers splayed. Asleep.

Tom bent to extinguish the candle-stubs, mindful that they were precious and not sure that his visit had proved a worthy enough occasion to light them. He should have known better than to touch even these puny objects— perhaps did know better, subconsciously, for he changed his mind and tried to pull away a split second before the nuggets of wax attached themselves to his fingertips like leeches and began to suck.

'*Oh no! Get off! Get off me!*' Frantically, he slapped his hands against his jeans. To his relief, each burning stub fell away easily; yet the shock of having them chomping at his flesh, however briefly, left him trembling. I can't touch anything here, he realized. Nothing. It's all against me.

'Oi! Mind me glimsticks. Don't step on 'em!' Astra was up now, scrambling to rescue her bits of candle. 'What's up wiv yer?'

'*I can't touch stuff,*' Tom told her. '*Everything hurts. It . . . It's horrible.*' He backed away from the mirror, fearful suddenly in case it should shift, fall, and . . . what? Knock him senseless? Jab at him with shards of pointed glass? Nothing would surprise him. Not now.

Astra stopped picking melted wax off the floor, sat back on her haunches, and scowled in his general direction. 'A pox on yer fancies,' she said. 'We needs your 'elp. There ain't no one else can do it. Not wivout being seen.'

Tom squatted down and gazed, helplessly, at the tiny, stubborn face in front of him. He wished she could see his own expression, so she would know how scared he felt, and how sorry he was not to be able to help her. '*Who's "we"?*' he said. '*Not that it matters. I can't help anyone, can I? Not if I can't touch anything.*'

Her eyes, pale green and as blank as water, stared through and beyond him. ''Tis the Giant needs you most,' she said. ''E's the one you've got to 'elp.'

'*The Giant?*' said Tom. '*What Giant? Where?*'

Behind him . . . a sudden grating noise. A movement of bricks in the basement wall like the beginnings of a demolition job. He whirled round, panic-stricken.

''S all right,' said Astra. 'No need to piss yerself.'

What was it then? Rats? Some kind of earth tremor? So far as he knew, the Black Raven's cellar was all that lay beyond that wall. He turned back to Astra.

'*Someone's coming in,*' he said. '*From the pub next door. Who is it, Astra? Is it him? Is it the Giant?*'

'No,' she said. 'It ain't. For he ain't goin' nowhere, poor sod.'

A sudden crash and clatter, and it seemed to Tom as if the whole basement was about to cave in on itself. He spun round, his eyes smarting from the cloud of dust being thrown up. A large, jagged hole had appeared in the wall. The first thing he saw, coming through it, was a candle. Then he saw the hand around the candle's stem—a hand so thickly matted with hair that he assumed, at first, that this visitor was wearing black woolly gloves.

Then the arms came through. Then the top of the head.

Tom gulped.

''Ave a care, Angel,' said Astra, her voice gentle behind him. 'Don't tear the lace off that pretty gown or there'll be hell to pay.'

The person inching its way into the basement was grumbling and wheezing too much to hear. Its rump caught, but it strained forward, grinding its teeth with the effort. Then, with a rip of broken wind, it landed on all fours, in a shower of brick dust, at the foot of Astra's straw heap.

It was a woman, yet it wasn't. And Tom was glad that no one could see the look on his face as she rose up on her hind legs. For a couple of seconds he and the new arrival took stock of one another, across the candle flame. It was all the time the Gorilla Woman needed to decide that Tom was a loathsome scut, come down after hours from Bartholomew Fair, with evil intent towards the Child. She moved fast, in spite of her bulk.

'No, Angel!' Astra's voice pealed, uselessly, across the room. ''E ain't a bad 'un.'

Tom willed his legs to shift. To shift now. Immediately.

Towards and over the gap. The woman-monkey-thing was right in front of him. Teeth bared. Arms raised. Lace frills and embroidered lilies straining across the great hairy slab of her chest.

'Don't touch 'im, Angel. 'E's a poor monster, like us. Only a poor monster. Don't 'urt 'im!'

Tom's whole body twitched, shocked into action by a blast of the monkey-woman's terrible breath as she leaned forward to cuff him.

He jumped backwards. Then to one side. Ducked underneath one threatening, silk-sheathed arm. *Did it*, he thought, for a single triumphant second, before tripping on invisible feet over the trailing ends of his all-too-visible shoelaces.

5

All quiet. House in darkness. Gentle patter of rain against the front door. Faint scent of polish on the banister as Tom hauled his aching body upstairs. On the first floor landing he stopped to check his reflection in a full-length mirror. Pale face. Startled eyes. Beginnings of a stonking bruise beneath his fringe, where the side of a packing crate had broken his headlong fall across the gap. At least I'm back, he thought. At least I'm not being torn limb from limb by an ape in fancy dress. At least I'm still me.

Exhausted, he staggered into his attic room and collapsed, fully clothed, on the bed. Tomorrow, he thought. Tomorrow I'll talk to Declan . . . Find out what went on here . . . What else? . . . Oh yes . . . Get Astra something to eat.

He twisted, fretfully. Felt a twinge as his forehead brushed against the pillow. Was he mad? Was he seriously considering going back?

No way. Forget it.

He closed his eyes. Nice soft mattress . . . Breakfast soon. A fried egg sandwich. With ketchup . . . Everything back to normal . . . Rain hitting the skylight just above his head, like the tapping of tiny fingers.

'I'm 'ungry. I'm 'alf starved . . . '

He scrunched his fists against his ears. No good. It was no good. She would only follow him into sleep.

'All right,' he muttered. 'All *right*. Tomorrow. I'll come tomorrow, but only for a minute and only if it's safe. That crazy ape could've killed me.'

He covered himself with his sleeping bag; burrowing right into it so that only the top of his head stuck out. 'And don't go on any more about that giant.'

He pulled his bedding tighter, like a cocoon. 'I said I'd bring you some food and I will, but I'm not helping any giants. I'm sorry, but you'll have to tell him. The answer's no. It's my decision and he'll just have to live with it.'

A final sprinkle of raindrops, like a peal of laughter, and she was gone.

Good, thought Tom. Sleep now. And tomorrow . . . Get some food in . . . and an air freshener, or some pot pourri, for that stinking basement. No, on second thoughts, not pot pourri. He never wanted to set eyes on any pot pourri again. Scented candles, then. Loads of scented candles. For worthy occasions . . . For Astra . . .

'Tom. Thomas, love. Can we talk?'

Tom opened his eyes. His room was full of sunshine. The hands on his travel clock grinned ten to ten at him. His head hurt. A lot.

His mother was calling from the first-floor landing. She sounded too out of breath to come all the way up, and was probably too embarrassed, anyway, about last night to come barging in on him with complaints about fuggy bedrooms and terminal lazy-itis.

He was tempted not to answer, only then she might come in after all.

'I'll be down in a minute,' he croaked. 'I'm only just awake.'

He could sense her relief at having got a reply out of him, and a surprisingly chirpy one at that. It was more than she deserved.

'Oh—good,' she said. 'I . . . I thought we'd take

40

croissants to the park for a brunch. Just you and me. What do you think?'

Tom thought croissants might be a fitting snack for Astra, being soft and squishy and presumably fairly easy on toothless gums. Tom thought his head might be fractured, so painful was the egg-shaped swelling under his fringe. Tom thought that, in the great scheme of things, dropping his mother's false boob in a bowl of dried flowers was not that big a deal after all. He hoped she wasn't going to worry about its effect on his psycho-sexual development, or spend the whole morning being tragic. There was too much else for him to think about today. Too much he had to do.

'Fine,' he said. 'Whatever.'

'Good.' He heard the stairs creak as she moved away. 'Oh, and Tom?'

'What?'

'If you don't want to have supper at the pub tonight we don't have to.'

'No, it's OK.' He closed his eyes and kept his voice neutral. 'I don't mind going.'

'Oh . . . Good. That's good. See you in a minute, then?'

'Yeah.'

The park was somewhere Tom's mother remembered from her childhood—a small wedge of green near St Paul's Cathedral; as surprising to suddenly come across as blades of grass on a Monopoly board. Lime trees, heavy with late-summer leaves, screened the place from the roads and muffled the sound of traffic flowing through the City. There were benches set at intervals around a circular path; flowers in gaudy spurts of red, pink, and orange. From a central plinth reared a statue of a minotaur, its bull-head and man-body splattered with bird droppings.

'Come on! Let's check out the wall of fame!' Tom's mother led the way to a quaint wooden verandah where rows of plaques, pale as toilet tiles, recalled the untimely deaths of long-forgotten Londoners. *In Commemoration of Heroic Self Sacrifice* read a sign above them all.

Tom scanned the wall, uncomfortably aware that his dealings beyond the gap had given him a special relationship to long-forgotten Londoners. Pausing in front of one small epitaph, he read aloud:

'Sarah Smith—Pantomime artiste at Prince's Theatre. Died of terrible injuries received when attempting in her inflammable dress to extinguish the flames which had enveloped her companion. 24 January 1863'

'Poor Sarah,' murmured his mother. 'Mind you, when I was your age I thought that was a *brilliant* way to go. I used to lie awake at night, imagining myself as Sarah Smith, blazing away on stage, like Joan of Arc. I used to picture your gran, and everyone else I knew, sitting out in the audience calling me the bravest girl that ever lived. And weeping buckets too, of course.'

'Mum,' said Tom, 'you're a sicko . . . Hey, listen to this one:

"Frederick Alfred Croft—Inspector, aged 31. Saved a lunatic woman from suicide at Woolwich Arsenal Station but was himself run over by a train. 11 January 1878"

How's that for bad timing . . . Mum . . . hey, Mum?'

His mother had wandered out of the verandah and was pacing the curve of the path, deciding where to sit.

Tom could see that there was nobody else around. 'Are we safe?' he called after her, testily. 'What about dossers

42

and drug addicts. I bet they hang out here. Aren't you worried about being mugged?'

His mother stopped beside a particular bench and turned, sharply, to look at him. 'I try *not* to worry about things that haven't happened yet and probably never will,' she called back. 'But I *am* worried about you. Come here.'

Oh cack, thought Tom. Here we go.

He ambled across the grass, preparing to appear attentive. His shoulders went automatically into a hunch as he sat beside his mother, leaving enough space between them for at least two drug addicts or a very large dosser.

'I'm so sorry, Tom, about last night,' his mother said. She was pleating the croissant bag between her fingers. 'I don't know what came over me. Do you want to talk about it?'

Tom raised an eyebrow. Did he have a choice then? This was a first. 'No, actually,' he muttered. 'It's all right. I'm all right about it now.'

His mother smiled. 'Your gran sent me to my room,' she said.

'Not surprised,' he replied. ' . . . Does she want us to leave?'

'Yes and no. It's more complicated than that. My relationship with your gran is more complicated than that, I mean.'

Tom eyed the breakfast bag. 'I'm hungry,' he said. 'I'm half-starved.'

She passed him a warm, dented, croissant, then sat quietly for a while, contemplating a bed of roses while he chewed. (*Could Astra really manage one of these without teeth? he wondered. Should he be thinking soup, yogurt, mushed apple—the kind of slop babies eat?*)

His mother was deep in thought. There were things on her mind he couldn't fathom. Private things. Secret things. He wasn't sure he wanted to know what they were, but

43

could tell, from the way her fingers were still shredding and folding the paper bag, that she was about to tell him anyway.

'You know,' she said at last, 'I'm really proud of you.'

'Oh,' he said. 'Cheers.'

'No, I mean it.' She began scuffing at a patch of gravel with the toes of her strappy sandals, tipping her feet so that tiny stones tumbled down inside and out at the heels. 'You're a real tower of strength. I don't deserve a son like you.'

Tom shifted, suspiciously. There was a catch to this, somewhere.

'The thing is, Tombola . . .'

Yep, here it came.

'The thing is, we can't go home yet. I need to spend time with your gran. We've a lot of emotional baggage to sort out. A lot of bridges to mend. Are you following me?'

'Not really,' said Tom. 'But it doesn't matter. I don't need the gory details.' (*The pink drink, he thought. Mum's pink drink. Full of minerals and vitamins . . . Astra might go for that. It might do her good.*) 'Mum,' he said. 'Do you remember the last time we were here? When I got lost in the house?'

His mother tilted her face towards the mesh of leaves, sky, and branches above their heads and half-smiled. She hadn't eaten her croissant. It wasn't healthy enough—too much saturated fat.

'Your dad and I were going frantic,' she said. 'We called and called. We searched everywhere. In wardrobes. Under beds. Up the chimney, even. Everywhere.'

'Who found me?'

'No one. You just appeared in the kitchen, with your thumb in your mouth, and bits of straw in your hair. Your dad was *this far* from calling the police.'

44

A pigeon flew down onto the path, scenting breakfast. Tom looked at the uneaten food in his mother's lap, then back at the pigeon, then away.

'Did I say anything?' he said. 'About what happened? About where I'd been?'

The pigeon was fat. A fat, piggy pigeon, advancing in fits and starts.

Tom's mother closed her eyes against the sun's rays. 'No,' she said. 'Although from the state of you, it was clearly somewhere filthy. The basement, probably, although we'd looked in there. Twice. You must have been hiding in a box, you rascal. Why. Can *you* remember?'

'No,' said Tom. 'At least . . . Oh, watch out!'

The pigeon had made a sudden, flapping lunge for the croissant. Startled, Tom kicked out, sending the bird wheeling away into the shrubbery. Thick flakes of pastry spilled from his mother's knees onto the gravel. 'Bloody thing,' he said. 'You nearly had it land on you.'

His mother laughed, shakily. 'Oh,' she said. 'Goodness. A fate worse than death. Thanks for saving me.'

She shook the rest of her breakfast onto the path, then turned to smile at him.

Tom smiled back. Pale face. Startled eyes. Stonking bruise . . .

'Tom! How did you get that?' She raised a hand towards his forehead. He flinched away.

'It's nothing,' he told her. 'I fell, that's all.'

'Fell where? When?'

'Last night . . . I fell out of bed. Landed against one of Grandpa's boxes—a big heavy box, full of old books. I'm all right though. Don't fuss.'

She continued to stare.

'What?' he said. 'What's wrong?' His heart gave a sudden lurch. Her eyes . . . She was looking straight through him, just the way Astra had. She was looking through and beyond him, as if he wasn't there.

'What's the matter?' he cried. 'What is it, Mum? Can you see me? Can you?'

She snapped out of her trance, startled by the fear in him.

'Of course I can see you,' she said. 'Of course I can. What's the matter? What is it?'

Her face. She had frightened him. She hadn't meant to. She hadn't meant to scare her son. It was the books, that was all. Hearing about the books had unnerved her. Patting his back, as soothingly as she knew how, she began to talk about plans. Supper at the Black Raven tonight. The Science Museum tomorrow . . . A barbecue for all his mates as soon as they got home. Not long to wait, before going home. Not really.

And Tom, weak with relief that time hadn't faltered after all; that he was still as clearly visible as his mother's yellow hat and the crumbs on the path; Tom stopped freaking out and allowed himself to be hugged.

6

Four p.m. Still warm. Still humid. The sign outside the Black Raven casting a shadow on the pavement like a black hole. Petunias in hanging baskets, gasping for a drink. *Stewed Eels*, someone had chalked on a board beside the entrance. *With Chips*.

Tom hummed a little tune as he unlocked his gran's front door. He had been shopping. Alone. Two carrier bags, which he now had to hide, bulged with groceries and other treats for Astra.

His mother had been surprisingly cool, he thought, about letting him wander around by himself all afternoon. She must have understood that he needed time out, after all that heavy emotional stuff in the park. Anyway, she had given him the *A to Z* and a generous wad of cash, pointed him in the general direction of some shops and left him to it. No sweat.

'Mum? Gran? Anyone home?'

No answer. Great. He scampered upstairs to stash Astra's supplies under his bed. He felt pretty good, he realized. Light-hearted, even. Browsing round the shops had perked him up; made him feel normal—if you could call shopping for a centuries-old elf-girl with no teeth normal.

The sitting room door was closed, but the sound of raised voices beyond it slowed him down. They were at home after all. Treading carefully, to avoid creaky floorboards, he crept along the landing.

'I don't care. They should never have been put there in

the first place. Goodness only knows what kind of filth . . . '

'But, darling . . . '

'I mean it. Get rid. Tonight. We can sort through the other stuff later. Honestly, why you ever agreed to . . . '

Still tiptoeing, Tom reached the attic and put his bags down on the bed. The room looked different, he noticed—brighter, and more spacious, without all the boxes.

'Tom? Hey, Tommy-rot? Is that you up there?'

He went quickly down.

'Have you been up to the attic?' he asked.

' 'Fraid so.' His mother placed her empty pink-smeared glass on the coffee table. 'I know I usually respect your privacy, and I promise not to invade it again, but Gran and I thought you'd be happier with all those boxes of books out of the way.' She was watching him carefully.

'Oh,' he said. 'OK.'

'High time I had a bit of a sort out,' said his gran, a little shakily. 'After all these years, I mean. Silly to hang on to things, just for the sake of it.'

'Right.' Tom slouched against the door frame. He was bored, now, with the subject of Grandpa and his books.

His mother pushed herself up out of the armchair. 'I'm off to get tarted up,' she said. 'We'll go early to the pub, Tom, if that's all right with you.'

'Fine.' He was impatient to cross the gap; could hardly wait to see Astra's face when she unpacked all the things he had chosen for her.

He hung around in the doorway for a while, listening to his mother's bath running. Her empty glass was still on the coffee table. Had she left any pink drink in the blender? Maybe Astra would like some right now. He could pop it across the gap while his mum was getting tarted up and be back in no time. While he was at it, he would make sure that Astra's hairy friend knew to stay well clear tonight . . . *Well* clear, otherwise he would never go back, and there would be no more presents.

'Don't loiter, Tom,' said his gran. 'Either sit down and watch Sir Charles sweep the American girl off her feet or go and get ready to go out.'

Tom bounded across the room and picked up his mother's empty glass. 'I'll take this down,' he said. 'Can I get you anything, Gran? More ice?'

'No, thank you, darling.' She gave his arm an awkward little pat. 'You're a good boy, Tom. Catherine's lucky to have you. Oh, I say!' She waved towards the television screen, sending a slosh of gin over the rim of her glass and trickling down her forearm. 'The silly little thing's playing hard to get. Still . . . he'll charm her in the end. They always do. Sure you won't stay and watch?'

'No, thank you,' said Tom.

Down in the kitchen he grabbed the jug from the blender and poured what was left of the pink drink into a glass. A straw. How about a straw? And one of those dinky little paper parasols? And a glass stick for stirring? Gran kept that kind of stuff in the cutlery drawer, all jumbled up with sharp knives and silver spoons.

By the time he had finished, Astra's drink looked like something you would serve after sunset, at a cocktail bar in Tenerife. It was pretty, though, thought Tom. A pretty present.

Quickly, he carried the glass down to the basement, pushed open the door, and steeled himself to jump.

Nothing.

Come on, he muttered. Come on, come on . . .

Sunlight dribbled through the window, to play against the patch of wall where Astra's mirror had stood last night. Tom took this as a sign; a prelude to the slipping of time. When he realized that it wasn't, that it was only

49

weather, he felt cheated. So where was she, then? Why couldn't he sense her?

He crouched low, and tried willing the gap to appear. But he soon felt stupid, hunkered down on the cold concrete with a glass of crushed fruit and soya milk growing warm in his hands. Stupid and suspicious.

'Astra! Can you hear me?' The words seemed to bump around in his head. 'Astra!' He was angry now. 'Astra! 'Iznibs! Ugly Great Ape Thing! Answer me, somebody, will you?'

Nothing. No voices, no static in his brain and no gap. Just cobwebs and packing crates and a bit of a crack in the floor that any fool with a trowel and a dollop of gloop could fix in a trice.

'Astra!'

It was no use. Tom stood up, defeated. He might as well forget it. His mum would be out of the bath soon in any case, and then they were going out. He turned away; had one hand against the door, half a mind on supper, when someone tapped him on the shoulder.

'What the—!' He whirled round, conscious of a sliding and slewing sensation in his head. The room grew dark and cold, all in the blink of an eye. He couldn't see a thing.

'Astra? Is that you? Stop messing around!'

'Patience, young fellow my lad, patience. The Changeling Child will admit you shortly . . . '

It was him. The man with the smarmy voice who had called to him yesterday, and the day before that. Where was he? Where was he hiding?

A thick gurgling sound made him jump. Down on the floor the gap was forming, but sluggishly, lurching along in fits and starts like a snake having trouble shedding its skin. Peering into it was worse than checking out a sewer. Retching, Tom backed away.

'Stay awhile, sir. No need to hop the twig. 'Tis only a shilling extra to touch this miracle of nature.'

There was nothing bright or beguiling this time about the lumps taking shape in the gap. Tom flinched as the first one split. He heard a woman's scream; saw the cloaked figure of a man emerge through fog and gaslight. The man threw him a startled glance, before vanishing into the smog, and Tom knew he had become the only person to have ever looked, with certainty, upon the face of Jack the Ripper—and lived.

He did not want to see more; refused to stay put while murderers and other villains went floating past like turds in a drain. All he had to do was push open the basement door and make a run for it . . . and quickly, before the next shape turned into someone gross.

Too late. A pasty blob of matter had detached itself from the flow to become a sly, pockmarked face, its mouth calling him back.

'Ye'll regret leaving with such undue haste, my friend, indeed ye will. For it gives great satisfaction, this creature of mine; great satisfaction . . . '

The man's tone was hypnotic, intent on enticing him down. Tom, already disoriented, felt himself moving forward, so much against his will that it was as if his legs belonged to someone else. Teetering on the brink of the gap, ready, if not willing, to jump, he forced himself to look down; to make eye contact with the nasty piece of work cajoling him over.

The jolt that he got, as the man leered up at him, was as awful as it was unexpected. Without thinking, needing only to blot this moment out, he raised the glass still clutched in his right hand and sent its contents swilling into the gap.

The man's curses were awful, but mercifully short-lived as his face became pink porridge then boiled over into nothing. Other shapes festered for a second before dropping away, like scabs, as the gap began to close in on itself.

Tom backed towards the door. His heart was bumping. You're OK, he told himself. He didn't get you. You're OK. It took a while for the gap to heal completely, and for his heart to slow to normal. Feeling less threatened, at last, he found himself wondering where the cocktail stirrer and the little paper parasol had ended up. As splinters, he hoped, jabbing at that scumbag for all eternity.

He stayed where he was, with his back pressed against the door, until the gap had become, once again, the smallest of cracks at his feet. Only then did he turn away, silently pledging to Astra that he would try again later. Definitely. No question. He was feeling more than a little pleased with himself now. And why not? Hadn't he just zapped a villain single-handed? Oh yes; he would jump the gap tonight all right, come hell, high water, or every villain in history. He would give Astra the things he had promised her. And he would help the wretched Giant, if that was what she wanted. Only, the ape had better watch out. The ape had better show him some respect. Or else.

7

The small dining area at the Black Raven was deserted as Tom and his mother took their seats. There were fresh flowers on their table and peppermints in a little saucer.

'Sorry, Declan,' said Tom's mother as she moved their vase to another table. 'It's my hayfever . . . '

Tom frowned. His mother didn't suffer from hayfever. She didn't suffer from anything, except cancer. She was just funny about flowers, that was all. Blue and red ones, in particular.

Declan poured Coke and mineral water with a flourish. 'Avoid the stewed eels. I would,' he said. ''Tis a gimmick of a dish but not worth defrosting, for all the taste that's in it. The chicken and the chips now—would you fancy those? We can do you proud with the chicken and the chips.'

'I'm a vegetarian,' said Tom's mother, gently.

Declan's face fell. 'Eggs, then,' he said. 'We can fry a couple of eggs up with the chips. And tomatoes. We've a few of those left in a tin.'

Tom and his mother agreed that eggs and tomatoes sounded lovely. The words 'free range' and 'organic' hovered between them unspoken.

'Are you joining us, Dec?' Tom's mother was wearing a silky top, with a pattern of tropical flowers. She had tied a silk scarf around her head and put make-up on for the first time in ages. She looks almost like her old self, thought Tom. Almost.

'I will,' declared Declan. 'Before the rush.' He pulled up a chair; called across to the bar for a pint, then turned his attention to Tom.

'I've a book you can have a lend of, Tom. For school. For the history. It mentions this auld pub somewhere and your gran's house, too. Remind me, before the night's out.'

'I will,' said Tom. 'Is it to do with the things you told me about yesterday? The freak shows and so on?'

' 'Tis.'

'Oh, brilliant!' The excitement in his voice sounded ghoulish, as if he could hardly wait to start drooling over pictures of bearded ladies and Siamese twins. 'What I mean is, I need something interesting to read while we're here. There isn't anything at Gran's.'

His mother threw him a strange look. He lowered his eyes and took a swig of his Coke. What *was* her problem? He sat quietly until their food arrived, carried in by the curly-haired waitress. His mother stared wistfully at the girl as she positioned plates just so.

'I love your hair, Madeleine,' she said. 'Is it permed?'

The girl, Madeleine, began doling out chips. 'No,' she said. 'It's natural. Terrible to get a comb through though. I could cheerfully chop it all off, at times. Oh . . . I'm sorry. I didn't mean . . . ' She raised a hand to her mouth, pink with embarrassment.

'No, no, don't apologize.' Tom's mother reached for the salt. 'My own's growing back thicker and stronger than ever. Give me six months, then call me Rapunzel. Pass the ketchup, Tom.'

Declan's big hand beat Tom's to the ketchup bottle. 'Sure, you're a pretty sight in that head-wrap, Catherine,' he said heartily. 'You've the skull for it.'

Madeleine placed Declan's empty glass on the tray. 'More drinks,' she spluttered. 'I'll fetch more drinks across.' She sped to the bar, returning, a few minutes later, with a straight face and a heavy tray.

'That's quite a bonfire blazing away, over the wall,' she said, setting the tray down on the table. 'Is she having a big clear-out, your mam?'

Tom looked up from his meal. His mother put a forkful of fried egg in her mouth and began to chew. Tom frowned. 'Mum!' he prompted, irritated by her silence and embarrassed for Madeleine. 'What's Gran up to? She's not burning all those books, is she? She can't. They might be worth a bob or two. She told me.'

His mother stabbed a chip. 'Leave it, Tom,' she said, quietly.

Declan cleared his throat. Then he placed a hand on Madeleine's arm in a way that said 'don't worry your head'.

'We've a grand drop of ice cream out the back, Tom,' he boomed. 'The mint choc-chip, how about that?'

Tom pushed his dinner plate aside. Leave *what*? What did Mum mean? How dare she treat him like a four year old in front of these people? And how dare she be so rude to Madeleine?

'Yes please,' he said. 'Ice cream will be fine.' His voice sounded small and ungrateful. He hadn't meant it to. He had been trying to make up for his mother's bad manners. What was the *matter* with her?

Madeleine hurried away, thankful for the excuse of serving pudding. The mint choc-chip was rock solid; would need a pickaxe to turn it into dainty portions. Half a minute in the microwave would do the trick.

She slammed around the kitchen, searching for bowls. That Catherine. What a weirdo. You had to feel sorry for her, with the cancer and all, but still . . . Declan clearly doted on the woman, but then, he had known her at secondary school, and was a big softie anyway. As for the boy; you had to pity him with a mam like that. Still . . . he'd have the girls all over him like a rash in a year or two. Those eyes of his—wow!

Staring through the kitchen window, waiting for the microwave to ping, Madeleine noted that next door's bonfire was still going strong. And this a smokeless zone too! The old witch was probably pissed. Great charred flakes of something were spiralling skywards like severed crows' wings. She watched them rise, a sudden shiver sliding down her back. Good job there's no breeze this evening, she thought, to puff those cruddy black bits over the wall. For you wouldn't want smut like that in your own backyard now, would you?

Indigestion. Typical. Tom lay on top of his sleeping bag, waiting. Beside him, on the bedside table, was Declan's book. He would read it later, when he no longer felt as if he had eaten stones.

His mother was taking her time in the bathroom. His gran, he knew, was already in bed.

The carrier bags containing Astra's presents rustled at his feet and he couldn't help but grin, like a boy waking early on Christmas morning.

'Wotjer got in them sacks?'

'Never you mind. I'll be down in a minute . . . '

He could have danced with relief. She was all right then. She was all right and she was waiting for him.

At last he heard footsteps padding out of the bathroom, followed by the click of a bedroom door being shut. He wasn't sure how well his mother slept nowadays. Perhaps she lay awake for a long time, feeling all lopsided and worrying about death. He couldn't bear to think of her like that. It was too sad. It was beyond sadness. He tried sending kind thought-waves through the floorboards, towards his mother's bed. What was it hypnotists said? Your eyes are getting heavier and heavier . . . you are very very sleepy . . .

Mum, he thought. You are getting better and better . . . you are very, very healthy. He yawned. His own eyes were drooping . . . And Mum, I have to tell you, that pink drink of yours has serious magic powers. It got the better of something really evil today. So keep knocking it back and you'll be fine . . . just fine . . .

'Oi! Wake up, you idle drone. We ain't got all night.'

Oh . . . Tom sat bolt upright, rubbing sleep from his eyes. He must have dozed off. He glanced at the clock. A whole hour had passed. Cack and double cack. He might have slept the night away . . .

Grabbing the bags from the end of his bed, he crept out on to the landing and stood for a minute, listening. All clear. He held his breath as he passed his mother's door, then bounded the rest of the way downstairs.

Momentarily, as the gap began to form, he cursed himself for a fool. He should have come prepared with at least another hit or two of pink drink. What if that sleazebag of a man reappeared, out for revenge? The gap had a different air about it tonight, though, as it tunnelled, purposefully, towards the opposite wall. The shapes were moving slowly, avoiding collisions. After you, they indicated. No—after *you*.

A rhombus shattered to form a miniature Wat Tyler, calling for an end to serfdom. He had a nice face even though he carried a burning brand and wanted John of Gaunt's head on a pole.

Neighbouring shapes nudged Wat Tyler gently but he had a lot to say and was in no hurry to leave. Queen Victoria had to push him, in the end. *'Yes, yes, move along . . . '* she scolded, laughing so uproariously that the gap quivered. She wore widow's weeds and a severe parting in her hair, yet the eyes she raised to Tom had a twinkle. *'It is not true that we were not amused,'* she said, her image dissolving as softly as Highland mist. *'On the contrary, we were often highly amused . . .'*

The next shape exploded like a firework. *'Votes for women!'* shouted Emmeline Pankhurst, rattling her chains. Tom crouched down, the better to communicate with this small, angry, suffragette in the narrow space at his feet. 'Was it you threw yourself in front of the king's horse?' he said to her. She stared up at him, uncomprehending. 'Because if it was, I can tell you that it all worked out. Women *did* get the vote. And we've had feminism since then, and a woman prime minister. We're all equal now.'

'OI!'

Moving swiftly along in the flow came Astra, although, until she spoke, Tom barely recognized her.

'What *are* you wearing?' he exclaimed, staggering to his feet and tightening his grip on the shopping bags. 'And what are all those marks on your face?'

'Hush yer clackin' and git across,' she snapped. *'And 'ave respect in yer heart and yer wits fine-tuned when ye gets 'ere. The Giant's dead. 'Tis time for you to be of service.'*

8

There were candles burning, lots of them, and a sweetish smell in the air. Tom, a little dazed after his jump, peered anxiously round, half expecting to see a twenty-foot corpse, in seven league boots and a shirt the size of a duvet, laid out on the basement floor.

The beings that met his gaze, however—or at least the blank space that passed for his gaze over here—were all very much alive. One of them—oh, cack—was the ape lady. He tensed as soon as he clapped eyes on her, but she made no move towards him. She was sitting, hunched up, beside Astra's bed of straw, her hairy face expressionless, both swarthy arms clasped around the froth of her skirts.

Beside her was someone who looked as if he ought to be in pain; someone with his bare feet planted firmly on the ground and his spine bent over at such a fantastic arc that he was able to gawp, full-faced, back through the space between his legs.

'I see you!' jabbered this strangest of sights. 'Leastways, I see there is nothing to see and I sense there is nothing to fear. Malachi Twist, sir. Bendy Man. At your service.'

The rubbery limbs curved up and around to become a lanky individual of medium height, twitching compulsively in an ill-fitting suit of mouldy cloth. 'I won't shake your hand,' he said to Tom. 'For I have no more grasp than a herring's membrane. And besides, any touch, I am told, torments thee beyond endurance.'

59

'*Right,*' said Tom, still anxiously eyeing the ape. '*Where's Astra?*'

The Gorilla Woman made a small movement towards him. With an involuntary '*eek!*' he stepped backwards, treading all over his bags of presents.

'Be still with all yer stampin' around. Angel ain't after yer,' piped Astra, visible now, perched on the Gorilla Woman's lap. 'She knows y' ain't a bad 'un, for all ye look the part. Now . . . the Giant's dead, Gawd rest him, and there's rogues and all manner of miscreants after 'is bones. We gotta lay a reckoning. There ain't no time to waste.'

Tom couldn't take his eyes off her. She looked so . . . so *strange*. Her dress was beautiful, he couldn't fault that. Scarlet and gold it was; the full skirt caught up in bows at the sides to show the dainty front of a petticoat. Her wig, too, was extraordinary—an elaborate pile of curls decked out with so many imitation flowers and fronds that it looked in danger of toppling. No, it was Astra's face— chalk white, *deathly* white, the cheeks and mouth daubed crimson—that appalled him. The marks he had noticed earlier were, he now realized, tiny black patches stuck to her skin; one the shape of a crescent moon and two teeny stars. She wore false eyebrows which looked, for all the world, like strips torn from the pelt of a brown dog. Her eyes, beneath them, glittered feverishly.

'Wotjer gawpin' at?' she snapped. 'And don't tell me you ain't. I can feel it.'

'*You look . . . I don't know . . . different,*' he stammered.

She regarded him imperiously. 'I ain't 'ad an opportunity to change me garments,' she said. 'For 'Is Nibs is indisposed.'

Malachi Twist gave a whoop of laughter. 'Oh my . . . indeed he is,' he chortled. 'He has fled, sir, like a scalded cat, calling upon every upright man in London to bear witness to the mischief done to him this day.'

''Tis I will pay the price,' sniffed Astra. 'When 'e rolls back sozzled, wiv a score still to settle and every man from 'ere to Jack Ketch's warren mocking 'im for a halfwit.' She sagged a little against the Gorilla Woman's chest, her mouth and her adornments quivering.

'He'll be in no state to torment thee, I'll warrant,' soothed Malachi Twist. 'I hear that his face swelled like suet the second he was doused and that the sight of it along Duck Lane, not half an hour since, was enough to frighten the dead.' He twirled blithely on chipolata-toes, his face a gleeful scrunch. 'I would give much to know the secret of such a potion,' he mused. 'And I would call the gentleman who threw it both a saint and a friend. I would shake such a one by the hand, I would, if my grasp had more of a clinch to it . . . '

Tom cleared his throat. *'Er . . . did they catch the "gentleman" who threw this potion?'* he asked.

'They did not,' replied Twist. 'He vanished clean away, taking his magic and his motives with him.'

''Cept for 'is toothpick and 'is scratcher,' said Astra, 'which, according to Angel, ain't worth a bent farthing between 'em . . . Now then!' She raised herself bolt upright on the Gorilla Woman's knees, like a marionette with the strings pulled suddenly taut. 'What we gonna do about the Giant? For if we don't set our wits to it, that arch-rogue Rafferty Spune'll 'ave 'im out of 'is grave and sold to them doctors at St Bart's afore we can thwart 'im.'

Tom had a feeling he was losing the plot. *'I'm not with you,'* he said. *'You'll have to explain. Who is Rafferty Spune? And why would he sell your friend's body to a hospital? They can't do much for him now can they?'*

The Changeling Child, Malachi Twist, and the Gorilla Woman considered this response. It wasn't helpful. Maybe this monster's brains were missing, along with his head. Maybe they would be better off without him.

Angel groped for a muslin pouch attached to her skirts by a length of ribbon, pulled its neck open, and plunged the whole of one dark hand into its depths. Chuntering softly, taking care not to jolt the poor abused little mite on her lap, she drew out her new toothpick and began prodding the sharp end between her molars. It helped her to think.

'Oh . . . ' gasped Tom, recognizing the miniature parasol from Astra's pink drink, its torn paper frill dangling like spinach from the Gorilla Woman's mouth as she jabbed away at her fangs.

Astra sank back, snuffing for comfort and reassurance at the ripe Angel-odour of sweat and fur seeping through the layers of silk and lace against her cheek. 'You tell 'im, Twist,' she muttered. 'You explain. I ain't got the vitality . . . '

Gurning so wildly that his bottom lip almost swallowed his nose, Malachi Twist leant towards Tom, bending from the waist and offering up his face as an earnest reflection of sincerity and good character. 'You are from foreign parts, sir, am I right?' he said. 'From the Spice Islands, maybe, or from realms even further beyond? For though we have mapped the world enough to know it is shaped like an orange, not like a plate, there remain creatures upon it, so I am told, with no more notion than a cuckoo of the workings of Christian society.'

Tom shifted from one foot to another. There were pins and needles in his invisible calf muscles. He would have liked to sit down on Astra's straw heap but knew it would only bite his bottom, or become a shaggy swamp intent on sucking him in. *'I'm from the future,'* he said. *'From another time and place altogether.'*

He expected gasps of amazement but Twist merely nodded, humouring him. Astra and Angel did not even look up.

'Well then,' continued Twist, 'I see I must enlighten you. Rafferty Spune, sir, is of that vile breed known commonly as the sack-'em-up men. No churchyard, sir, is secure against the shovels of these fiends, for they move swift, driven by greed, and can plunder a man from his final resting place in under twenty minutes. In short, sir, Rafferty Spune is a grave-robber.'

'Poor Giant,' keened Astra, rising from the crook of the Gorilla Woman's left arm with her wig all askew and a red rose shedding petals down her bodice. ''E'll be dug up for certain. There ain't no grave deep enough to stop it. There'll be a price on 'im so 'igh that Rafferty Spune'll 'aul 'im up were 'e twelve foot down and under solid rock.'

Tom cleared his throat. *So why do the doctors want him, now that he's dead?'*

The Gorilla Woman began to moan; a low, pitiful sound that made Tom's skin crawl.

'Don't fret, Angel, don't fret,' begged Malachi Twist. 'For our friend here has a kindly heart, I'll vouch for that, and will help us if he can.' He turned back to Tom. ''Tis no life for a monster, sir, in this time and place,' he said. 'Death, you might think, comes to us as a blessing, for hasn't our Lord promised eternal life in Paradise to all good creatures, however foul of face or strange of limb?'

A tear rolled from his left eye. He caught it, deftly, with a flick of his tongue, before continuing: 'Alas, sir, we monsters are denied even that happy prospect. For when we die the doctors—those cold-hearted men of science—cannot wait to get their hands on us. If they can barter with our owners as we take a final gasp all the better for them. If we have friends to give us a Christian burial, why they send the likes of Rafferty Spune to tug us up like parsnips . . .'

Angel's moaning rose a tone and she began to rock backwards and forwards, clutching the Changeling Child to her bosom.

'Hush now,' Astra commanded. 'Ain't no one gonna hang *your* skellington up in their drawing room. Worst thing can 'appen to *you* is they'll stuff yer, and cart yer around Europe for a bit.'

Tom was beginning to feel queasy. *'Is that the kind of thing they do, then?'* he said. *'These doctors?'*

Malachi Twist started pacing the floor. The tatters of his jacket brushed dangerously close to the candle flames and the bones in his feet squeaked. He slicked one trembling hand over the sparse strands on his head, then twizzled to face Tom, his arms outstretched, his fingers clasped as if praying for mercy.

'Men of science have no pity, sir. They probe our strangeness with their scalpels; they boil our heads in their kettles; they display our very bones to the gawping masses.' He began to weep, noisily, tears rolling from his eyes and bouncing off the balls of his cheeks like tiny drops of quicksilver.

'Imagine, sir, if you can,' he sobbed, 'the bitterness of knowing that come the great Day of Judgement you will not rise, you *cannot* rise, to stand before your Maker as He Himself intended—whole in body and spirit. You cannot do it, sir; not if your skull has been left to moulder on a surgeon's mantelpiece, your lungs are in a jar, and your soul . . . ah, your soul . . . who can say where your soul has gone?'

Tom rummaged in the pocket of his jeans. He had a handkerchief somewhere. He found it, pulled it free, and passed it to Malachi Twist. The smallest tingle passed between them as Twist nipped the handkerchief from his grasp, taking care, even in his misery, not to touch this fellow-monster and cause him pain. 'I'm obliged,' he said and shambled back to the straw heap, blowing his nose as he went.

Seconds passed; the silence thick in Tom's ears. He knew he ought to say something—anything—to make these creatures feel less dismal. He was from the future, after all, and knew far more than they could ever imagine about all kinds of things. Death, though . . . that was a tricky one. And life after death—what could he tell them about *that*? He could talk to them for hours about the miracle of electricity; about aeroplanes and washing machines; CD Roms and astronauts. But he knew no more than anyone—how could he?—about what happens when people die. It was the one great mystery, he realized. The one big puzzle which no living person, however brilliant, had ever come close to unravelling. As for the religious stuff . . .

'I'm not . . . not sure about the Resurrection or . . . God and things,' he faltered.

Three pairs of eyes regarded him with pity. Twist shook his head. 'You're a savage, friend,' he said. 'We must forgive you your ignorance.'

It was like having a trio of particularly intense Jehovah's Witnesses in front of him. His mother would have invited them in, plied them with herbal tea, and bamboozled them with passages from *The Spiral Dance: A Rebirth of the Ancient Religion of the Great Goddess.* She did that to lots of people, but had yet to win over a Witness. Tom could always tell, from their faces, that Witnesses thought his mother was mad. Mad and bad and about as likely to get into Paradise as win the Lottery. He was always relieved when they gulped down their tea, so fast it burned their mouths, and left. And yet . . .

Malachi Twist looked a bit like a Witness; the same fervent expression on his face, the same sorrow in his eyes over Tom's pagan state. And Tom wondered, not for the first time, who was closest to the truth? His mother or the Christians? It was too big an issue for right now, though. He decided to change tack.

'Look,' he appealed to Angel and Astra, '*even if there is a Day of Judgement, I don't think you should worry too much about not being, you know, whole for it. Where I come from, lots of people are organ donors.*'

Angel blinked.

'Wotjer gabbin' on about?' snapped Astra.

'*I'm only saying,*' continued Tom, patiently, '*that in a while from now lots of people will actually want their kidneys, or hearts, or whatever, to go to science after they die. They'll be happy for doctors to take them out and put them into people whose own bits and bobs aren't working properly . . . It's like . . . like a gift. A gift of life, they call it. People give blood in my time too, a pint every few months, to help people who lose a lot in accidents and so on.*'

'How so, friend?' Twist's mouth gaped like an open purse. 'Do these unfortunates swallow the blood like ale? Or must they suck like a leech from the benefactor's veins?'

Astra jumped, suddenly, from the Gorilla Woman's knees, stamped both feet, and glared. 'Enough!' she commanded. 'This ain't helpin' the Giant.' She whirled to face Tom, her green eyes glittering. 'You!' she said. 'Tomorrer night. You gotta get yerself to The Fortune of War where Rafferty Spune and 'is rabble do carouse and get maudlin drunk regular. You gotta sneak in there and listen out, so we'll know the night and the hour set aside for nabbin' our Giant from the earth.'

'*You've got to be joking,*' said Tom. '*No offence, but you've got to be out of your tiny mind.*'

They stared, mutinously, at one another in the flickering candlelight while Malachi Twist sighed and dabbed his eyes and the Gorilla Woman slid her toothpick

66

carefully back into her muslin bag. Tom was the first to look away, uncomfortable with the intensity of this eye contact, however one-sided.

'I can't go out on the streets,' he muttered. *'How can I? I'm invisible, in case you hadn't noticed. People will take one look at my clothes, moving along by themselves, and there'll be a riot.'*

He looked back at Astra, saw amusement and exasperation written all over her painted face. It was clear what she was thinking; so clear that he blushed.

'Oh no . . . ' he said. *'No, no, no. I'm not stripping off. Not for anyone.'*

9

Tom expected the Changeling Child to argue; to stamp her foot again and call him a whey-faced dolt. But she said not a word, only licked her crimson lips and began to simper. He didn't like it. It made him feel uncomfortable.

'What?' he said. 'What? *Why are you looking at me like that?*'

She clicked her fingers, the sound barely louder than a pin dropping. Instantly Malachi Twist and Angel got to their feet, fell into line, and shuffled across to the hole in the basement wall. Angel climbed through first, without so much as a backward glance. Twist followed more slowly, wringing his hands and darting worried little looks back at the invisible savage upon whom so much depended.

'Be not ashamed, sir, to go naked,' he ventured. 'For wasn't Adam so, in the Garden of Eden, before sin entered the world? And if I offended thee by calling attention to your Godless state then I beg your pardon. Only take heart, sir, for no savage is beyond redemption. Why, the little black pigmy being shown at the White Horse in Fleet Street can recite Psalm 23, so I'm told, and takes a glass of ale in his hand like a true Christian. He also plays the harpsichord . . . '

'GO!' yelled Astra and Twist went, wriggling like an eel through the jagged opening in the wall and waggling his heels in a farewell salute.

Left alone, Astra picked her way to her strawstack,

hitched up her petticoats, and, wincing, sat herself carefully down. She hurt all over; wanted only to lose herself in sleep, to forget the day's procession of gentlemen with their stale breath and their extra shillings at the ready. But this silly monster needed winning over and she knew of only one way to do that.

'So . . . ' she said, spreading and smoothing her skirts. ''Ave you brought me some presents?' Her voice was as sweet as strawberry jam; her smile like a butterfly, pinned to her face.

She's *flirting* with me, thought Tom. *Yuck*. He bent down to pick up his carrier bags, uncertain, suddenly, about the things he had bought and what she would think of them. He wished she would stop smirking and preening herself in such a stupid way. It was ridiculous. It was spoiling everything.

He opened one of the bags and pulled out the first thing he touched. A packet of ham. Ten slices.

'Here you go,' he said, passing it across. *'It's food. You can eat it straightaway.'*

She pounced like a cat, snatching so quickly that he barely had time to wonder—too late, anyway— whether touching stuff from his side of the gap would hurt or horrify her as much as any contact over here did him.

He watched, anxiously, as she turned this gift over and over in her hands. It was all right, he decided. She wasn't traumatized—only fascinated by the pictures and words printed on the plastic wrapping.

'This ain't food,' she jeered. ''Tis some kind of book, only it don't open.' She slid to the floor, set the packet down in a pool of candlelight and crouched low on her heels to examine it in greater detail. 'Wot's it say?' she said, prodding at the label with fingernails as small and sharp as thorns. 'This bit 'ere?'

Tom, resigned to humouring her, knelt down beside the billow of her skirts and squinted at the packet of ham. He had to press his nose to it to make out the information on the label. The candle flame was a little too close for comfort. So was Astra. He read as quickly as he could, given the bad light and the small print:

'Ingredients: Pork (83 per cent), Water, Salt, Dextrose, Stabilizers (Disodium Diphosphate, Sodium Triphosphate, Sodium Polyphosphate), Antioxidant (Sodium Ascorbate), Preservative (Sodium Nitrate.)' He turned to Astra. *'It's meat,'* he said. *'Basically.'*

''Tis a spell straight from Satan's almanac,' she snapped back, her eyes wide and wary. 'And I ain't eatin' no devil words for all I'm 'alf starved.'

'Oh, for crying out loud . . . ' Irritated, Tom picked up the packet, ripped it open and pulled out one of the slices. *'Here,'* he said, waggling it in front of Astra's face. *'Meat. Take it.'* She cringed against the strawstack, wrinkling her nose.

'All right, then. Watch me . . . ' He sprang to his feet, tipped back his head and made the slice of ham disappear, bit by bit, into the portion of thin air that was his mouth. He chewed noisily, gulped theatrically, and patted his stomach. *'See?'* he said. *'Delicious.'*

Astra clapped her tiny hands and giggled. 'That's funny,' she said. 'Do it again.'

He ate another bit, gave a conjurer's bow and offered a third slice to her. This time she took it, wolfing it down so rapidly that he had to look away, shocked to discover that what, for him, had been a pretence of hunger was, for her, a genuine need. She was ravenous. He waited, politely, while she polished off the remaining seven slices.

'All right?' he asked, as she wiped her mouth on the lace frills around her wrists.

'Middling bad,' she said. 'Deal with such a butcher no more. Wot else y'got?'

Tom passed her the carrier bags, content to let her rummage. With luck, she would forget about the Giant now and he would be off the hook over the small matter of wandering around Smithfield stark naked to eavesdrop on a band of lowlifes in some dodgy tavern.

He watched, smiling secretly, as Astra unpacked her presents. First the candles, which she sniffed, rapturously, before thrusting them out of sight in the smelly depths of the strawstack. Then the soft bread rolls and the punnet of raspberries which she devoured in a trice. The can of air freshener puzzled her, until he showed her how to press the button that hissed invisible lemons.

The hair ribbon was of little interest. Gentlemen were forever giving her hair ribbons—silk ribbons, velvet ribbons, embroidered ribbons, and, once, a ribbon as fine as spider-thread trimmed with tiny pearls, the exact shape and size of her own missing teeth. No. She had enough hair ribbons tucked in her strawstack to plait a rope from here to Vauxhall Gardens and back again.

The tin of biscuits made her gasp.

'A picture,' she murmured, stroking the lid with fluttering fingers. 'You brought me a picture.' And she gazed and gazed at the cheap, mass-produced image of a sunlit forest as if she might somehow enter it.

Tom was surprised. He had filched the biscuits from the back of his grandmother's food cupboard. They were nearly past their use-by date, so he had assumed they would never be missed and that Astra might as well enjoy their sweetness, dunked and softened in a cup of milk. He had thought the trees on the lid, and the words '*A Present From The New Forest*' tacky. Still . . . there was no accounting for taste. And anyway, he had forgotten to bring any milk. She would have to dunk the biscuits in water—if she had any water. There was a rusty-looking jug over by the wall, but what it contained was anybody's guess.

'I didn't bring you a drink,' he said. *'Are you thirsty?'*

She wasn't listening. Her wig had fallen off and her own hair stuck out in patchy clumps, like a partially blown dandelion clock. Most of her lipstick had been wiped away and the flounces of her beautiful skirt were getting all crushed as she sat among breadcrumbs and plastic bags, feasting her eyes on the lid of the biscuit tin.

'Astra?'

She looked up then, her face so bleak and hopeless that something of the true horror of being trapped down here touched Tom for the first time. The trees on the lid. When had she last seen a real tree? Had she ever seen one? Did she know how it felt to breathe fresh, clean air . . . to run through grass . . . to be free? *Had she ever been free?*

Suddenly Astra stiffened, her pointy ears detecting a particular sound through the constant clatter and din outside. Leaping to her feet, she began shoving presents and bags and plastic wrappings into the straw.

'Quick!' she hissed over her shoulder. 'Go. Go now! You gotta go!'

Tom, too alarmed to ask why, bounded towards the gap, confident that it would be waiting; bubbling quietly in the dark.

It wasn't.

He jumped anyway, only to find himself flat up against the rags and splinters of the blocked-up window with all the candles still flickering and Astra down on her knees, clawing apart two big wodges of straw in a desperate attempt to completely conceal her picture.

Beyond the basement door: the dull thump of someone lurching down the stairs.

'Hide!' yelped Astra, appalled to see her monster-friend still dithering next to the very place through which 'Is Nibs was about to come blundering and raging, like a hog with its throat half slit. 'Hide yer stupid self if ye can't get out. Only do it now, for pity's sake, or 'e'll swing for the both of us and that's the truth.'

'Is Nibs. Drunk as a skunk. Eyes awash with pink pus. His pride as sore as his face. He would be in no mood for biscuits and a bit of a chat, Tom knew that much for sure.

Quickly, he turned to the only other means of escape he could think of—the hole in the wall leading through to the Black Raven. In the gloom he thought it was still there and began to move towards it, his legs dragging in slow motion, as if through an invisible river, as if in a horrible dream . . .

Oh no!

His sight had deceived him. The hole had been filled in; each brick retrieved and replaced, carefully and quietly, by the long arms of Malachi Twist while Astra was opening her presents.

In mounting panic, Tom scanned the room. Where to go? What to *do*?

With a crash and a curse, 'Is Nibs tumbled down the final few steps and began prodding around with a key, damning the door and the key and the step and the lock for slipping and sliding like instruments of Satan.

Tom's thoughts were jumping like nits. He was desperate now. The mirror. Could he hide behind the mirror? Prop it at an angle and wedge himself in against the wall? Oh, but it would hurt to touch those things. It would hurt . . . *Astra* . . . She was huddled on her strawstack. Curled tight. Mute. Maybe if he crouched low in a corner . . .

It came to him then. The only option left. The most obvious thing, really. Ripping his T-shirt up over his head, he sprinted across to the furthest, darkest, part of the room. Hopping and trembling, he kicked off his trainers and pulled off his socks.

Ouch! Ouch! Ouch! The floor . . . It was sticking like hot tar to his bare feet. *Nightmare. Nightmare. Should have realized* . . . He jumped on to his discarded T-shirt. Better. Much better.

His fingers were shaking so much he could barely undo his flies. The key was in the lock now. Turning. Down came the jeans. Off came his underpants. No time to hide these things, only to kick them into the corner with his socks and trainers as the door swung open and 'Is Nibs fell into the room.

For a moment or two the very air seemed to recoil from this intrusion, pressing hot against Tom's bare skin as 'Is Nibs found his feet. The candle flames dotted around the walls and floor continued to dance; their brave little lights looking suddenly provocative—just asking to be snuffed out.

Tom held himself very still. He felt like a statue. Nude boy on crumpled T-shirt. Nude boy about to piss himself with fear.

'Is Nibs lifted his head and sniffed the air. 'Whereareyer?' he bellowed. 'Don't think ye can hide from me. Make a sign, damn ye.'

Tom heard a faint rustling as Astra raised herself. He swallowed, carefully. His left buttock itched. Something— a flea, probably—must have bitten him. He hoped it was only one flea and that it hadn't decided to go walkabout around his bits and bobs.

'Is Nibs swayed. He held a candlestick, like Wee Willie Winkie, but there was nothing wee about the shadow he cast as he staggered a little further into the room. His face, above the candle's steady flame, was a mess. It reminded Tom of Hallowe'en; of badly-carved pumpkins and lumpy rubber masks. It made him think of the traitors' heads Declan had described with such relish . . . *Up on London Bridge they'd be, rotting like turnips . . .*

'A sign, I said, so I know it ain't just the rats I'm wastin' me breath on.'

Wearily Astra reached for her empty cup and knocked it, twice, against the basement wall.

'Right. That's better. That's a good creature.'

Tom risked a quiet scratch. *Not rats*, he thought, his toes curling. *Please not rats . . .* The very idea of rodents nibbling at his extremities made him catch his breath.

All at once he was hiccuping. Loudly. Uncontrollably.

'Wassat? Who's there?' 'Is Nibs turned and glared straight at him; his left hand raised in a fist. Tom got ready to duck. The man was so close to him now that he could smell the ale on his breath; observe his eyes, flashing vivid blue between the soreness; hear the sick, heavy wheezing in his chest. He wasn't a big person, not really. He was all swagger and stomach with pathetic bow legs beneath a ridiculous nightshirt and strands of greasy hair worming out from an even more ridiculous nightcap.

Across the room, Astra began banging her cup, loudly, insistently, against the wall. Distracted and confused, unable to see much of anything through the pink haze blurring his vision, 'Is Nibs stepped away from Tom and shook his still-raised fist in the direction of his creature.

'You ain't gettin' nothin', you hear me?' he shouted. 'Nothin' . . . nothin' at all.' His eyes began to water. He rubbed them, violently, with the knuckles of both hands, wishing death in a ditch upon the rogue who had doused him; and upon all from here to Pye Corner who had dared to laugh at his plight.

'Whereareyer?' he called above the drumming of the cup. 'I'm 'urt. I'm 'urt bad. Give us a kiss an' I'll fetch ye a scrap of mutton. Come 'ere now. Come on . . .'

The cup kept banging, only not so loud. Tom held his breath. His hiccups had stopped, thank goodness. Poor Astra, he thought. Who would ever want to kiss that piece of filth? Surely she wasn't going to? Surely he wouldn't make her? A sudden thought, a terrible thought, brought the blood rushing to his face. What if 'Is Nibs wanted more than just a kiss? What if he . . . ? No. It was too revolting to think about . . .

One more despairing little knock and Astra went quiet. Tom could just make out the shape of her, curled like a foetus on the straw. 'Is Nibs began inching towards her.

No, thought Tom. *Don't touch her. Don't hurt her. Don't go anywhere near her or I'll . . . I'll . . .*

Intuitively, without thinking or caring about the risk to his feet, his life, or anything else, he ran to the corner of the room . . . *ouch, ouch, ouch* . . . snatched up one of his training shoes and threw it.

'Have mercy!' shrieked 'Is Nibs as the shoe smacked against the side of his head, its lace whipping along his left cheek. ''Tis a rat! A rat straight out o' Hell's kitchen!'

He dropped his candlestick and blundered back across the room. In the doorway he stopped and turned, one hand clutching his face, the other pointing and jabbing towards the strawstack where Astra remained face down, quivering with relief.

'A pox on yer,' he spat. 'The rats can 'ave yer, and welcome. You ain't so special, not any more. There's a Geek eats live chickens over Ludgate Hill rakes in more shillings than you. You're spoiled fruit now, that's what y'are. And spoiled fruit ain't got no choice but to rot . . . '

A bang of the door, a rasping of the key in the lock, and he was gone.

10

Tom waited, needing a moment or two to gather his wits and recover from his sprint across the floor. The soles of his feet were tingling hot, but it had been worth it. He would do it again if he had to. After a while he noticed that the gap had reappeared.

Good.

He was tired now. Going back, he knew, was easier than crossing over. He didn't have to wait; could jump at any time. Astra hadn't moved. He would make sure she was all right, then he would leave.

'Astra? Are you OK?' He shuffled himself across the room, the T-shirt bunching beneath his toes. *'He's gone now, don't worry. I chucked my shoe at him and he panicked. He thought it was a rat, the plonker.'*

With an effort, the Changeling Child looked up, her face turning to the sound of his voice, like a flower towards the sun. Tom, realizing he was still naked, stopped abruptly and covered himself with his hands.

'I can't see yer,' whispered Astra. ''Ave ye gone?'

Reassured, Tom shuffled a little closer. Astra, sitting up now, watched the T-shirt slip-sliding towards her along the floor and smiled, wanly. 'See?' she said. ''Twasn't nuffink to get all prissy about, were it? Tomorrer night. The Fortune of War. Twist'll show ye the way . . . '

Tom spread the T-shirt flat with his toes and knelt clumsily down on it. She might not be able to see him, but all the same . . . he felt better with just the upper half of his body on show.

'Forget the Giant for a moment,' he said. *'Why did 'Is Nibs call you spoiled fruit? What did he mean?'*

She didn't answer straightaway, only scrunched herself smaller, like a poked sea anemone, in the red velvet folds of her dress. Her mouth began to tremble, but she held her head high.

'I ain't pure,' she said at last. 'That's what 'e meant. I ain't . . . pure . . . no more.'

Pure. Tom turned the word over in his mind, concentrating on the concise, sweet, sound of it.

Pure.

Untarnished.

Unspoilt.

A field of snow before people walk all over it. A glass of milk with no additives. He wanted to carry on thinking about safe, beautiful images, but it was no good.

I ain't . . . pure . . . no more.

The words hung between them, demanding recognition and understanding but meeting only silence. It wasn't that Tom was stupid, or slow on the uptake. It was just that the words were too loaded, their implications too shattering, for him to accept their full meaning.

He thought of a group of girls at home who, he knew, were no longer pure either. They were a sassy bunch and although he acted cool around them, they frightened him half to death. Matthew had bragged, fairly recently, about going with one of them in the long grass behind the scout hut. But Matthew had lied, for they scared him half to death too.

It was wrong, Tom knew, to compare Astra to those girls.

Only an extra shilling, sir, to touch this miracle of nature . . .

No. Astra didn't ask to be mauled around every afternoon by so-called gentlemen. She didn't take their shillings—'Is Nibs pocketed those, leaving her to earn

78

them. She didn't have a *choice*, so how come he felt so . . . so let down. Why was he so *angry* with her?

It gives great satisfaction, this creature of mine; great satisfaction . . .

His heart raced as he remembered how she had flirted with him earlier, trying to get her way with him over the Giant. What kind of a creep had she taken him for? Did she really think all men and boys were the same?

Spoiled fruit.

Used goods.

Tart.

Slut.

He wouldn't touch her with a ten-foot bargepole, even if he wanted to. Even if he dared.

'Say somethink, will yer?' she whispered. Her expression was no longer defiant. She looked vulnerable—and scared.

'I can't,' he replied, looking away towards the gap. *'I can't . . . '*

In the silence, before he moved away to gather up his clothes, and jump, he risked a quick glance at her face. Big mistake. She looked so lost; so tiny and sad that he felt terrible for judging her. Truly terrible. Still, he couldn't wait to get away; couldn't wait to put the gap and several centuries between them.

In his guilt and confusion, he had neither the heart nor the energy to wipe away the few tears that fell as he picked up his T-shirt. *What a pillock you are, Tom Cotterill,* he thought. *Always blubbing nowadays. Good job she can't see you. Good job she'll never know.*

And the Changeling Child's mouth fell open, in astonishment, as she watched each teardrop form; then hang luminous for a second in mid air before rolling unchecked along the invisible curves and planes of her monster's features.

'E's cryin', she thought, for *me*. 'E's cryin' for me . . . Ain't no one ever cried for me before, 'cept Angel, and she cries for all humanity . . .

As Tom moved away, preparing to jump, she reached deep into her strawstack until her hands struck tin. Too worn out to tug, she closed her eyes, leaving her fingertips to trace and draw comfort from the trees, the earth, and the sunlight on her picture.

'Tomorrer,' she croaked, her voice faltering as sleep pressed down on her. 'You'll come tomorrer won't yer? For the Giant's sake?'

No answer. He had gone.

* * *

And not far away, as the crow flies; in a room jutting like a peculiar growth from the side of St Bartholomew's Hospital, Dr Jeremiah Flint rubs the gore from his fingertips, sits down at his desk, and reaches for his journal.

It is ridiculously late. He stifles a yawn.

Across the room, a large green macaw, perched on the back of a chair, tilts its scabby head and opens its beak.

'Blister and purge!' it shrieks. 'Blister and purge!'

It is a tiresome bird, but a clever one. The students who pay ten guineas apiece to attend Dr Flint's lectures on basic anatomy bring it slices of fruit and handfuls of nutmeg, for its fluttering presence and sudden pronouncements provide light relief from the stomach-churning business of cutting up corpses.

Dr Flint is so tired that the quill pen between his fingers trembles and splutters. A scalpel would never have slipped. A scalpel, in Dr Flint's hand, is always as steady and precise as the point of a sundial.

Wearily, Dr Flint blots the page in front of him, and begins to write:

August 22nd, 1717: Did take delivery of a highwayman hanged yesterday at noon. A fine specimen, the muscles rounded but free from fat. Busy anatomizing with three students until first light. Must conclude dissection of the limbs with some haste for in this infernal heat the stench grows quite fearsome.

Outside, beyond the thick hospital walls, he hears the sound of a fight breaking out. Common men, he sniffs, driven wild by strong drink and the arrival of Bartholomew Fair.

The next few days will, he knows, be hell out there, as fire eaters and fortune tellers, rope dancers and puppeteers tout for business, and all manner of cripples and frauds go prancing around the taverns and coffee houses, masquerading as miracles of nature.

Dr Flint is nobody's fool. He can spot fakes a mile off. No silver-tongued showman will ever convince him that a talking centaur is anything more than a legless soldier attached to a stuffed decapitated horse. The real miracles of nature now . . . they are something else; rare as hens' teeth and a joy to behold.

He writes:

Am anxious for news of my next specimen.

It HAS to be a good one, he knows that. An extra-special specimen. None of your run-of-the-mill paupers or another woman dead from childbirth. Women dead from childbirth are two-a-penny round here. He's had three in a row and his students are bored.

No. The next specimen to land on Dr Flint's dissection table is going to have to be exceptional; something to amaze the students and send his own reputation, as a teacher of basic anatomy, rocketing sky high. A miracle of nature, that's what Dr Flint is hoping for. A corpse that his colleagues in the competitive world of medical science would give their right arms for.

Restless now, he flings down his pen and strides across the room to a small, square window overlooking Cock Lane and the Fortune of War Tavern. The crowds have thinned, now that day is breaking, yet the street, even at this hour, remains a thoroughfare for beggars, drunks, and women of ill-repute.

As he stands there watching, the door to the Fortune of War swings open and out steps a great hulk of a man. A man roughly dressed, yet as upright and arrogant as any Lord of the realm. Rafferty Spune. King of the sack-'em-up men. Grave-robber extraordinaire.

Dr Flint narrows his eyes and steps away from the window. He despises Spune for a low-bred oaf, yet cannot help but admire the tactics and low cunning which have earned the man a reputation as the best body-snatcher in the land. It is said there isn't a burial ground from here to Edinburgh that Spune, armed with crowbar, sack, and wooden shovel, cannot plunder successfully. It is said that, given a dark night, softish soil, and no interruptions, he does the job in less than twenty minutes. Dr Flint respects such professionalism. He himself can amputate the leg of a living man in three minutes flat. Speed is of the essence, it seems, to both the digger and the cutter. It is a small thing to have in common, but there it is . . .

The macaw skitters and bobs. Its claws catch, and tear, in the chair's tattered upholstery. Its beady eyes are fixed on Dr Flint's brooding back. 'Hey you!' it shrieks. 'Bring me the head of John the Baptist!'

Dr Flint allows himself a wry smile. It will take more than a head, even a famous head, to keep his career on track. Ideally, each of his students should work on two specimens to learn the structures of the body and a third to practise surgery. But once the highwayman is finished with there isn't so much as a sniff of another decent corpse. Not yet, anyway. Not yet . . .

He steps forward again and scans the street. Rafferty Spune, having lingered a minute in a doorway, with a woman of ill-repute, is striding away into the morning. Fie upon him, thinks Dr Flint. Look at him go, his step as steady as can be, for all his head's fuller of snuff than brains, and he's been tossing back rum as if it was water.

It riles Dr Flint, it riles him terribly, that Spune is making a pretty penny out of body-snatching. Rival surgeons are desperate for corpses to tinker with, for there is much to learn, still, about the workings of the human body. If there were enough hanged felons to go round, all would be well, but there aren't. Little wonder that Spune can charge by the inch for an ordinary specimen and name his own exorbitant price for something a little . . . what shall we say? . . . different . . .

A knock at the door.

Dr Flint wheels round to find his assistant, Johnny Moffat, already in the room, too excited to wait for the customary invitation to enter.

'Well?' snaps Dr Flint. He is annoyed at the lad for barging in, yet too impatient for news to take him to task. 'Come on, boy, spit it out. Is everything arranged?'

Johnny grins. He is well-pleased with his night's dealings in the Fortune of War. 'Aye,' he replies. ''Tis exactly as we hoped. The price and everything. The first specimen to be delivered to the usual place on Friday, late of the clock.'

'And the second?' Dr Flint's heart is beating faster. He hardly dares to hope. If he could shake a reply out of Johnny Moffat a split second sooner than he's going to get one, he would do it.

'Well, that's trickier. Irregular, you might say, but not impossible.'

'When then?'

'Friday night, if time allows. Saturday if not.'

'Good. Excellent.'

It is hard for Dr Flint to keep the glee out of his voice. He would like to grab Johnny Moffat and dance a jig around the room, but that would not be proper. Instead, he returns to the window and makes a show of checking the street.

Rafferty Spune has reached the corner. He is about to disappear down Hosier Lane, when he turns, suddenly, and looks back, straight up at the hospital. Dr Flint ducks out of sight, but not before Spune, the impudent wretch, has doffed his hat to him in an exaggerated display of servility. Grinding his teeth, Dr Flint returns to his desk and picks up his pen.

'Go away,' he tells Johnny Moffat. 'And remember: not a word to a living soul. If this gets out before time I'm ruined. And you . . . you're worm fodder.'

Johnny Moffat slips from the room. Dr Flint writes:

They are mine. I have them both. God-willing, I will dissect the two together, to the wonder and amazement of all who attend. I will charge each witness a guinea—a trifling price to pay for the most unique display of anatomizing ever performed in this institution.

He dips the quill in the inkwell. He will go home soon, to his house in Charterhouse Square. He will sleep like a babe, and dream of a statue, carved in his honour and erected here at St Bart's amidst a thicket of roses, their petals the purple of venous blood, their thorns as sharp as blades.

Quickly, he scratches a few more sentences:

Specimen 1. Grossly over-sized male. To arrive Friday. Rafferty Spune to deliver, the regular way.

Specimen 2. Grossly under-sized female. To arrive Saturday at the latest. Rafferty Spune to arrange collection and delivery, the irregular way.

'Blister and purge!' screeches the macaw. 'Spit it out! Spit it out! Not a word! Not a word! Or I'm ruined!'

One of these days, thinks Dr Flint, that bird will go too far.

He blots the page, closes the journal, and beams. They are his. A perfect couple of specimens. So different, yet so delightfully complementary. True miracles of nature—the Giant and the Changeling Child.

11

The Science Museum was bigger than Tom expected, and about ten times busier. He couldn't get near the flight simulator for the queues, and the first three floors were swarming with little kids, whingeing for sweets or the toilet. Dutifully, he trailed behind his mother as she toured the Secret Life of the Home exhibition, zooming in on ancient-looking paraffin heaters, and radiograms as bulky as baby dinosaurs.

'I *recognize* most of these things,' she laughed, darting around like a butterfly in her bright embroidered dress. 'I suppose that makes me a right old fossil. Look at that!' She pointed to a hairdryer attached to a length of hose with a plastic shower cap stuck on the opposite end. 'Your gran used to dry my hair with one of those. I'd sit there with the cap on feeling as if my scalp and my ears were about to ignite.'

Tom stifled a yawn. 'Why didn't you tell her it hurt?' he asked.

'I did try,' she said, 'but she never listened.'

In the section about cookers, Tom stared for a while at a model of an eighteenth-century spit being turned by a dog running round and round on a treadmill. It seemed to him a very long way from that spit to the end of the display, where a fibreglass chicken glowed red in a microwave.

Up on the fifth floor, there was hardly anybody about.

'That's better,' said Tom's mother. 'I couldn't hear myself think down there . . . ' She was walking purposefully towards The Science and Art of Medicine.

85

'What are you looking for?' asked Tom.

'Cancer,' she said. 'I can't see Cancer anywhere. Can you?'

Tom slowed right down, pretending to be distracted by Cardiac Pacemakers. 'Maybe it's not here,' he faltered.

His mother gave a harsh little laugh. 'What?' she said. 'The biggest challenge ever known to medicine? It had better be.' She looked round, spied an attendant and shouted across: 'Excuse me! Hello! Where's Cancer?'

Tom flinched. He should have stayed in the queue for the flight simulator. He should have stayed in the eighteenth century. He should never have left Dorset.

The attendant directed them to a far corner. 'Well,' said Tom's mother. 'It hardly jumps out at you, does it?'

Tom glanced, briefly, at the picture of a human lung, the cancer cells stained purple. He skimmed the bit of text that went with it, and shrugged. *140,000 people die each year* . . .

'No,' he said. 'It doesn't.'

They moved away, back to the place they needed to start at, to follow the development of science and medicine through the ages.

'Mum,' said Tom, after a while. 'I don't want a huge discussion or anything, but do you believe in life after death?'

His mother was contemplating a toothbrush which, according to the label, once belonged to Napoleon.

'I believe in life *before* death,' she replied, without turning round. 'In living it to the full, every hour of every day. Remember that.'

Napoleon's toothbrush was made of silver gilt and horsehair. It was amazing, thought Tom, that it had survived all this time without getting lost or broken.

He followed his mother into Childbirth in the

Eighteenth Century. 'You're going the wrong way,' he told her. 'You're going back in time, not forward.'

'So?' she said. 'Who cares?'

There was a strange-looking chair in this display, broad and squat, the wooden slats decorated with ornate images of Jesus on the cross.

'Weird,' mumbled Tom.

'It's a birthing chair,' said his mother. 'Women sat on it to deliver their babies. When the pain got really bad they were supposed to look at those pictures of the Crucifixion and remember that their suffering was nothing compared to Christ's.'

Tom took her arm. 'Mum,' he said, hesitantly. 'Do you ever worry that if there *is* a Heaven, you and I won't get into it?'

His mother swung round to look at him. Surprise, then sadness, then something brave flickered in her eyes. 'No,' she said, resting both her hands, gently, on his shoulders. 'I never worry about that. And nor must you.'

It wasn't enough. Tom frowned at the birthing chair. All those thorns . . .

'But there has to be something . . . ' he muttered. 'When you die. It can't just be nothing.' Tears prickled his eyelids. Mustn't cry, he thought, biting hard at his lower lip. Not *again*.

He felt his mother's hands clench; sensed her own struggle to keep her face from crumpling.

'Tom,' she said at last. 'Look at me.'

He looked.

'I don't intend to die just yet, if that's what you're worried about,' she said. 'Not for years. Do you believe me?'

He nodded.

'I'm going to be a loopy old lady who wears a T-shirt saying "You Go Girl", and wakes her grandchildren up at midnight to look at the moon. Right?'

87

He nodded again.

'Good.' She gave him a swift hug. Tom rested his chin on her shoulder. He would soon be taller than her. Off to his left, in the corner of his eye: a sudden movement behind glass, a flash of green dipping and disappearing like the wing of a bird.

'Let's get out of here,' said his mother. 'I need the loo.' She punched his arm, playfully, then blew her nose on a bit of old tissue.

Tom blinked. The flash of green, so bright and vivid, seemed indelibly fixed on his retinas.

'You go on,' he said. 'I just want to look at something.'

His mother touched his arm once more, lightly this time, then turned away.

Tom waited a minute. Then he went to the showcase where, he was certain, one of the exhibits had moved. There was a bird in there, all right, a parrot by the look of it, but it was clearly no more capable of flight than Napoleon's toothbrush.

He pressed his forehead against the glass. The bird was a fine specimen, considering how long ago it must have been stuffed and stuck on the back of that tatty old chair. It regarded him now, with peculiar glazed eyes, as he examined the things that went with it.

There was a big desk next to the chair, and on it a wax model of a female figure, its body divided into anatomical zones and regions. The muscles, diaphragm, and lungs were layered like a trifle. There were tabs you could lift, to expose the heart, the kidneys, and the uterus. It was a teaching doll, said the accompanying blurb. For dissection.

Beside the doll was a book, a great thick book lying open, with a thin strip of leather marking the place. The pages were yellow with age, the spidery writing faded to brown. It was hard to make out the words.

'Specimen 2 . . . ' Tom read, squinting at the strangely-formed letters. 'Grossly undersized . . . fe-something . . . '

The writing here was smudged. The third letter looked like an 'n', or maybe an 'm'. Femur. That was probably it. That made sense.

'Grossly undersized femur, to . . . arrive . . . Saturday . . . at the . . . latest. Rafferty Spune . . . '

Rafferty Spune! Tom felt a leaping in his ribcage as he recognized the name.

' . . . to . . . arrange . . . collision? No . . . collection . . . to arrange collection and . . . delivery . . . the . . . ir-something-or-other . . . the . . . irr-eg-u-lar way . . . '

Rafferty Spune to arrange collection and delivery the irregular way.

Well, there's a thing, mused Tom. One of my people is in the Science Museum! One of my people delivered a leg bone to whoever wrote this diary! He felt almost proud. If he ever clapped eyes on the infamous Rafferty Spune, if he decided, after all, to eavesdrop on the man, it would be as if they had already been introduced. He wondered what the irregular way meant . . . The irregular way of collection and delivery. It sounded dodgy.

He looked again at the bird. *No . . . Surely not?* It had crapped on the chair. There was bird poo on the chair. Fresh bird poo. A big gunky dollop of the stuff sliding down towards the seat. And the bird. The bird had moved. It was further along the chair back, he was certain it was.

Tom stared, hard, through the glass partition. The bird gazed fixedly back. Stuffed. Definitely stuffed. His mind, he decided, was playing tricks. The droppings were a special effect, that was all. Somebody's idea of a joke.

All of a sudden, he felt shivery. It was really freezing now, up on the fifth floor, and still nobody else around. He ought to go. His mother would be waiting for him. She would need a lie down this afternoon, and he could do with a kip himself.

His thoughts turned to Astra, down in the basement. Best not to dwell on her. Not even for a second. If he *did* decide to go to the Fortune of War tonight it wouldn't be on Astra's account. Not any more. It would be because he didn't want that bendy man thinking he was a coward as well as a savage. It would be because he was up for an adventure. It would be because, if there *was* a Heaven, doing a good deed, like saving the Giant, might give him more than a cat in hell's chance of eventually getting in. His mother would have to plead her own case. She'd be good at that. Whoever was on Pearly Gate duty when his mother arrived would probably wave her through just to shut her up.

Rubbing some warmth back into his arms, Tom turned towards the lift. He'd got as far as Leech Cages and Enema Syringes when he heard the piercing shriek.

'Hey, you!'

He spun round, the tiny hairs on the back of his neck tingling.

'Blister and purge. Blister and purge. You go girl!'

The call, so shrill and urgent, had come from overhead. He looked up. There. There it was. The bird. Wheeling in crazy emerald arcs across the ceiling.

'It's all arranged!' it shrieked, swooping low behind a display of tongue depressors, probes, and lancets. *'Irregular, but not impossible. Remember that! Remember that!'*

Tom opened his mouth, then closed it again and stumbled back. For the bird had appeared right in front of him. Just inches from his face. Hovering like a hawk on outstretched wings and crapping all over the floor.

Instinctively, Tom raised both arms.

'Friday night if time allows. Saturday if not. Remember that! Remember that! Let's get out of here!'

Droppings and feathers were flying everywhere now, as the bird flapped and flapped its wings, determined, it seemed, to stay in one place and fill Tom's head with squawk after squawk of nonsense. Tom kept his arms up over his eyes and his head lowered. He neither knew nor cared how a tropical bird had got into the museum. But it had clearly gone wild. It might go for his eyes.

'All right, mate?'

The sound of a human voice made Tom jump. He turned, dizzily, to find a museum assistant hovering at his elbow. It was the man who had shown his mother where Cancer was.

'I . . . I think so,' he replied. 'There's a bird loose up here. It gave me a fright.' He glanced up, warily. 'It's gone now. It must've seen you coming.'

The attendant seemed puzzled.

'A green bird,' Tom told him. 'It was in the case with the dissection doll and the book about Rafferty Spune.'

The attendant shook his head. 'Come on,' he said. 'Out.'

'It's true,' Tom persisted. 'It's flying around and crapping everywhere. Look!' He pointed down at the floor. Nothing. There was nothing there. 'That's strange,' he said. 'It was definitely here, and most definitely pooping.'

The assistant took him firmly by the upper arm. 'You're winding me up, mate,' he said, as he frog-marched him towards the exit. 'And I don't need it.' He jabbed the button beside the lift and waited for the doors to open, whistling testily between his teeth.

'Crazy kid,' he muttered, as the boy stepped into the lift and the doors slid shut on the disconcerting blue of his gaze. 'Crazy little tyke. I'll give him green birds . . . '

And he trod heavily away, in the general direction of Mind and Brain, completely oblivious to the bright green feather clinging, like a sprig of goosegrass, to the seat of his trousers.

12

Tom had been right about one thing. His mother was shattered after their morning out, and spent the rest of the day in her room. At five o'clock Tom tapped on her door with a glass of pink drink and a slice of banana bread.

'Come in, Tom-ato Paste,' she said. 'You don't need to knock.'

She was lying on top of a double bed in her hippy kaftan, flipping through a pile of interior design magazines. Her prosthesis was on the dressing table, next to her perfume bottle and peacock feather earrings.

'Thanks, love,' she said, as Tom placed the tray with the drink and the banana bread carefully down beside the magazines. 'I thought we'd decorate your bedroom when we get back. Make it more grown-up for you. What do you think?'

'Cool,' said Tom.

'I thought a really zingy orange would be good, with a black ceiling and a sort of gothic shelf for your CDs. Or would you prefer blue and white?'

'Blue and white,' said Tom. 'Definitely.'

She smiled.

'Not because of blue for a boy,' he added, seeing the smile, 'but because of the sea. I'd like a bedroom like the sea.'

He glanced around, looking for some memento in this room of his mother's own childhood—a doll, perhaps, or a pair of ballet slippers, dangling by their ribbons from a hook. There was nothing; nothing at all.

'Was this your room, when you were growing up?' he asked.

'Nope.' His mother slapped banana breadcrumbs off the duvet onto the floor. 'This is the spare. Mine was the little one along the corridor. The one overlooking the yard.'

Tom thought for a moment. Then: 'Can't I sleep in that room?' he said. 'I'm getting roasted to a frazzle in the attic. There's no air up there.'

His mother lay back against the pillows and closed her eyes. 'No,' she said. 'I don't think so. It . . . it hasn't got a very nice feel to it.'

'Why not?' said Tom. 'Did somebody snuff it in there?'

She smiled, weakly. 'No,' she said. 'Nobody snuffed it in there.'

'Well then . . . ' Tom's voice trailed away into a yawn. He couldn't be bothered to argue. It didn't seem important. 'I'm off out to the video shop,' he said. 'Do you want anything?'

'No thanks, love,' she replied. 'I'm going to read my book after supper and get a decent night's sleep. Will you be OK, staying up by yourself?'

'I'll be fine,' he said. 'I'll talk to Gran.'

His mother snorted. 'Well, good luck with *that*,' she said. 'I'd get at least three videos out if I were you, in case there's a lull in the conversation . . . '

10p.m.: Credits rolling silently on the TV screen. Apricot lamps glowing dim against the walls. Tom half asleep on the settee; the evening one big lull.

'I'm *so* sorry to abandon you, darling,' his gran had said, shortly after seven, 'but I always play bridge on Wednesdays.' A hoot of a taxi horn, a final swig of gin,

93

and she had gone, leaving Tom to clear the supper dishes and then to do as he pleased.

The video had been a disappointment. He had seen it before, round at Matthew's, and was cross with himself for having forgotten. He didn't usually forget things like that. He switched the television off and began prowling the sitting room, looking for distractions. His mother was asleep. He knew where he ought to be, but was biding his time. He would go when he was ready.

Beneath the far window stood a bureau, one of the old-fashioned kind with a front that pulled down to make a writing desk. It wasn't locked, so he opened it. *And why not*, he thought. He hadn't intended to pry. He was just bored. Clutter, that was all he could see anyway—dog-eared envelopes, boxes of notelets, and a load of old gas bills stuffed into little cubby holes.

Casually, he flipped through a wodge of Christmas cards. There was one from him. It had a scribble on the front that may or may not have been a robin and *'seesons greetings from yor grandsun Thomas'* printed inside in different coloured crayons. When had he done that then? He couldn't remember.

He put the cards back and began rummaging at the very back of the bureau, behind the notelets and the rest of the junk. Evidence; that's what he was looking for. A piece of his mother's childhood. Something to reassure him that her young life hadn't been half as gloomy or as boring as he'd been led to believe.

His fingers closed around a brown envelope, its edges sealed down with Sellotape. He tugged it towards him. It was just a plain old envelope. No name or address written on it; no labels. The tape was old and easy to pick off with his fingernails. Carefully he lifted the flap and pulled out three photographs.

The top one was of a child. His mother. She was sitting

on a swing, holding tight to the chains; her hair in two thick plaits, her skinny legs trailing from her shorts. The sun must have been in her eyes, for her laughter, frozen in time, looked more like a grimace. Two of her front teeth were missing. She must have been about six, thought Tom. The gappy age.

He turned quickly to the middle photograph. A studio portrait. Mother. Father. Daughter . . . Gran. Grandad. Mum . . . All dressed in their best against an artificial backdrop of trees . . . all smiling for the camera . . . Grandad's hands resting lightly on Mum's shoulders . . . only, someone had blacked out Grandad's face, scrawled all over it with a biro so that his head looked like a panscrub. Tom frowned. This wasn't a child's scribble, done carelessly and without malice. Someone had de-faced Grandad deliberately, pressing so hard with the pen that the point had gone through his left eye.

It seemed a terrible thing to do to a man who had died of some blood thing before he was very old. Who had done it? Tom wondered. His mum, or his gran? And why?

The third photograph was instantly recognizable. Tom smiled, a little self-consciously, at his own nine-year-old face. It was like checking out a younger brother. His cheeks had been pudgier then; his hair shorter and in no particular style. Cute, though, he thought: *a cute little mannikin*. His eyes hadn't changed, that was certain. People—women mostly—had been cooing over his eyes for as long as he could remember. Embarrassing, really. He wondered, suddenly, whether Astra would think he had nice eyes, but blocked *that* thought straightaway.

Frowning, he shoved all three photographs back, and banged the Sellotape back down with his fist.

Right, he thought, slamming the bureau shut, Twist will be wondering where I've got to. Time to go . . .

* * *

95

The gap, to Tom's surprise, was waiting for him this time, bubbling across the basement floor like the tributary of some turbulent brook, and sending little spurts of phosphorescence up into the dark. Quickly, he went to the edge and peered down.

The shapes were moving at high speed tonight, linked tight in a fluid chain with just a moment or two each to change, speak, and move on. The first one was huge and squelched, impolitely, as it became a woman of such vast proportions that her body looked fit to burst from its great marquee of a dress.

'Hurry up,' she called. The flesh of her upper arms wobbled like blancmange as she beckoned Tom closer. *'Hurry up, lad. They need you . . . '*

Before Tom could respond she had disappeared, chivvied gently along the gap by a couple of dwarfs, identically dressed in leather knee breeches, buckled shoes, and little green jackets. One of them turned a somersault, splashing Tom's trainers with a shower of sparks. *'Oh fee, fie, fo, and fum,'* squealed his companion. *'Ye be as clumsy as a loaded wagon and as giddy as a maid . . . '*

A clatter of hooves and the dwarfs dissolved, making way for the oddest looking creature Tom had seen so far. A creature with the head, arms, and torso of a man but the lower body and legs of a horse. A creature that reared delicately to a halt and fixed Tom with a gaze so melancholy, yet so wise, that Tom fell to his knees, bending close to the gap to hear what it had to say. A centaur, he thought to himself. A real live centaur . . .

The creature sidestepped to the right, driven on by the flow. 'What?' prompted Tom. 'What is it you want to tell me?' Too late. The image of the cantering man was gone; and now here was Astra, drifting along like waterweed, her face a luminous disc, drained of all its courage.

'*Are ye there?*' she whispered. '*Are ye there, monster . . . and will ye cross?*'

'Yeah, yeah,' grumbled Tom, staggering to his feet. 'I'm on my way. Don't nag me.'

He jumped clumsily, landed awkwardly, and cursed.

'Upsy-daisy, friend.' Malachi Twist came to meet him, flapping like a scarecrow in the gloom. 'No bones broken, I trust?'

Tom righted himself. '*I'm fine,*' he growled. '*Let's go if we're going.*' He unbuttoned his shirt, pulled it over his head and threw it over Astra's mirror. Then he kicked both training shoes into a far corner. His jeans went the way of his shirt, the fly button striking the mirror with a sharp twang.

'Oh my!' Twist wrapped his arms twice around his own body to give himself a pat on the back. 'Didn't I say this monster would come good in the end? Didn't I say to Angel this very morning, ''Have faith, fellow-sufferer, for just as fine wine may lodge in a shoddy flask, so, I'll wager, does a brave heart beat beneath that savage's missing breastbone . . . '' ' He leapt high into the air, his coat tails swirling, his knee joints creaking like door hinges. 'Didn't I say—'

'*Mind out,*' ordered Tom, flinging his pants across the room.

'Wait! Just a jiffy.' Astra had slipped from her strawstack and was tottering towards the gap, clutching something against the front of her shift. She staggered a little as she walked. Tom's heart went out to her for a second, then hardened again. He bent down and began easing off one of his socks.

'Don't . . . don't 'urt yerself. Put these on. For walkin' in.'

Tom looked up. There she was, an arm's length away, holding out a couple of clear plastic bags—the ones he had brought her the fruit and bread rolls in.

'Your sacks,' she said, in a small, hopeful voice. 'You can stick 'em over yer feet and tie 'em on wiv bits of twine. Ain't nobody goin' to notice a couple o' nips of twine trailin' around. Not in the Fortune of War anyway. Ain't nobody sees much in *there* beyond the bottom of a blessed tankard.'

Tom considered the plastic bags and the bits of hairy string trailing from the Changeling Child's outstretched fingers.

'Thank you,' he said, stiffly. *'But I've already thought of that.'*

He reached into the pocket of his jeans and pulled out the rough and ready slippers he had made, in his gran's kitchen, out of freezer bags, clingfilm, and elastic bands. He'd had the sense to bring a pair of transparent plastic gloves too—the kind that came free with packets of hair dye.

His mother, before she got ill, had started dying her hair bright red, to cover the first traces of grey. 'My roots are showing!' she would grumble before colonizing the bathroom to emerge, an hour later, with flowing copper locks and a satisfied face. Tom would find the gloves she had used all scrunched up in the sink dripping red gunk down the plughole. 'Mum!' he would yell. 'It's like someone's been stabbed in here. You've sloshed it all over the tiles *again* . . . '

In the chemist's Tom had bought, without thinking, the exact brand and colour of hair stuff his mother used to use. The gloves were just the job for protecting his hands, but the supply of Cherry Auburn was no good to him, and a fat lot of use to a woman with stubble.

He had hovered over a litter bin, the small bottle of dye warm in his hand. *Give me six months then call me Rapunzel.* Tossing that bottle in among apple cores, empty fag packets, and old tube tickets had made him feel terrible, as if he had slapped his mother's face or—worse—somehow triggered another tumour. Less than ten paces away he had spun around and gone back. The hair dye was in his sponge bag now, and his mind felt easier.

'*Right!*' he said, flexing his toes in their plastic bags. '*I'm ready.*'

With an audible 'ping' one of the elastic bands round his ankles snapped. *Cack*. It was one of several, but what if the others went the same way? Astra had left the lengths of string beside him on the floor. Quickly, grudgingly, he picked them up and tied them on.

Astra had returned to her strawstack. She said not a word as Malachi Twist went capering across to the hole in the wall, beckoning Tom to follow.

Tom kept his eyes on Twist's coat-tails as he ducked his head beneath the jagged arch of bricks, and left his gran's basement for whatever lay beyond.

He refused to look back at Astra, and he did not say goodbye.

13

The buzz Tom had felt, at the thought of going properly into the past, lasted about as long as it took him to follow Malachi Twist through the Black Raven's inky cellar and on to the rough flight of steps leading up towards the light.

Each step was slimier than a rock at low tide. His plastic slippers seemed suddenly about as durable, and sensible, as a paper parasol in a downpour. *What if they get torn?* he thought. *What if they fall off?*

It was pitch dark on the steps. Pitch dark and foul-smelling. Tom, dragging his plastic-wrapped feet, was in no great hurry, now, to be a hero. His nakedness worried him. A lot. Every bit of his skin shrank from the touch of nothing more than the air around him. Really, he thought, he should have cling-filmed his willy. He had never felt so vulnerable in his life.

'All right, friend?' Twist paused on the top step, outside the squat, heavy door that led through to the main bar.

Tom bent to feel the elastic bands around his ankles. They were bitingly tight. His slippers were secure.

'All right,' he whispered back.

Beyond the door: the noise of men's laughter, great rough gales of it, interrupted by girlish shrieks and what sounded to Tom like a lot of spitting.

'I will clear us a path,' murmured Twist. 'Only, first you must give me your hand.'

Slowly, reluctantly, Tom lifted his right hand in its clammy plastic glove. Nodding encouragement, Twist waited, his fingers outstretched, his facial tic slowed by sheer willpower to a gentle tremor.

'Have faith, friend,' he murmured. 'Take my hand, for all a herring's membrane has a better clinch, and let me lead you. For I dread what might happen if I lose thee among the rabble.'

Holding his breath, Tom clasped the outstretched fingers.

It was OK. No pain. No nasty shocks. Just a certain amount of difficulty hanging on; for Twist's fingers were certainly odd—odd in a boneless flabby way, like plasticine snakes which, with too firm a squeeze, might squelch out in all directions.

'I hope I don't . . . ' Tom began. He was cut short, the words catching in his throat as Twist kicked open the door and went bounding across a room so thick with pipe smoke that Tom believed, for one panic-stricken second, that the place was on fire.

'Yee-ha!' whooped Twist, one mad arm whirling, the other yanking Tom along. 'Make way, gentlemen. Make way for the Bendy Man!'

Tom, his heart pounding, his vision distorted by sweat and fear, saw only a blur of red faces as he trotted and skidded along in Twist's wake. One of the faces loomed closer. A hand shot out, waving a tankard.

''Ere!' called a man's voice. 'A mug of ale to moisten the monster's droughty carcass!' Something slopped. Tom twisted sideways, narrowly avoiding a spill of ale which, he knew, would have eaten into his flesh like acid.

'Forgive me, sir,' piped Twist, pushing at the door which led out to the street. 'But this poor monster's innards are messier than a slut's cupboard, and looser than a gossip's tongue. Ale—even a thimbleful—plays havoc with 'em.'

101

He held open the door, let go of Tom's hand and flapped his fingers to let Tom know that he should go on ahead. 'Wait for me,' he murmured. 'Wait for me, friend.'

The man who had proffered the ale was looking thunderous. He had expected Twist to be grateful for a sup of something stronger than river water or rancid gruel. A monster at Bartholomew Fair was supposed to stop a while when noticed, and put on a bit of a show—not shoot through like some la-di-da Lord of the Manor. Twist knew this too; had known it since he was little more than a gangling baby boy, tying his little legs into double knots to earn a living for his keeper. There would be trouble here, in the Black Raven, unless he appeased his audience.

The door swung shut. Tom, finding himself alone outside, opened his mouth to protest. He didn't understand. What was Twist up to? He wasn't stopping for a quick pint after all, was he? The crazy loon was jittery enough sober. Half cut, he would be a serious liability. And anyway, there wasn't time.

'Twist!' he yelled. *'Come on. We've got to hurry.'*

A woman, passing dangerously close, glanced up, startled. She had a weird face—small, yellowish, and not quite right. She paused for a second, then hurried on. Tom bit his lip. It had been stupid of him to call attention to himself. He wouldn't do it again.

Breathing as carefully as a man on the moon, he shuffled forward a little, the better to see his grandmother's house. It looked strange; like a person you only vaguely recognize when you ought to know them well. He stumbled a little on the slippery cobbles. Careful. He would have to be very careful out here.

More people—two men and a woman—hurried past in a gust of chronic body odour. One of the men carried a kind of shepherd's crook with a lantern swinging from it.

The other was waving a bottle around and singing a song about bidding farewell to a bonny lass. Tom watched them go. There were no street lights to see by, yet the night sky had its own peculiar radiance. Of course, thought Tom, the tower blocks are missing. Everything's more open when you look up. Less . . . filled in.

But it wasn't just that. The sky, with its swathes of stars and waning moon, was brighter and closer than Tom ever remembered seeing it. There had to be millions of stars up there. Trillions. All glittering away like . . . like . . .

'Yee-ha! Here I come! Make way for the Bendy Man!' The Black Raven's door flew open, and out tumbled Malachi Twist.

'I'm over here,' said Tom, sternly. *'And you'd better not be drunk.'*

Twist shook himself upright and held out his fingers. ''Tis mere affectation, my friend,' he replied. 'A necessary act. And now—I must convey thee to the Fortune of War before Rafferty Spune concludes his night's business. Come!'

Stepping gingerly across the cobbles, Tom took Twist's hand and they were off, capering down a dark, stinking alleyway towards the clamour of Bartholomew Fair. A few steps in, the alley grew so narrow that Tom's naked shoulders came close to skimming parallel lines along its dank green walls. There were things underfoot that he was glad he couldn't see. He thought of rats, and clutched Twist's fingers as tightly as he dared. The slice of light, laughter, and music up ahead grew closer, brighter, louder . . . Then they were out there, running through it all, and Tom would have bartered the bags on his feet to be back in the relative comfort and security of the alley.

'Buy a mousetrap! A mousetrap! What lack you, sir? Little doggies for your daughters? A fiddle for your son . . . ?'

'Strawberries! Ripe strawberries!'

'Step smartly, good people! This way for the finest bottled ale at the Fair . . . '

'Gentlewomen, what do you lack? A velvet cap? A fine singing bird . . . ?'

Mind my toes, thought Tom. *Don't jostle me. Don't tread on me. Don't drench me in beer or clout me with a bone.*

Nearly everyone they passed, it seemed, was swigging from a bottle, or eating a great chunk of meat. The smell of roast pork was thick in the air; so thick that Tom could taste it. So many people . . . So many dirty, jostling, greasy-faced people . . . He would never get through this lot unscathed . . . Someone was bound to bump into him . . . bound to send him flying, his skin blistering from the impact . . .

All at once he noticed a group of men pointing in his direction, pointing, and laughing, and slapping their thighs. Could they *see* him? Was he visible after all, trotting stark naked across the cobbles, his wobbly bits wobbling, his legs bandy with fear?

But no . . . He heard shouts of 'Look! There goes the Bendy Man!' and 'There he is! There's the monster what can wrap hisself round a pole like a snake!' And he felt the tug and pull through his plastic gloves as Twist bowed and scraped to his audience, his free hand waggling, cheekily, towards women's chests and men's pockets.

'Oh! Oh!' shrieked the women, jumping away. 'Har-har!' laughed the men, slapping their thighs all the harder, but taking a few steps backwards themselves. No man among them wanted his purse lifted by those abnormal, probing fingers. Not for half a second. Not even in jest.

Then: 'Here we be,' announced Twist, skidding to a halt outside a rough-looking ale house. 'In ye go, friend.'

Tom gulped. *'You're coming with me, aren't you?'* he said. *'I can't go in there by myself. I . . . I don't know what Rafferty Spune looks like.'*

Twist turned to face his audience. Slowly, solemnly, he began fashioning his limbs into different shapes. A heart. A lover's knot. A bow and arrow.

'Spune will be the one holding court,' he whispered, swivelling his head at a fantastic angle, in the direction of Tom's voice. 'His minions cluster round him like flies around dung. Ye cannot mistake the man.'

Tom stood his ground. *'Come with me,'* he said. *'Please. Just until I get my bearings.'*

Malachi Twist sighed. A woman in the crowd threw him a flower. He caught it, deftly, between his toes. The crowd cheered. 'No,' he told Tom. ''Twould be the cause of much suspicion. Spune would clam up like an oyster.' Carefully, he brought the flower close to his face and made an exaggerated show of smelling it. Then, in one quick movement, he sniffed the whole thing up his left nostril.

The crowd shrieked with delight.

'Right,' said Tom, trying to sound indifferent. *'I'll see you later then.'*

A snort, a sneeze, and a shower of petals erupted from both barrels of Twist's nose. Bowing low to the howl of applause, he peered back between his knees. 'Have courage, friend,' he urged. 'Remember. God is with you.'

Tom did not hear him. He was in the Fortune of War, his eyes adjusting to the gloom. Rafferty Spune—where was he? The place was rough all right—real spit and sawdust on the floor, a few enormous barrels for tables, a couple of tapers providing barely enough light to see by. The ceiling was low, the walls the colour of moist earth. Not crowded though. That was good. Just a huddle of men around a barrel, a one-legged soldier in a stupor against the wall, and a couple of women in bright, ragged dresses, serving ale.

Rafferty Spune—who was he?

Tom scanned the faces of the men in the room, looking for qualities of leadership. Each face, partially obscured by hair, or a dark three-cornered hat, bore at least one scar, or a nose bashed out of kilter by a sailor's fist. They were as mean as meat axes, the whole lot of them, but not remarkable. There was no one here, so far as Tom could see, who was being clustered round, like dung.

So, what now? Should he report back to Twist? Or wait and see? His legs ached. It was torture not being able to sit down. He daren't even lean against a wall, like the one-legged soldier. Amazingly, though, the soles of his feet seemed in pretty good shape. In fact, he could hardly feel them. Worried, suddenly, that the elastic bands around his ankles were cutting off his circulation, he bent down to ease them a little.

The brush of someone's clothing against his bare bottom caught him, horribly, by surprise. Stifling a yelp he straightened up and spun round. Someone had come in—and so quietly that no one, least of all Tom, had so much as noticed the door open.

Spune. Rafferty Spune, moving in a sure, straight, line across the room, his coat as soft and black as moleskin, his boots encrusted with the soil of a young girl's grave.

Tom rubbed his buttocks, sickened, as well as hurt. The atmosphere in the tavern had altered with the arrival of this man. It was all charged up, like the air outside Gran's the other night, before the storm broke. He watched the women's faces brighten, listened as a group of thugs in the furthest corner murmured a respectful greeting.

'What, no copper clinking?' called the newcomer. 'All hearers and no buyers? Come, Molly—a jug of ale, if you please. And Ned—'tis as gloomy as a monarch's crypt in here, for all the Fair's in full swing. A song, my lads, a song!'

The woman called Molly ran, pink-faced, to fetch more drinks. The one-legged soldier produced a fiddle and all the villains in the room cleared their throats, like a chorus of bullfrogs.

Tom, hanging back beside the door, still feeling as if he had sat on a wasps' nest, gazed, with grudging admiration, at the one who had walked into this place and, within seconds, got everyone dancing to his tune. This was Rafferty Spune all right. No doubt about it.

> Good people give ear,
> Whilst a story I tell,
> Of twenty black tradesmen,
> Were brought up in hell.

The soldier's voice was high-pitched, like a woman's, and he kept his eyes tight-closed while he sang. The chorus crashed in, with every man present, except Rafferty Spune, roaring out the words:

> Mark you well,
> Hark you well,
> See where they're rubbed,
> Up to the gallows,
> And that's where they're nubbed.

At a nod from Rafferty Spune, Molly began a hip-swaying tour of the tavern, filling tankard after tankard to the brim. Three people weren't drinking—a ginger-haired man built like a shed, a weaselly-looking character with sores on his face, and Spune himself. Tom watched this trio carefully. They weren't standing together. They weren't doing much of anything until, without a look or a word to anyone else, they detached themselves from the merriment and disappeared into a back room.

107

14

Quickly, Tom darted across the tavern, dodging a man dancing a hornpipe and narrowly avoiding a poke in the eye from the fiddler's leaping bow. Luckily for him there was no heavy door to push open, just a low, narrow opening in the far wall which he slipped through like a phantom.

The place he found himself in was a store room, small and fusty, without so much as a grating to let in light or air. Barrels, piled one on top of the other, were leaking, darkly, onto the earthen floor. In the gloom they looked like boulders in danger of toppling. Spune and his cronies were gathered round one of the bigger ones, their faces rancid above the glow of a lantern.

The ginger-haired crony was rubbing his hands together. ''Tis well contrived,' he was saying, 'well contrived . . .' His hands were the size of shovels. Tom heard his knuckles crack, and winced.

Rafferty Spune fixed the ginger man with a look that would have silenced Parliament. 'Keep gloating like that,' he said, quietly, 'and I'll have ye by the throttle. There'll be time enough for gloating on the Sabbath; once both specimens are up on Flint's table being carved up finer than geese at Christmas.'

The ginger man shuffled his feet, and looked contrite. 'Name the time,' he said. 'And the place.'

Tom tiptoed forward, holding his breath.

'Dark night,' said Spune. 'Twelve of the clock at St Andrew's.'

Dark night? thought Tom. *When's dark night? What DAY?*

''Twill be a heavy job,' mused the ginger man, 'the specimen being such a big 'un, as it were.'

'Eight foot tall, I believe,' replied Spune. 'With hands that could cradle a hog. But he ain't buried any deeper than usual, so 'tis a regular task so far as you're concerned. There's no extra brass in it, so don't expect none.'

The skinny man with the spotty face licked his lips. 'The Fairy Child,' he whined. ''Oo's takin' care of that? I ain't keen on no brawl wiv its keeper. Not at any price.'

Tom frowned. *What? What was this?* A bad feeling took hold of him, a premonition of something far worse afoot here than the trading of dead bodies.

Spune, smiling dangerously, clapped an arm round the skinny man's shoulders and yanked him close in a tight embrace.

'Now then,' he murmured into the filthy crevices of the man's left ear. 'How long is it, Mattie Ladd, since I took thee off the streets and into the trade?'

'Five moons,' came the muffled reply. 'And a bit.'

'So when will ye learn, Mattie, that in this business we leave nothing to chance? Hmmm?'

The man, Mattie Ladd, said something inaudible against the cloth of Spune's shoulder.

'No loose ends,' continued Spune, hypnotically. 'Everything planned. Every step and stage to run as precise as a clock's innards . . . ?'

'Yep,' squeaked Mattie. 'Thassit. Course it is.'

'Well then!' Spune flung both arms out so hard that Mattie went reeling, painfully, against a pile of empty barrels. 'Well then, muck-worm, spare me an earful of your ignorance! The keeper is prepared. The keeper wants rid of his Fairy Child and for the clinking of a few coins will swear that it choked on a fish bone. Does that calm ye somewhat? Does that lessen the fear in yer cowardly gut?'

Struggling to his feet, Mattie swore that it did. Indeed it did.

The ginger man cleared his throat. 'This second specimen,' he said. 'This Fairy Child. Want me to see to it? After we've bagged the big 'un?'

Spune brushed down the front of his coat.

'No need,' he replied, his lip curling as he picked something off his collar and squashed it between finger and thumb. 'No offence, my friend, but this ain't one of yer run-of-the-mill specimens, to be dispatched in a shower of blows. The good doctor wants this one unmarked.' He adjusted his cuffs, picked up his hat, and made ready to leave. 'I shall deal with it myself,' he added softly. 'But one of you will sack it up and make the delivery. The house next door to the Black Raven. Be there before first light, and look for the sign. A red ribbon on the railing so ye'll know the deed is done. Are we clear?'

'Aye,' said the ginger man.

'Aye,' squeaked Mattie Ladd.

'Then come—let's drink on it.'

Picking their hats from the barrel in front of them, the men turned to leave. Tom forced his legs to move, to get him out of the store room and back into the bar ahead of these murdering . . . evil . . . He could hardly believe what he had just heard, could barely breathe for the horror of it. *The Fairy Child . . . Astra . . . They were going to kill Astra . . . Kill her and sell her body. For dissection.*

He remembered the doll at the Science Museum, its waxy body marked and labelled like a slab of meat. He remembered the words in the journal: *grossly undersized fe- something to be delivered Saturday at the latest . . .* Not 'femur', as he had thought himself so clever to work out, but *female*. And not any old female either, but Astra.

They were going to kill Astra.

110

For one awful second Tom thought he might throw up. Mercifully, the moment passed, leaving him only a little curious as to whether the contents of his stomach would have been visible on the floor.

The Fortune of War was crowded now, with folk drawn in by the sounds of fiddle playing and wild laughter. Taking a deep breath, Tom started to move, weaving carefully past the prod of an elbow here, the swirl of a petticoat there, until he had the tavern door in his sights. Behind him, Rafferty Spune, keen to cavort now that business was sorted, seized the lovely Molly round the waist and spun her round. 'More ale!' he called. 'And a bucket of oysters!' And he lifted the black, three-cornered hat from his head and tossed it, carelessly, across the room.

Tom, his eyes fixed on the tavern door . . . his mind set on getting back across Smithfield . . . back as fast as his numb, cling-filmed feet would carry him, to warn Astra . . . to get her out of the basement . . . Tom did not notice the hat spinning merrily through the air. He only felt it land, like a jackdaw, on his head, where it stuck fast and began to tickle and itch at his scalp, as if a thousand tiny spiders were escaping from the brim.

'*Nyaaagh!*' he yelled, beating with both hands at whatever demon had roosted so unexpectedly, and so horribly, in his hair.

'Oooooh,' moaned the scoundrels, the pickpockets, the women, and the fiddle player, scrambling in terror from the sight and sound of Rafferty Spune's hat careering round in circles, more than five feet off the ground, and wailing worse than a ghoul around a plague pit.

Rafferty Spune stood still as stone.

''Tis a curse!' yelped Mattie Ladd, whipping off his own hat and wedging it, tight, beneath his left armpit. 'A curse on all grave-rob—'

111

Whoomp.

A single blow from Spune's left fist sent him crashing, with a bloody nose, flat on his back.

'Off! Off! Can't . . . get . . . this . . . thing . . . off . . . '
The hat was twisting itself into all kinds of shapes as Tom, using all his strength and both his hands, struggled to dislodge it.

Mouths gasped and boots jostled. Mattie Ladd raised himself up, spitting red froth. The brave and the foolhardy began edging forward.

'Sounds like there be someone under there,' declared the one-legged soldier. And he leaned forward, to prod the air beneath the hat with his fiddler's bow.

'Get away! Stay away from me!' Tom, made reckless by relentless itching, lashed out with his feet and snapped the bow in half.

'Whoooaaah!' Everyone reared back. They looked at the bow, lying in two pieces on the ground, then back at the hat, contorting in mid-air, then over at Rafferty Spune, still standing there, as calm as you like, while a piece of his clothing whirled around and around, like a thing possessed.

A curse. It might easily be a curse. Some gibbering spirit come to carry the grave-robber's hat off to Hell. To carry it off in front of witnesses, so all who watched would be left in no doubt as to where the souls of Rafferty Spune, and all other sinners, were bound. Every woman who had ever swooned over a highwayman, fallen for a swindler, or wished for a kiss from Rafferty Spune made a silent promise to say her prayers from now on. To pray fervently every night. And to make do with a nice steady clerk for a sweetheart. Or a shoemaker.

Every man present thanked his lucky stars that his own hat was clamped safe over his own two ears.

Spune, who could never bear to fall, even a little, in

people's estimation, scowled and spat contemptuously. ''Tis a trick!' he shouted, surveying the swell of onlookers through narrowed eyes. 'A hoax done with mirrors by some arch rogue from the Fair. A plot to scare honest folk.'

Everyone shifted, doubtfully. Then: 'He's right,' squealed one of the women, pointing down. 'See . . . See that bit of twine there. A bit of twine movin' around. That ain't come from beyond no grave. There's someone out there pullin' on that, I reckon . . . '

'Right!' roared Spune, producing a truncheon from beneath his coat, and brandishing it so vigorously that Mattie Ladd, swaying around beside him, almost got a black eye to match his bloodied nose. 'Right, my lads. Let's trounce the rogue. After him!'

With one almighty yell, the scoundrels, the pickpockets, the women, and the fiddle player surged forward, stamping the ground in a bid to trap the pieces of string flailing around Tom's ankles. At the same instant, Tom made a lunge for the tavern door.

No time to look for Malachi Twist. No time to think about anything except saving his own invisible skin as he stumbled into the street with the mob hard at his heels.

'The hat!' someone shouted. 'There it goes! Over there!' And the mob was after him, baying for blood, as he ran, faster than he had ever done in his life, in what he hoped was the general direction of the Black Raven. His plastic slippers, already puckered, filthy, and torn in several places, flapped alarmingly. His toes would be through, any second, he just knew it, and then what would he do?

'Stop the hat! Grab the hat!' bellowed Spune.

'Out of the way! Out of the way!' panted Tom. He jumped, clumsily, over a beggar sprawled on the cobbles, and veered left into a street crammed with booths, sideshows, and the dark, swinging shapes of shop signs. It was

crowded in this part of the city; too crowded for comfort, for all the sight of a hat zooming along all by itself had so far cleared a path just as effectively as Twist's antics had done. Scared of being bumped, driven almost wild by the itching on his head, Tom lifted the awning of the first booth he came to, and slipped inside.

It was hot in the booth, hot and strange and smelly, but Tom didn't care so long as he had shaken off Spune and his rabble. It took a minute or two for the trembling in his legs to subside, and slightly longer than that for him to be certain that no one had seen him come in, that no one was going to come bursting through the awning of this booth to clobber him with truncheons, or to hack with knives at the strings around his ankles.

As soon as he dared, Tom turned to see what was going on in this temporary refuge of his. The booth was packed, but with people too busy craning their necks towards a makeshift stage to notice a hat wavering around behind their backs. Outside, Tom could hear other folk being turned away:

'Full house, ladies and gentlemen. Full house. Take a bottle of ale at Pye Corner, why don't you, and come back for the next performance. Full house, sir, full house. Everyone wants to hear the angel sing tonight.'

Tom passed a still-quivering hand over his face, and began pulling weakly at the hat. The itching was no longer unbearable, only unpleasant. Maybe it was wearing off. Maybe all the horrible sensations he was prone to here wore off in time. Maybe that's why the soles of his feet were OK, even though his slippers were torn to ribbons. All the same . . . the hat was a liability. The hat could be seen. He had to get it off. Somehow.

A disturbance behind the booth—a flurry of movement and the loud, hawking sound of someone's throat being cleared—sent a murmur through the audience.

'She's comin',' someone said. 'She's out there.'

Tom wasn't listening. He didn't give a monkey's who or what was about to sing for its supper. He just wanted to get Spune's hat off his head and be away. It was no good, though. Pulling the hat this way and that only made the itching worse. One final, vindictive tug and he let go, defeated. Making a dash for it seemed the only option left. He was about to lift the flap and chance it when he sensed he was being watched.

A girl, a little girl, had detached herself from the audience and was staring towards the peculiar dancing hat with solemn eyes. It was clever, she thought, very clever—but alarming. When it bent, suddenly, in her direction, she backed away, and clutched her father's legs.

'It's all right,' said the hat. *'Don't be frightened. Just . . . do me a favour, will you? Please? See if you can get this thing off?'*

She didn't understand. She hid behind her father's sailcloth trousers and peeped out. Everyone around her was applauding wildly. She didn't want to miss the show. Her father would pick her up in a minute, so that she could see. The hat was inches away, tilting itself forward as if it wanted her to have it. Shyly, tentatively, she reached out a small, dirty hand and stroked the brim.

'Go on,' said the hat. *' Go on. It's all right.'*

Reassured, the girl patted the hat. Then she gathered it up, like a kitten, into her arms. She thought she heard it say *'Thank you'* before it went all floppy and still. It must be tired, she thought, as her father whooshed her up on to his broad shoulders for a better view of the angel. From time to time, as she thrilled to the sight and sound of the thing on stage, she gave the hat a little squeeze. Nothing. It must have died, she decided. And she flung it away, in disgust.

* * *

Being completely invisible again was, Tom discovered, a mixed blessing. OK, so the mob wouldn't catch him; he was safe on that score. But getting through the crowds unscathed was going to be a problem. It didn't help that he had no idea which way to turn to find the Black Raven. It would be best, he decided, to return to the Fortune of War. With luck, Malachi Twist would still be there, waiting for him, as arranged.

The street was seething. It was tempting to stay put, untouched and unnoticed in the space he had found between two booths; to give it until dawn broke and the crowds thinned before trying to move. He couldn't, though. Of course he couldn't. He had to warn Astra. He had to get her out of the basement to some safe place, where Spune would never find her. Dithering about wasn't helping anyone. Dithering about was not what he should be doing.

Deep breath . . . Flex the toes, numb as pebbles in the tatters of those slippers . . . Ease the elastic bands . . . Focus on Astra . . . on the spark that is her strength, her mischief, her indomitable will . . . on the spark that nothing, not even the worst of things, has ever stifled . . . Focus on that . . . Hang on to that . . . And now GO.

'Stand back! Stand back! Make way for the invisible monster!' Tom hadn't planned to shout, let alone those particular words, but it was what he found himself doing as he struck out, blindly, for Pye Corner. Waving his arms, every bit as wildly as Twist had done, he used his gloved hands to push aside anyone too slow, drunk, or infirm to get out of his way.

'What? Where? 'Oo's shovin' me?'

'A monster! A monster! There's a monster comin'.'

'Mind outer the way, Nell! Mind out, I say!'

Fathers whisked their families down alleyways; young men ducked, hastily, into the nearest booths; and the slow, drunk, and infirm fell over one another, like bad acrobats, in their haste to give this invisible monster plenty of leg room.

Relieved to reach the corner unharmed, Tom took a left.

'Make way! Make way!'

Within minutes he was hopelessly lost. The Fortune of War might as well have been on the Kentish coast, given the fat chance he had of finding it again. He took another left, taking him further still from the merry chaos that was Bartholomew Fair, and still further from the place where Malachi Twist stood, wringing his hands until the knuckles squelched, convinced that his invisible friend had come to a sticky, unseen end.

For what seemed like hours, Tom dragged his aching feet and legs down one backstreet after another. Once or twice, he thought he recognized the road he was in, only to find that it didn't come out where he thought it should, or ended in some nasty little courtyard.

He came to a canal so chock-full of rubbish that the water wasn't moving, only bubbling slightly, like some foul broth that would kill you in seconds if you swallowed so much as half a mouthful. He passed three sailors, six pickpockets, a prostitute, and a composer called Handel. He was sniffed at by a dying dog, tripped by a beggar's leg, and almost drenched by the contents of a chamber pot being emptied from an upstairs window.

Finally, in complete despair, he stopped walking. It was pointless . . . pointless and exhausting going in and out of the same alleyways just in case they led somewhere. Placing his gloved hands against the grime of a wall, he sagged, wearily, against them.

Useless, that's what he was. No good as a messenger and total cack as a hero. Tipping back his head, to look up at the sky, he let his eyes fill with tears. The stars—paler at this hour, more like pearls than diamonds—winked and swam. So many stars, he thought . . . and nothing to block them out, except for Saint Paul's . . .

Saint Paul's. There it was. Glorious. Magnificent. Only recently rebuilt after the Great Fire, and looming over the city like a great, domed spacecraft.

It was a landmark Tom could home in on. A place he recognized. So he wiped his eyes against the back of one arm and made his way slowly, but surely, to the cathedral steps. From there, keeping his wits about him, and the tatters of his slippers clenched between his toes, it took just five minutes and only one false turn before he recognized the railings of his grandmother's house, and, just a little further along, the sign of the Black Raven.

With a sigh of relief, Tom plodded the final few steps to the tavern door. In the queer half-light that comes just before dawn, the painted raven looked almost purple.

'Caw, caw,' whispered Tom, pressing both hands flat against the heavy door and pushing. *'See you back in the twenty-first century, you . . . you vulture.'*

He felt, rather than noticed, the breaking of the dawn. Felt it in his guts as the ground slewed beneath his feet and the door, his hands, the tavern—the whole street— became lost, suddenly, in a great swirl of something. Mist . . . Smoke . . . Tom couldn't tell what it was, only that it was eddying all around, covering him up in what felt like a second skin made out of somebody's breath.

'Astra!' he called, as the first birds began to sing, and the unmistakable sound of a passing car came filtering through the softness wadding up his ears. *'Astra, get out of the basement. You've got to . . . get out . . . '*

Just as quickly as it had swaddled him up, the soft, misty feeling unwound itself and went away. He stood there, with his eyes scrunched shut, feeling his body exposed, once again, to the elements. He didn't need to look around to understand what had happened. He could tell from the sound of the traffic, from the smoothness of the pavement beneath his feet, even from the way the morning air felt against his skin, that he was back in his own time.

Eventually, he opened his eyes. Yep. He was back all right. Back outside Declan's Black Raven, with its baskets of wilting flowers and the chalkboard advertising *satellite football* and *lasagne*. Back in good old, busy old, twenty-first-century Smithfield—stark staring naked in what was rapidly becoming broad daylight.

15

Tom had been starkers before, in public places—but only in his dreams. Asleep, he might have solved the problem by being able to fly. If he could only fly *now* he thought, in mounting panic, he would flap like crazy up to the rooftops. Then he would crouch awhile among the pigeon droppings and TV aerials, and come down in his own good time—preferably on a dark winter's night with all the streetlights on the blink, and the whole population of Smithfield in bed with the flu.

He glanced, warily, up and down the street. Nobody about. *Thank you . . . thank you . . .* Grateful for small mercies, but keeping a sharp lookout, all the same, for joggers, milkmen, and early-morning dog-walkers, he ran, full-tilt, to the steps of his gran's house.

Looking down at himself, as he scampered along, he was struck by the amount of filth on him. He looked like a beast, he thought, with his limbs, his chest, even his poor old dangly bits covered in soot, dust, and splashings of goodness-knows-what. Tearing the filthy plastic gloves from his hands he touched his face. Then his hair. Yeuch. Disgusting. Never mind being arrested for indecent exposure, anyone seeing him now would think he had escaped from a zoo.

Shivering, he ran up the steps to his gran's front door, hunkered down and wondered what to do. It was bliss being able to sit, despite the less than brilliant circumstances. It was a relief, too, to have got back all right; to know that there were planes flying overhead, trains rumbling underground, and people easing themselves into the day with bowls of cornflakes and warm showers. These were comforting thoughts—or would have been if only he had some clothes to put on.

And Astra . . . Astra . . . He hadn't had time to warn Astra . . .

Twisting his aching body, he peered between the railings towards the basement window. What if he was too late? But no. Dark night, they had said. It was daylight now. She was safe. At least, until tonight.

The concrete step felt cold against his buttocks. His thighs were sore with grit and dirt. *This is crazy*, he thought. *I can't let Mum, or anyone else, find me like this.*

Focusing, now, on the immediate problem of hiding his nakedness, he began looking around for something—anything—that might do the job. What though? His eyes fell on his gran's dustbin, squat and grey on the pavement.

Bin day. Brilliant.

There had to be something in there he could use—old newspapers, a carrier bag . . . even last night's pizza box would do. You'd have to be desperate, he knew, to cover your bits with a box advertising a pepperoni special with extra toppings. But that's what he was at the moment. Desperate.

He jumped to his feet, ran down the steps, and wrenched off the dustbin lid.

Nothing. Empty. The bin men had already been.

Cack, he thought, peering in. There was a single cabbage leaf stuck to the inside of the lid. Better than nothing, he decided, peeling it off.

He went and sat back down, then positioned the cabbage leaf, very carefully, between his legs. *Ridiculous*, he thought, scowling down at the wilting bit of greenery on his lap. *Ab-so-lute-ly ridiculous.*

Then he noticed the black plastic bin liner tied loosely round one of the railings. A new, unopened bin liner left by the refuse collectors for next week's rubbish. A big, strong, body-bag of a bin liner which he snatched at so gratefully that it almost tore. Opening it up, he slipped into it up to his neck, not caring that the plastic stuck, squelchily, to the muck on his body. His mother, he knew, would be only slightly less horrified to find him on the steps in a bin liner than stark naked, but it would be a lot less humiliating for him. A *lot* less.

It was warm in the bin liner. So warm that Tom thought he might drift off to sleep for a while . . . just drift off, with his head against the railings . . . drift off and leave it to chance as to who found him and what they did about it. He would tell his mother he'd been sleep-walking . . . having nightmares . . . all so unreal . . .

'Keep the change, darling. And thanks everso . . . '

The slam of a car door, the revving of an engine, and there was Tom's gran teetering along the pavement, head bent over her handbag as she fished around for her door key.

Oh-oh.

Slowly, carefully, Tom slid his bottom to the very edge of the top step. Curling his toes and hunching his shoulders, he scrunched himself as far down into the bin liner as he could possibly go. His gran had found her key. And now she was at the steps. Taking a deep breath, Tom tugged the liner up over his face and held it there, loosely scrunched between his two hands, with just a little space for air.

'Oh—darn it!'

She had dropped the key. Tom exhaled, slowly. *Get a move on*, he thought. *Hurry up, you sozzled old trout, before I suffocate* . . . There was something jabbing at his left thigh—the cabbage stalk. He shifted a tiny bit, as much as he dared, and took a little, gulping, breath of air through the space between his hands.

His gran's high heels came clacking, falteringly, up the steps. He could tell she'd had a skinful. No one walked like that normally. He held himself rigid as she reached the top step.

Don't faff about. Don't look down. Keep going.

Her key was in the door. *Good . . . Good . . .* She was turning it. *Good . . .* Then she stopped.

He held his breath . . . counted to four . . . felt a sudden, sharp pain in his knee. She had *kicked* him. Kicked him hard on the leg! What was she . . . ?

The door banged open and he heard the toc-toc of her heels going away along the corridor. *What was she doing? And why had she kicked him, the cow?*

Cautiously, he wormed his head out of the bin liner. He could hear his gran rummaging around in the kitchen. There was a clink and then a scrunching sound, as if she was sorting stuff out. Rubbish. She was sorting rubbish. She thought the bin men hadn't been yet. Any minute now she would be back on the steps, lobbing tea leaves into his liner or breaking empty gin bottles over his skull.

The open door was more than a relief. It was a mercy and a blessing and the best thing to have happened all night. With no time to waste, Tom thrust both his feet through the bottom of the bin liner and gathered its folds around his waist. Then, hobbling like a hen, he half ran, half stumbled, into the hall and up the stairs.

'Is that you, Catherine?'

Quickly, he dived into the first-floor bathroom, locking the door behind him.

'It's only me,' he called back. 'I need the loo.'

'All right, darling,' trilled his gran, from the bottom of the stairs. 'Don't forget to put the seat down. Then back to bed.'

It seemed to Tom that she paused a while, before shutting the front door. He could picture her bewilderment. It made him smile as he began to run a bath. *Yes, Gran*, he chuckled to himself. *The rubbish has legged it! The trash has walked!*

9a.m.: 'Well, I don't know,' Tom's mother said. 'Look at you. You look totally washed out. Should I call a doctor?'

Tom shook his head.

'I just need some sleep,' he said. 'I . . . I watched videos all night. Sorry.'

He stretched and yawned, appreciating the softness of his sleeping bag and the smell of the shampoo he had used to rinse gobs of eighteenth-century muck from his hair. His attic bedroom felt safe, like a nest or a den. The sky, beyond the slanted window, was a deep, late-summer blue, zipped across by the faint, white trail of a passing aeroplane.

'I hope you're not going down with something,' said his mother. Her right hand landed on his forehead.

'No. I told you. Stop fussing.'

'Hmmmm.' She dangled her fingers over his face, making spider-runs across his cheeks and over his nose. 'Impsey-wimpsey spider, Tom,' she said. 'Remember?'

'Oh, *Mu*-um. Quit it.' Laughing, despite himself, he grabbed his pillow and biffed her with it.

'Ouch! Unfair. Where's the other pillow?'

'Tough, there isn't one.' He biffed her again, on the shoulder. Then again, a little harder. Each biff was really a hug in disguise. Each biff said 'You . . . are . . . infuriating . . . but . . . '

'Ow! Peace, peace . . . I give in . . . ' She grabbed a book from his bedside table, raised it like a shield—then froze.

'What's this?' she said, all the laughter gone out of her. 'What's this you're reading?'

Confused, Tom lowered his pillow. 'It's Declan's,' he said. 'It's the book he lent me about Smithfield . . . about the freaks at Bartholomew Fair. I haven't read it yet. Why? What's the matter?'

His mother relaxed, visibly. 'Oh, nothing . . . It looks good,' she said, putting the book back on the table.

Tom watched her, carefully, as she straightened his alarm clock, patted his pillow, and sat back down in the chair beside his bed. She was smiling again, but not like before. Something's worried her, he thought. Something about the book. She was worried about the book, only . . . it isn't anything to get upset about. It's just a book.

'Mum,' he said. 'It's just a book.'

'I know.' Her eyes were wide. Unreadable. 'I know it is. I just thought for a moment . . . Never mind. It doesn't matter. Get some kip. But don't sleep all day, OK? I'm going out at lunchtime, but Gran'll be around for a while. I'll tell her to wake you up.'

'OK.' Tom closed his eyes. Felt himself drifting.

'Where are you going?' he mumbled. 'At lunchtime?'

His mother was opening the door. He heard it creak.

'A support group meeting,' she said. 'For women who've had mastectomies.'

'Oh,' said Tom. 'OK. Have fun.'

'I think I will, actually,' said his mother. 'You'll never guess what it calls itself, this group. Go on. I'll give you twenty quid if you get it in three.'

Tom squinted up at the skylight. The aeroplane trail had faded to nothing.

'Dunno,' he said. 'Can't think. Too tired. Tell me.'

'Bosom Buddies,' she told him.

Tom groaned. 'That's terrible,' he said. 'That's *really*

terrible. Why can't they just be . . . I don't know . . . the Mastectomy Mob or something?'

His mother's laughter echoed up the stairwell.

'Nice one, Atomic,' she called up to him. 'I'll suggest it.'

16

It was mid-afternoon when Tom awoke. He had been dreaming—a vague, troublesome dream in which Malachi Twist had been trying to use a toothbrush. 'NO,' Tom had snapped. 'Put it down. It's not safe.'

His mother had walked into the dream and told him not to be so bossy; to let his friend brush his teeth if he wanted to. Her hair had been long and freshly washed. It had smelt of flowers. She had wanted to go to the beach. She had wanted Tom and Malachi Twist to go to the beach with her, to swim in the surf and eat ice cream.

'GO AWAY,' Tom had shouted at her. 'THIS HAS NOTHING TO DO WITH YOU. GET LOST!!' He must have really shouted this last bit, because he had woken up with the words ringing in his ears and his mouth open, drooling saliva.

Bleary-eyed, he looked at his alarm clock. 3.10. So much for Gran's wake-up call.

He dressed quickly, turning over in his mind the scheme being hatched by Rafferty Spune. It took more than a little effort to keep believing in it. The pack of low-lifes in the Fortune of War . . . the leer on Spune's face as he looked forward to the kill, '*I shall deal with it myself*' . . . the blood streaming in ribbons from Mattie Ladd's nose . . . it all seemed so fanciful; the memory meshing with dream-images of Twist brushing his teeth, and Mum wanting ice cream.

Astra, Tom said in his head. *Are you there?*

Left in silence, tugging on his socks, he wondered

how long he would have to wait before crossing the gap again. How long before he could get Astra away from the basement? Six, maybe seven hours?

Trying to cross in daylight was not an option. He knew that. Astra would keep him away by the sheer force of her will; protecting him, even now, from what was happening when gentlemen came to call. 'Is Nibs might try luring him over again, but he wouldn't bet on it. Not now that he'd half-blinded the man with pink drink.

Trainers. Where were his trainers?

His eyes fell on Declan's book: *Bartholomew Fair: A History*. It looked heavy-going, but he picked it up anyway. It might be worth skimming after he'd had something to eat. There might be an old map of Smithfield in it. There might be some reference to 'dark night'.

Still no sign of his trainers. Then he remembered. He'd flung them off, hadn't he, along with the other stuff he'd been wearing, before going out to eavesdrop. Would he have to go round all day in just his socks then? But no. He knew, instinctively, that he would find all his clothes waiting for him, down in the basement, among the cobwebs and the boxes.

In the kitchen Tom found his gran, wiping surfaces. She was wearing a cotton dressing gown—white with a big pink flamingo embroidered on the back. Her hair needed combing and she had no make-up on. Her face, as she turned to see who had walked in, looked different without its camouflage of paint and powder. She looks like Mum, thought Tom. I can see my mum in her.

'Oh . . . Tom. Darling. Did I forget to wake you up?' The flamingo contorted as she turned to switch the kettle on. 'Coffee?'

Tom put *Bartholomew Fair: A History* down on the breakfast bar and reached for the Weetabix packet. 'No thanks,' he said.

His gran wrinkled her nose as he helped himself to cereal. 'Tell you what,' she said. 'Since we've both missed breakfast—and lunch come to that—why don't you and I have a splendid fry up? Eggs, tomatoes, fried bread—mushrooms if we've got some. How about it?'

Tom looked at her. 'OK,' he said, warily.

'Good chap. But don't tell Catherine. She'll only be cross with me for stuffing you full of cholesterol.'

Tom smiled. 'Mum does lose it sometimes,' he agreed. 'She can't help it. She gets stressed.' He paused, noting the way his gran's hands trembled slightly as she cracked eggs into a pan of hot fat. Then: 'I heard her giving *you* a hard time,' he said. 'Over Grandpa's books. What was that all about?'

His voice was light. Conversational. But the question seemed to hang, like gas—invisible yet explosive. For a while, Tom's gran said nothing, only prodded their fry-up with a plastic utensil until the eggs, tomatoes, and mushrooms hissed and spat, like a panful of curses.

'Toast,' she said at last. 'Brown or white?'

'White,' said Tom. He gripped the edge of the breakfast bar until his knuckles paled. No. He wasn't going to *let* her change the subject. Whatever the big deal was, about those books, he wanted to know. It hadn't bothered him before. Too much else on his mind. But his gran had ignored a perfectly reasonable question as if he had no right to *ask* it.

He waited until she was sitting beside him at the breakfast bar. Waited until they were both tucking into their food.

'I could've had Grandpa's books,' he said, his voice cold between mouthfuls of mushrooms. 'You shouldn't have burned them. You and Mum. Why did you?'

His gran put down her knife and fork. Carefully. Deliberately. The breath she drew in was ragged and uneven. 'Tom,' she said, 'does your mother *talk* to you about your grandfather?'

'Of course,' he replied. 'All the time.'

She threw him a startled, sideways look.

'I have his eyes,' Tom added, quickly. 'But not his temperament.'

His gran gave one of her snorts.

'What?' Tom was angry now. 'Just tell me! Tell me why you burned his books.'

His gran got down from her stool and began scraping crusts and tomato skins into the pedal bin. For a long while there was just the sound of a knife scratching the plate. 'Because . . . ' she said at last, ' . . . they weren't worth anything after all, darling. Load of old rubbish, really.'

She snapped a tea towel from a plastic hook and began drying up. The flamingo trembled in the folds of her dressing gown as she polished a teaspoon way beyond the point of being dry, then flung it into a drawer.

Tom stared at her. 'But that's no reason to *burn* them,' he said. 'You could have taken them to Oxfam. Or to a jumble sale. You could have given them to *me*.'

'Well, I didn't,' said his gran. 'I just didn't. All right?'

It wasn't all right. Whatever his grandfather's reading habits had been, it didn't seem at all right, to Tom, to send the whole collection up in flames. 'Old rubbish' probably meant murder stories, or stuff about war—things his gran and his mum would never want to read in a million years. He probably wouldn't have been all that interested either. But all the same . . .

'You should have kept those books,' he muttered. 'They'd been knocking around here long enough. I might've liked them.'

No answer.

Defeated, Tom took *Bartholomew Fair: A History* and slid down from the breakfast bar.

'I'm going out,' he told his gran. 'I'm going to sit in the park and read for a bit.' He held the book up. 'History,' he said. 'In case you were wondering.'

It was the start of the evening rush hour, yet the park, behind its screen of trees, was peaceful. Deserted. Tom lingered by the wall of fame. He could smell the roses and hear pigeons burbling. It was a good place to know about, he thought. A good place to be. He read a memorial:

> **Thomas Simpson died of exhaustion**
> **After saving many lives from the**
> **Breaking ice at Highgate Ponds.**
> **25 January, 1885**

A hero, he told himself. Thomas Simpson was a hero. A man with ordinary eyes, probably, and a nice temperament. Bet nobody burned his stuff up. Bet *his* stuff got passed on to his children, and his children's children, and maybe even his children's children's children. Thoroughly out of sorts, now, he plodded round the path and sat down on a bench. Leaning back against wooden slats still warm from the day's sun, he opened *Bartholomew Fair: A History* and began to read:

Bartholomew Fair has its origins in the twelfth century, when Henry I allowed a monk, who had once been a court jester, to hold a fair outside the Priory in West Smithfield.

Smithfield, in those days, was literally a 'smooth field', overhung by great elms. Beyond lay open countryside bounded, in the distance, by the great boar-infested forests of Middlesex . . .

Boring.

Tom flipped ahead. There was some gory stuff about heretics being burned alive outside the Priory gates. In Tudor times, he read, Bartholomew Fair's tumblers and actors would often cavort on ground still black with the ash of human remains.

Gross.

He read about the plague years when the Fair was cancelled due to an understandable lack of interest. He learned that the Great Fire of 1666 sent flames two miles long and a mile broad crackling through the City—and then stopped at Pye Corner, within a lick of the Fortune of War. Then he came to the chapter on monsters.

Men who could dance without legs . . . dwarfs . . . giants . . . scaly boys . . . Such wonders, human or bestial, held a tremendous fascination for visitors from all walks of life . . .

He read about the Clever Mare, admired by the diarist Samuel Pepys, and about the German Woman without hands or feet who could thread needles, spin fine thread, and fire pistols. These 'monsters' were real, he read. Whatever trickery lay behind their strangeness, whatever made them odd, they were living, breathing creatures. No doubt about it, for they were advertised in genuine handbills and seen by the public. Nature's oddities, to be gawped, marvelled, or sneered at. To be touched, perhaps. For a price.

3d to see the most amazing pig . . . Counts his audience and tells the hour, to a minute, by a watch.

Now showing at the sign of the Golden Lion: a man-child having in his right eye the words Deus Meus *and the same written in Hebrew in his left eye . . .*

To be seen next door to the Black Raven in West Smithfield, during the time of Bartholomew Fair: A Living Skeleton . . .

Also showing . . .

Tom dropped the book; picked it up again and began leafing, quickly, clumsily, through its pages. *Where was it? Where had he seen . . . ?* His heart was jumping. There. Found it. He spread the book flat on his knees. Small shadows, cast by a nearby tree, poked at the page, dappling and flecking first one sentence then another, as

Tom's eyes flicked from line to line and his face grew hot with both the pleasure, and the sorrow, of recognition:

A Changeling Child

Notice: To be seen next door to the **Black Raven** *In* **West Smithfield,** *during the time of Bartholomew Fair: A Living Skeleton taken by a Venetian Galley from a Turkish vessel in the Archipelago. This is a Fairy Child, supposed to be born of Hungarian Parents, but chang'd in the Nursing, Aged Nine years or more; not exceeding a foot and a-half high. The Legs, Thighs and Arms so very small that they scarce exceed the bigness of a Man's Thumb, and the face no bigger than the Palm of one's hand; and seems so grave and solid, as if it were Threescore Years old. You may see the whole Anatomy of its Body by setting it against the Sun. It never speaks. It has no teeth, but is the most voracious and hungry creature in the World, devouring more Victuals than the stoutest man in England. Gives Great Satisfaction To all that ever did, or shall, behold it.*

There. He smoothed the page with the flat of his hand; smoothed it the way his mother sometimes smoothed the hair from his forehead—gently, sweetly, holding the moment so that it would always mean something. This was Astra's memorial, he realized. This was all that was left of her. However her life had ended, whatever had happened to her down in Gran's basement, she no longer existed. She had been dead for nearly three hundred years.

He read the handbill again, and shivered. Poor Astra. Poor girl. How dare they refer to her as an 'it'. How dare they write about her as if she had no feelings. It was true that she had no teeth, true that she was always hungry.

But whoever wrote this had twisted everything. It made Astra sound more like a wild animal than a starving child. She was more than a foot and a half high too—albeit not much. And she *did* speak. She *did*. Hadn't anyone heard her?

From where he sat, Tom could see the wall of fame. Its rows of plaques seemed to glimmer in the thick, early evening light. Those people . . . you were supposed to admire them. They had died noble deaths. Their deaths marked them out as special, like saints or soldiers.

He smoothed Astra's page again, his mind busy. Thomas Simpson, for all anyone knew, might have been a right old git—the kind of man who walloped his kids and got blotto every night. Or he might have been unremarkable; no better or worse than anyone else. Only, that day, when the ice began to crack at Highgate Ponds, when Thomas Simpson saw women and children flailing in the freezing water, calling out for help . . . that day he did what he had to do. He did it because he was there. And because, git or not, unremarkable or not, he couldn't stand around while other human beings froze or drowned.

Memorials lied, thought Tom. Memorials told you nothing real, or important, about anyone.

The pages on his lap began to flutter. The scent of roses grew stronger, like incense.

Tom closed the book. Gently.

Astra was . . . had been . . . as brave and as good as anybody. If I could write about her, thought Tom, I would. If I was older, and could write, I would tell her story properly. Her true story.

He left the park, holding the book a little tighter as he approached a main road. In his mind's eye, he could still see the handbill on page 216. Astra's memorial.

Don't worry, he told her, in his head. *That wasn't all there was. I'll get you out of there. Tonight. I'll get you out . . .*

17

The telephone was ringing as Tom let himself into his gran's house. He followed the sound into the kitchen and traced it to a white touch-tone phone hanging, like a chameleon, on a white-tiled wall beside the fridge. There was a note attached to the fridge door by a magnet shaped like a pineapple. 'Back late, darlings,' it read. 'See you tomorrow.'

'Hello?' he said. The receiver's mouthpiece smelt musty.

'About time too!' yelled his mother. 'I was about to hang up.'

'Oh,' he said. 'Well, I'm here now. What's happening?'

'I'm staying in town for supper. With the girls.'

'What, the Bosom Buddies?'

'Yep, with them. Can I speak to Mu—to your gran?'

'She's not here. She's gone out. Until late, the note says.'

Silence. Tom shifted the receiver.

'Why?' he said. 'What do you want her for.'

'She said she'd join us. She *promised*.' His mother's voice was high-pitched. Over-wrought. 'I can't believe she's out. Unless . . . Oh, never mind.'

Tom moved the pineapple fridge magnet so that it snapped into place between an orange and a plum. All three fruits had faces painted on—smiley mouths and googly eyes.

'What would Gran want with all of that anyway?' he said. 'She's not a Bosom Buddy.'

His mother sighed. 'I know,' she said. 'But this is a support group, Tom. Your gran and I need to thrash some stuff out, and sometimes it's easier to do that in a group situation. It's too hard one to one.'

Tom turned the plum upside down.

'Well, she's bottled out,' he said, 'by the look of it.'

'Hmmm,' said his mother. 'Don't suppose you want to come, do you? You could get a taxi. I'll pay. Bonnie—one of the Buddies—has done a big veggie casserole. And her son's here. Guy. You could go on the computer together while the group does its thing.'

Tom tried to imagine the Bosom Buddies doing their thing. They would be sitting in a circle, probably, with scented candles burning. Some would have wigs on. One or two, like his mother, would be wearing a hat or a scarf. Then again, since this was one of those caring, sharing groups, they might be thinking, so what? They might be sitting around bald, or tufty-headed, comparing prostheses and letting rip about petrol fumes, men, dodgy beefburgers, or whatever else they blamed cancer on.

They would be like Amazons, thought Tom. Angry and wild. And scary.

'No thanks,' he said.

9p.m.: *'Is 'e coming? Is 'e? Is them 'is footsteps I can 'ear, patterin' along?'*

'No, it ain't. 'Tis just a rushin' of the water up and down. We 'as to wait for them pictures. When the pictures start, that's when 'e comes.'

'Tell me what the pictures are. Be they holy?'

'No, they ain't. They're people. Just people. Hush up now. Angel—sing to 'im will yer? 'Is eyes are givin' 'im jip, poor mite . . . And you two! Lummox an' Bantam! Git off me bed. Tell 'em, Chang. Tell 'em to stop jouncin' around on me bed. I got

*me glimsticks an' . . . an' me other bits in there. They'll break
'em . . . '*

*'Tell me. Tell me when the pictures start. Tell me when 'e gets
'ere.'*

*'IF he gets here, friend. IF he gets here. For there was precious
little sign of the poor fellow last night, after Spune and his rabble
gave chase along Cock Lane. Oh my! I fear for that missing
monster's skin, just as surely as I fear for his heathen soul. I do, I
do . . . '*

*'Hush yer gob, Malachi Twist. Hush a while, all of ye. See
that bit 'o stuff in the gap? The bit that do look like a shoe
buckle. It's changin'. See? The pictures are comin'. 'E ain't
snuffed it. I told you 'e'd get 'imself 'ere. I told you 'e
would . . . '*

Tom landed smoothly, like a cat. *Nice one*, he thought,
bouncing upright. Then he saw them.

Twist was there, grinning from ear to ear, his eyebrows
caterpillaring up and down in crazy lines. The Gorilla
Woman was at Twist's side, her swarthy hands resting,
protectively, on the birdlike shoulders of a little boy. The
boy himself looked perfectly normal, except for some
kind of bandage, or blindfold, over his eyes.

'Is it 'im?' the boy was asking. ''As 'e jumped?'

Further back, in the shadows, stood a foreign-looking
person tugging, thoughtfully, at the longest moustache
Tom had ever seen. Over on the strawstack, two stunted
men—or were they overgrown boys?—were tussling and
squealing over what looked like a bone.

And Astra . . . Tom's eyes sought her out in the gloom,
and fixed on her with relief.

'I'm here,' he said to her.

'So I see,' she snapped. 'I ain't blind. What news on
the Giant? Start blabbin'.'

137

Tom took a deep breath. *'They're digging him up on dark night,'* he said, *'whenever that is. But, there's worse . . . '*

'Tomorrow! Aaiee!' The foreign person stepped forward, his hands raised and fluttering in dismay. He was oriental, Tom realized, noting the slanting eyes, and hair pulled so tightly back in a pigtail that the flesh of the man's face was stretched as taut as the skin of a drum. He said the word 'tomorrow' as if it was 'tomollow' and his voice had the deep, sonorous note of a funeral bell. 'Tomorrow. No moon. See? Dark . . . very dark . . . '

Tomorrow.

The dwarfs, Lummox and Bantam, stopped fighting over a candle stub, slipped down from the strawstack and waddled across to the Gorilla Woman, their faces identical, splat-nosed images of dismay.

Tomorrow.

'Oh my . . . ' said Malachi Twist, softly. 'Oh my, oh my . . . '

'Wait,' said Tom. *'You haven't heard all of it . . . '*

'Shut yer trap!' Astra's chin was up; her tiny fists clenched as tight as embroidery knots. 'Now listen. This is it. We gotta get to the boneyard. Dig 'im up ourselves if we 'as to and get 'im down to the river, like 'e wanted . . . '

'Oh . . . Oh, but I cannot take command of a spade,' gabbled Malachi Twist. ''Twould slip from my grasp in less than a trice. 'Twould make no more impression on the sacred soil covering our beloved friend than the falling of a twig . . . '

'ASTRA!' Tom shouted. *'Listen! You've got to LISTEN to me!'*

Twist, surprised into silence, backed away to where Chang, the Exotic, stood winding strands of his beard into a complicated cat's cradle. The Gorilla Woman, the dwarfs, and the boy with the words DEUS MEUS throbbing around the iris of his right eye, huddled closer. Astra didn't move a muscle. 'Go on then,' she said. 'No need to piss yerself.'

Tom's lips were dry. He licked them. *'You've got to get out of here,'* he said. *'Let Twist find you a safe hiding place. That doctor. Flint. He doesn't just want the Giant, he wants . . . he wants . . . '*

The Changeling Child raised her chin a little higher; held her spine a little straighter. Only the slightest wince, a tremor that flickered across her face and then was gone, betrayed the fact that she knew what was coming. She knew what he was going to say.

Tom couldn't go on. His throat ached with sorrow and the words just wouldn't come.

'It's me, ain't it?' said Astra, quietly. ''E wants to boil me up in 'is kettle, don't 'e? Along wiv' the Giant? So 'e can show off me skellington?'

Tom swallowed, and managed a nod. Slowly, almost soundlessly, Twist and the others moved forward, surrounding the Changeling Child in a shambling circle. For a long time none of them spoke—only gazed and gazed at the Child in horrified empathy; struck to the core, each and every one, by this terrible reminder of how helpless they all were. How disposable.

The silence was broken by a low, droning lament as the Gorilla Woman, keening bitterly, flung the dwarfs and the damaged boy away from her lap, and held out her arms to the Child.

'No, Angel.' Astra stood her ground, although it seemed to Tom as if she swayed, just a little, towards the comfort of her friend's embrace. 'Ain't no point gettin' agitated. Ain't nuffink to be done . . . '

'Fiddle-faddle!' Malachi Twist broke from the circle and began pacing the floor. Tears and fleas dropped from his person as he shuddered and twitched in distress.

'There *is* something . . . the only thing . . . the one and only thing that can be done.'

He whirled round to face Tom. 'Our friend here,' he continued, wringing his hands until they squeaked. 'Our trusted friend and fellow-monster . . . He must take thee back with him. Back to the place he comes to us from. Just for a while. Until the danger passes.'

Tom felt his jaw drop. He hadn't considered this precise course of action. Not for a second. It made sense, in many ways, but he really, really, didn't want to do it. How could he? The responsibility would be awesome . . .

'*I don't know* . . . ' he began. Astra cut him short.

'This partic'lar danger ain't never goin' to pass,' she snapped. 'Never. For if Flint don't get me tomorrer, you can bet yer life 'Is Nibs'll sell me off to some other poxy quack in double quick time. 'E's 'ad enough of me, 'Is Nibs 'as. Reckons there's more money to be 'ad showin' geeks.'

Tom's mind was working fast. *It might work. It might. She could stay in the basement. She was used to that. Gran and Mum need never know. They never came down. Never. And, anyway, she'd be invisible, wouldn't she? Surely, if he couldn't be seen in her time, she wouldn't be seen in his? It might work. It just might . . . For a day or two anyway . . .*

He opened his mouth to speak, but Astra was moving now, moving and chattering, like a little lunatic. Across the room she ran and up onto her strawstack, waving her tiny arms and crying out: 'Listen! Listen to me! We're forgettin' about the Giant again. We still gotta save 'im. We promised. We did!' Standing ankle deep in filthy straw, with every line of her body held rigid, she looked like a warrior queen.

How can she be so brave? thought Tom. *Correction. How can she be so STUPID? What kind of girl thinks more about helping someone who's ALREADY DEAD than about saving her own skin?*

The other monsters had gathered around the strawstack

in a sad little huddle. The Exotic's beard resembled a strip of wire wool, so fiercely had he been twisting and tugging at it. Lummox and Bantam lay slumped against the Gorilla Woman, like big, ugly babies. Tom couldn't see the boy. Malachi Twist was looking back over one shoulder, blinking away tears. Do something, friend, said the expression on his face. Save the Child. Take her away.

'You!' Astra pointed straight at Tom, commanding his attention. 'We need fings. Anyfink that will scare Spune an' 'is lot in that boneyard tomorrer night. You're to bring it. I'm trustin' yer.'

They were all staring at him now. The look on the Gorilla Woman's face said: Do as she says or I'll rip out your liver. From somewhere in shadow, the boy began to whimper. 'I have to go soon. I have to go, Mr Twist, or there'll be Hell to pay.'

'Well?' Astra snapped. 'Can ye do it? Lip me an answer for pity's sake. These monsters'll get a whipping if they're away too long.'

Tom sighed. The germ of an idea was growing in his mind. It was a good one. It made him smile. It provided some relief from the gnawing anxiety he was feeling over what was to become of Astra. *'Yes,'* he said. *'There's stuff I can bring.'*

'No muskets,' interrupted Malachi Twist. 'No blades. No slingshots and no crossbows. No weaponry of any kind. We cannot stoop to murder, friend. Our Lord forbids it. And anyway, they'd hang us.'

'It's OK,' Tom said. *'I wasn't thinking about killing anyone. There's other things I can bring. Things from my time that will freak Rafferty Spune right out. Things that will make him think the Devil is right there in the graveyard, about to drag him down to Hell.'*

'Aieee!' Chang the Exotic bobbed his head, in respectful admiration.

Twist began to caper, his shadow ludicrous against the basement walls. 'Yee-ha!' he whooped, whirling his arms and shuffling his feet in what Tom had come to recognize as his Happy Dance. Twist used his whole body the way other people used their faces. His dance was a smile, only bigger.

'There's one condition,' added Tom. *'Astra's got to come back with me. Now. Tonight.'* He took several steps towards the strawstack and held out his hand.

Astra reared back.

'No!' she hissed. 'I ain't doin' it. I ain't budgin'.'

'You have to,' Tom told her, moving closer.

She waited until he was inches away, then sucked in her cheeks and spat. Her spittle stung Tom's left cheek, like fallout from a sparkler. He flinched, but stood firm.

'I. Ain't. Budgin',' she said, again.

'You are,' he insisted. *'Because, unless you do, I'm not lifting a finger to rescue the Giant.'*

Behind him Chang the Exotic shuffled forward and bowed. 'But, sir,' he said, 'if Rafferty Spune run away tomorrow night, like gutless dog, then the Child—she safe? No?'

'Yes,' nodded Twist. 'Yes, indeed.'

'Indeed!' and 'Indeed!' echoed Lummox and Bantam.

'No,' snapped Tom, without turning round. *'Not necessarily. I mean, losing the Giant might make Spune so mad he'll be all the more determined to get Astra. It's too risky. She needs to leave.'*

Swiftly, decisively, he pulled his T-shirt up over his head and down his right arm so that he could wrap his hand in its folds.

'There. Take my hand,' he appealed to Astra. *'Take it. Hurry up. We'll jump the gap together.'*

'Go with him, Child,' murmured Malachi Twist. 'Be not afraid.'

142

'It won't hurt,' Tom urged her, jiggling his arm around, in its loose sheath of cotton. *Look, my hand's completely covered.*

Still the Changeling Child remained backed up against the basement wall, her feet firmly planted in her bedding.

'No,' she said, averting her eyes from the waggling fingers. 'I ain't jumpin' nuffink. I'm stayin' 'ere.'

Tom felt an overwhelming urge to slap her. Had to dig his nails, hard, into the palm of his hand to stop himself.

You're just being a wimp,' he said. *'A coward. A chicken. You're pretending to be brave but I think you're scared. I think you're scared to death of leaving this basement in case you go somewhere worse. Well you won't. You can't. Your life couldn't GET any worse.'*

Silence.

'What's the matter with you?' he yelled. *'Why are you doing this?'*

The bandaged boy began to sob—a pitiful bleating which set Tom's teeth on edge.

'I have to go. I do . . . I really do . . . I have to get back.'

Now it was the boy Tom itched to slap. He heard Malachi Twist, or maybe it was the Chinaman, murmur, 'Shhhhh . . . shhhhh,' followed by the whisper of the Gorilla Woman's petticoats as she set about rocking the boy in her lap.

Then a new sound, a sound as familiar as it was unexpected, cut through the whimpering and the shushing and the rustle of starched lace, to sear itself into Tom's brain as effectively, and painfully, as a brand.

'Tom . . . Tom-ahawk. Where are you?'

It was like the breaking of the dawn had been, only worse. The slewing, dizzying sensation returned, along with the sickness in his stomach. Only, this time, he had the feeling of being turned around and pulled—pulled, quite literally, along the basement floor by an invisible cord attached to, and tugging at, his belly button.

'Tom! Answer me!'

He couldn't speak. Didn't want to. Couldn't. He dug in his heels and tried pulling against the force. It was no use. Slowly, inexorably, he felt himself being hauled towards the gap. Hauled inch by inch, like the loser in a tug-of-war.

'Are you downstairs? Tom! *Tom!*'

Twist and the others went lumbering and skipping into the shadows, out of the way. They were sorry, but not surprised, as they watched Tom disappear. Clearly, the boy with the writing round his eyes wasn't the only one who needed to be somewhere else. The invisible monster had to get back as well. His master was calling.

18

Still trembling, outraged at having been dragged back across the gap at such a crucial moment, Tom staggered into his gran's kitchen, grabbed a glass off the draining board and turned the cold tap on.

'Tom! Tom!'

'I'm in here.' His voice was sulky. 'Getting a drink.' He glanced over at the clock. 11.05. With luck, his mother would be in bed by midnight. He would do whatever it took, after that, to get Astra to see sense.

He gulped his water. The skin around his belly button felt sore, the way his grazed kneecaps used to do after he'd ripped off an Elastoplast.

'Tom, for pity's sake. I've been calling and calling. Why didn't you answer me?'

His mother, in the doorway, looked so terrible that he almost dropped the glass.

'What's up?' he said.

She sagged against the doorframe.

'Mum! Sit down. Shall I call Gran?' He grabbed one of the stools from beside the breakfast bar and started dragging it across the room. His mother waved it away.

'I hate those things,' she said, sinking lower and lower until she was sitting curled up on the floor, both sandalled feet touching one edge of the doorframe. 'And your gran's still out.'

She tipped back her head, as far as she could without cracking it on the frame. Then she closed her eyes and began taking deep, slow breaths. It was a yoga thing. It was what she did, Tom knew, when she was feeling particularly scared, or sick. She had done it a lot last year, after her treatments. But not indoors. Not if she could help it.

'I wish we were in our garden,' he said, for the want of something more helpful to say. 'Or on the beach. With your incense sticks on the go. Remember? Those nice ones in the purple packet.'

Her smile was faint. 'Lavender and sage,' she murmured. 'But you said they were cack, my incense sticks. You hated me burning them.'

Tom moved away to the sink, to rinse out his glass. 'They weren't that bad,' he said. There was a slice of lemon blocking the plug hole. He tried levering it up with a finger tip but it slithered, like a sea creature, and wouldn't come out.

'Tom?'

'What?' He opened the cutlery drawer, took out a fork, stabbed the lemon slice and shook it onto the draining board.

'I've had it here. Really. Enough's enough. We're going home tomorrow.'

Tom contemplated the lemon slice. It had three pips in the centre and tiny spots of mould around its rind.

'We can't,' he said, quietly. 'What about you and Gran? I thought you had stuff to sort out. Emotional stuff.'

'Pah!' His mother began to laugh and then to cough. She coughed so violently, and for so long, that Tom began to think she might choke. Quickly he re-filled the clean glass and took it over to her.

'Here,' he said, squatting down beside the doorway and holding the glass to her face.

She took a few spluttering sips. 'Thanks, love,' she croaked.

'We can't go home yet,' Tom repeated, more slowly this

146

time, as if to a child or a foreigner. 'Not until—until everything's sorted.'

His mother took his hand. 'I've realized,' she said, 'that some things can never be sorted.'

Tom frowned. 'You mean, family things?' he said.

'Yes. I wanted to talk to your gran. Really talk, heart to heart. I know where she's gone and it wasn't . . . urgent. She could have come to the meeting. It wasn't much to ask.'

Tom took his hand away. It was hard to feel sympathetic under the circumstances.

'I don't want to go home,' he said. 'Yet.'

Her eyes, which had been closed, flicked open.

'Tough,' she told him. 'We're leaving first thing.'

2a.m.: *'Astra. Are you there? Can you hear me?'*

He had been shouting, in his mind, for so long, that his head felt as if it had been kicked around the basement, like a football.

The gap hadn't happened. Nothing had happened.

He'd had a crack at his mother's deep breathing thing, so desperate had he been to get things moving. Deep breathing and visualization. That was the secret. That was the trick. Breathe slowly and deeply . . . focus your mind . . . and then WISH like mad for your heart's desire.

His mother had told him once how, having got her breathing right, she visualized the good cells in her body as specks of white light, doing battle with the bad cells. Blasting them to smithereens.

It had been known to work wonders, she'd said, this controlled way of breathing and thinking. Miracles even. You just had to believe. You had to get the breathing right, then focus your mind, and then believe, absolutely, in your power to effect change.

147

For over an hour Tom had breathed beautifully, convinced of his ability to part a concrete floor, whenever he wanted, and step across into the eighteenth century.

Now he was back in his sleeping bag. Defeated. Light-headed from so much breathing. Dreading what the coming day might bring. But still calling out. Still trying to believe.

The doctor came first thing. Tom heard his voice, rumbling behind the closed door of his mother's bedroom, and almost fell down the stairs. He found his gran in the sitting room. The shutters were closed and the telly wasn't on. She was sitting—just sitting—in the dark, a magazine lying unread on her lap.

'There's a man,' Tom said, indignantly, snapping on the overhead light. 'In Mum's bedroom. Who is he? What's going on?'

His gran jumped. 'I've had to call the doctor, darling,' she said. 'Catherine's not feeling very well.'

Tom turned and ran from the room, almost colliding with the doctor on the landing.

'Is it back?' he demanded, blocking the man's way.

'Ah. You must be Mrs Cotterill's son,' said the doctor. 'I'm sorry? Is what back?'

'The cancer,' Tom said. 'Is it back?'

The doctor looked at him for a moment, man to boy.

'She needs to rest,' he said. 'Her glands are up. I'm hoping it's just a touch of summer flu. There's a lot of it around.'

Tom continued to stare him out. The doctor swapped his bag from one hand to the other and cleared his throat. He was someone who believed in eye contact. It showed he cared. But the boy's eyes were so blue they were unnerving.

'And she's a bit low,' he added. 'Depressed. Only

148

natural after all she's been through. Try and cheer her up a bit, eh? Now—I just need a quick word with your granny.'

Tom let him go and went in to see his mother.

'How do I look?' she whispered from the bed.

She looked like death. She looked as if no amount of yoga breathing, incense-burning, or positive thinking would ever make her better.

'OK,' he said. 'You look OK.'

'Good,' she replied. 'Because that's one sexy doctor out there!'

She tried to laugh. Tom wasn't fooled.

'Can I get you anything?' It was hard to sound normal; to keep the fear out of his mouth. 'From the shops, I mean.'

'More fruit,' she croaked. 'You know the kind. For the pink drink.'

'OK. Anything else?'

'Ask Declan to pop round later. This afternoon, if he can.'

'OK. But it's just a touch of summer flu, right?'

'Yep.'

Knowing he would get nothing more out of her, Tom turned his attention to a portable music centre next to the bed. His mother listened to some terrible cack nowadays—new-age stuff with birdsong on it, and flutes making a sound like falling water. Before the cancer, she had preferred heavy rock.

'Do you need more batteries for the CD player?' he asked.

'It's plugged in,' she replied. 'Although there's always the faint chance I might go jogging with it later.'

Tom allowed some of the fear to seep away. She couldn't be feeling that bad; not if she could still be sarky.

149

'Actually, I wouldn't mind borrowing it,' he said. 'Tonight, after you're asleep, if that's all right.'

'Of course it is.'

'And that Sixties CD. The one with the song about hell fire, by crazy whatsisname . . . '

'The Crazy World of Arthur Brown?'

'Yeah. Did you bring it?' He crossed fingers behind his back.

'It's in the car . . . somewhere . . . '

She wanted him to go now. He could tell. Her energy was all used up. She didn't want to be bothered about songs, or shopping lists, or where the car keys were to be found. She needed to sleep, Tom told himself. A nice long sleep and she would be fine. He hoped he would be able to remember which size batteries the CD player took. It would be a fat lot of good in a graveyard, otherwise.

'I'm off out then,' he said. 'And Mum?'

'Mmm?'

'I'm sorry you're not well enough to go home.'

'No you're not.' Her head rasped against the pillow slip as she turned to face the wall. 'It beats me *why* you're not. But you're not. Anyway . . . go if you're going. I need my beauty sleep.'

19

The shopping list Tom wrote in his head, as he sprinted past St Paul's, went something like this:

four boxes of raspberries (organic if poss.)
strawberries (same)
loads of milk (soya)
batteries for CD player
torches
batteries for torches
another box of hair stuff (gloves)
plastic bags and clingfilm (loads)
ANYTHING THAT MIGHT SCARE THE LIVING
DAYLIGHTS OUT OF RAFFERTY SPUNE

He had a wodge of notes to spend—what remained of his holiday money, plus the twenty his mother had given him for the fruit and milk, and a handful of tenners his gran had pressed on him just before he left the house.

'You're a good boy, Tom,' his gran had said. 'Buy yourself some CDs, or a book, or something.' She had patted his arm, awkwardly, and even pecked him on the cheek. He hoped she hadn't left lipstick.

First thing, he bought the hair dye, batteries for his mother's CD player, and more bags and clingfilm for his feet. Then, stashing the rest of his money in the back pocket of his jeans, he headed down into the tube station.

The central line was heaving, but Tom didn't mind. At least he could trust the escalator not to scald his feet. At least he could sit down on the train knowing that the worst thing the seat could do would be to leave chewing gum on his trousers. At least he was in his own time, and knew what was what. The people sitting opposite stared right through him, but that, he knew, was how people behaved on the tube. Nobody wanted to make eye contact, or talk. This was modern-day London. This was how things were.

The shop he wanted was ten stops away, down a side street off a main road. A bell jangled as he pushed open the door. He slid in, past a dummy dressed as a spaceman, and looked around. There were no other customers, only more dummies, standing around in different disguises.

'*Go On. Be a Devil*', read a sign above Tom's head. '*Or a Princess, or a Clown, or Robin Hood*'. And underneath, in smaller letters:

'*Thieves beware. We always prosecute.*'

Most of the clothes for hire and for sale were hanging on rails. They were in no particular order, and so tightly packed that a mermaid tail brushed fins with the feathers of a canary costume, and a highwayman's coat had its sleeves caught up in the sequins of a ballgown.

There were wigs piled in an old-fashioned trunk, fairy wands stuck in a jar, like star-shaped lollipops, and a box full of plastic swords, cutlasses, and tridents. It was like being in the dressing room of some enormous theatre, during rehearsals for the biggest pantomime ever performed.

Tom picked his way to the back of the shop. The Hallowe'en stuff was tucked away in a corner, gathering dust. He spotted the masks under a table, all jumbled up and leering at the walls.

'Brilliant . . . ' he murmured, reaching down for the one he wanted.

'Can I help you?'

The shop assistant looked as if she was wearing some of the stock. Her dress was medieval, with trailing sleeves, and her hair so long, and such a bright, buttery, shade of yellow that Tom felt sure it was a wig. He looked at her face. She was old. Older than his mother. Too old to have hair like that.

'Oh,' he said. 'Yes, please. I rang earlier. About the party.'

'Ah.' She reached past him and picked up the mask he wanted.

'This lights up,' she said, pressing something. 'There you go. Look.'

Tom grinned as the mask's features flared and flickered.

'The horns are extra,' said the assistant. 'And the pitchfork. They light up too.'

'I'll have them,' said Tom. 'And this.' He had found a stretchy black bodysuit with a skeleton painted all down the front in fluorescent green.

'That glows in the dark, but you have to shine a torch on it for a few minutes first,' the assistant told him.

'Cool!' said Tom.

The assistant, fired by his enthusiasm, began rummaging beside him, along a rail. Satin wings, velvet jackets, and vampire cloaks got pushed aside, until her fingers fastened on something thick and shaggy.

'How about this?' she said, pulling something out, and holding it up for inspection. 'This is *really* scary!'

Tom considered the gorilla outfit. It was so heavy that the weight of it was pulling its metal coat-hanger out of shape. Its big feet dabbled on the floorboards, making marks in the dust. The assistant could hardly hold it.

'We've already got one of those,' he said, politely. 'But I'll take a couple of black cloaks. Oh—and torches. We'll need torches.'

The assistant moved to a glass cabinet. 'These are fun,' she said, indicating torches with detachable plastic skulls clamped on the ends. 'And we've got laser ones too. You can shine a skull and crossbones on to fences, or a wall, from quite far away, with one of those. Don't aim at people's eyes, though—that's dangerous.'

Tom said he knew that, and would be careful. He picked out a laser torch and three ordinary ones, and reached into his back pocket for his money.

'Well—I hope your friends approve,' said the assistant, ringing up the total with a sharp ping. 'Didn't they want to come and choose for themselves?'

'They can't,' Tom said. 'They . . . they don't live around here any more.'

He looked at the total, displayed on the register, and gasped. It was a lot. 'Oh,' he said, fumbling with the notes in his hands. 'I . . . I might have to put something back.' He bit his lower lip, wondering what to do without. The devil's costume was essential. So were the torches. And the cloaks.

He counted out his money onto the top of the cabinet. There was enough, but only if he went home without the things his mother needed.

'You're fine. That'll cover it,' said the assistant.

Tom shook his head. 'I've got to get fruit and things,' he said. 'My mum's sick. I've got to get strawberries and raspberries and about twenty pints of soya milk for this health drink she has.'

The assistant said nothing, only stared at him, through the fronds of her hair.

She doesn't believe me, thought Tom. *She thinks I'm trying to pull a fast one*. He looked back at her, blushing furiously. He thought of his mother, and about how disappointed she would be if he didn't do her shopping. She was already low. And clearly unwell. Depriving her of the pink drink, today of all days, would be cruel.

He reached out, and picked up the skeleton outfit—the most expensive item. 'I'll put this back,' he said. 'Sorry if I've messed up the till.'

'Just a minute.' The assistant took the outfit back again, tugging it away with both hands. Tom watched, in mild surprise, as she held it close to her chest and pulled.

Something ripped.

'Well, look at that . . . ' she said. 'A torn seam. You can have this at a reduced price. What shall we say—a couple of quid?'

She did something to the cash register, then picked up Tom's money—leaving a ten pound note out. 'There,' she said, pushing the bag with the costumes, the masks, and the torches in it across the counter. 'Don't forget your change.'

Tom put the ten pound note back into the pocket of his jeans, along with the handful of coins she had given him. Then he picked up the bag. He felt . . . happy. Elated, almost. This woman—this stranger—had done a kind thing. Not a huge, life-changing thing, but something that he would never forget. Ever.

'Thank you,' he said. 'Thank you very much.'

'You're welcome.' Her smile was gentle, like a blessing. She wasn't old and ridiculous after all, Tom realized. She was all right.

20

'Tom! Wait up!'

Juggling bags, doing his best not to squash the fruit, Tom turned to find Declan sprinting towards him. It was mid-afternoon. The basement railings cast faint shadows, like pinstripes, across the pavement. Somebody had watered the Black Raven's hanging baskets, in an attempt to perk up the petunias.

Tom put his bags down for a minute. 'Your plants are dripping,' he said.

Declan looked back to where great globs of water were falling from the baskets and landing, splat, on his chalkboard. Some of the letters spelling 'Dish of the Day' and 'Quiz Night' had been wiped clean away in the trickle.

D   h of the   ay   they said.

And   *z   Ni   t*

'Ah well,' said Declan, scratching his chin. 'Never mind.'

'I've finished your book,' Tom told him. 'Oh—and Mum would like to see you. She's a bit fed up.'

'Fed up is it? I heard she was sick.'

'Well, a bit. Just a bit.'

'Ah. Shall I bring her some flowers, Tom, to cheer her up?'

'If you like. But not roses. She hates roses—particularly red ones. And none of those blue things either. Cornflowers. She hates those too.'

'Ah.' Declan shuffled his feet. 'Ah, well . . . '

156

Tom picked up his bags, and started climbing the steps. 'Don't worry about flowers,' he said, kindly. 'Come in and see her now, if you like.'

'I will,' agreed Declan. 'Before the pub gets busy.'

Tom unlocked the front door and they both stepped into the hall. The air in the house smelt stale. Trapped.

'She could do with opening a few windows, the auld one,' said Declan.

'She's probably at Oxfam,' Tom told him. 'Working,' he added, noting the baffled expression on Declan's face.

'Ah.'

Tom nodded towards the stairs. 'Go on up,' he said. 'Second floor, second door along. Only, knock first. She might be asleep.' *I'll dump the costumes and things, in the basement,* he thought. *Ready to go. Then I'll make the pink drink.*

Declan was dithering, as if he wanted to say something but wasn't sure how to begin. Whatever it was, he thought better of it and turned away.

'Tell Mum I'll be up in a minute,' Tom called after him. 'With her drink.'

The kitchen was spotless, as usual. Tom chose the sharpest knife from the cutlery drawer and set about slicing strawberries into the jug that fixed on to the blender. He added raspberries, then a couple of organic bananas from the fruit bowl, peeled and chopped up small. Next, he poured in a whole carton of soya milk.

The Rescue Remedy was in the fridge. It was essence of boiled up plants, or something weird, sealed in a small brown bottle. His mother called it the 'magic' ingredient.

Tom took the bottle out of the fridge and over to the blender. The small weight of it felt cool and pleasant against the palm of his hand. What was in it again? What were the plants called? They had pretty names. Didn't one of them grow in their garden, every spring? *Clematis.*

That was it. Then there was the funny one that sounded as if it came from the Bible but was good for shock. *Star of Bethlehem*. Doing well . . . The third thing was from a type of rose. *Rock Rose*, that was the one. A small, yellow rose. Then there was the fruity-sounding thing. *Cherry Plum*.

Clematis, Star of Bethlehem, Rock Rose, and *Cherry Plum*.

There was a fifth thing, from a plant called something like 'impatience'. Tom couldn't remember what, exactly. But it didn't matter. It wouldn't matter. He had done well enough.

Twisting the stopper from the brown bottle, he let four drops of Rescue Remedy fall into the jug. *Clematis, Star of Bethlehem, Rock Rose, and Cherry Plum* . . . *Clematis, Star of Bethlehem, Rock Rose, and Cherry Plum* . . .

As incantations went, it sounded rather good. He put the lid on the jug and switched the blender to full power.

Clematis, Star of Bethlehem, Rock Rose, and Cherry Plum . . .

There's enough in there for later, he thought. For tonight.

Malachi Twist had said no weapons. But the pink drink wasn't a weapon. Not really. He would only throw it if he absolutely had to. In self-defence, or to save Astra.

Clematis, Star of Bethlehem, Rock Rose, and Cherry Plum . . .

He switched the blender off and poured a glass of the thick, milky potion for his mother. Then he put the kettle on. Declan, he knew, would prefer a cup of tea to anything pink that smelt of blossom.

10p.m.: All in order. Everything sorted. Hallowe'en stuff in a black bin-liner on the basement floor. Pink drink in a plastic beaker, with a lid on it. Batteries, and the *Groovy Sixties* CD, in place in the portable music centre. Tom wrapped in a vampire cloak, the green bones of his skeleton outfit glowing dimly beneath it.

The gap was moving slowly, less than an inch a minute. Tom willed it to hurry up—to zip across the floor and let him jump. He needed to keep moving tonight. He needed to get this thing over with, while he still believed that a sudden blast of rock music, and a bunch of torch-waving freaks in fancy dress, would truly scare the cack out of a man who dug up the dead for a living.

His mother was sleeping, peacefully. With luck, she would sleep until morning. Still, it was a worry. What if she woke up, and called out to him again? Tonight of all nights? Would he hear her? Would the sound of her voice go spiralling through time and across the rooftops of old Smithfield, to drag him, bumping and mewling, out of the churchyard and back into the house?

Block that thought.

The gap was complete, at last, and teeming. A bulging egg-shape cracked against the basement wall and out hatched a bird. A green bird. Tom recognized it at once. 'Blister and Purge!' it shrieked, flapping and skittering from one end of the gap to the other, its claws slipping on a shingle of shapes, its tail feathers catching in the spaces in between. 'Shut up! Shut up! Tonight's the night!'

A couple more squawks and the bird vanished, swallowed up by a thick, soupy fog that rolled all along the gap, hiding every shape from view.

Tom leant forward, straining his eyes.

WHOOMP!

The chariot, small as it was, almost took his nose off. A couple of horses passed in a blur; but the woman standing braced at the reins stared Tom straight in the eye as she tore through.

Go for it, man, said the look. *You can do it . . .*

Boadicea, armed to the teeth, her blue-painted skin marking her out as a Celtic warrior . . . Boadicea, about to put the wind severely up the Romans by razing London to the ground . . .

The fog thickened again, then parted, leaving the gap empty of everything except a slow rush of liquid. Suddenly they were there. Astra, Malachi, the dwarfs, the Gorilla Woman, and Chang the Exotic, their faces bobbing like peculiar flowers and their mouths twisting with relief, as they called out: *'Come on, come on . . . it's time, friend . . . it's time to rescue the Giant . . . '*

With the bag of disguises slung over his back, the pink drink held tightly in his left hand, and his mother's CD player clamped, awkwardly, under one arm, Tom jumped. His vampire cloak billowed out, as he landed, revealing his fluorescent bones.

'Oh my gawd,' squeaked Astra. 'Look at 'im! Don't tell me 'e's a bleedin' goner. Don't tell me Flint's got to 'im.'

'Speak to us, friend,' quavered Malachi Twist. 'Only speak . . . '

Tom put the CD player down, propping the beaker of pink drink next to it. *'I'm fine,'* he said, swinging the bin liner off his shoulders and onto the floor. *'It's a disguise.'*

'Aiieee,' breathed Chang. 'Our invisible friend has special power in the spirit world. We see his bones, but not his face.'

'They're not my bones,' Tom said. *'They're painted on my clothes. You have to shine a light on them, to make them glow, but they're pretty good—they last for ages. Now . . . Wait till you see what I've got in here.'* He dipped his hand into the bin liner, took hold of the devil mask—then hesitated.

The monsters were huddled together, on and around the strawstack. Malachi Twist had used his big toe to shove Astra's flickering candle stubs into a small line, like a barrier. Chang the Exotic was chanting something, in his high reedy voice. A prayer? A spell? Tom wasn't sure.

Astra looked as if she might cry at any second. Tom had never seen her looking so anxious, or so . . . so lonely. It was the bones, he realized. They weren't convinced about the bones. They honestly believed he had snuffed it, and jumped the gap to haunt them.

This clearly wasn't the moment for producing a mask that flashed tongues of fire at the press of a button.

Oh well . . . Only one thing for it.

Tom peeled off his disguise, becoming invisible, inch by inch. It was the only thing he could think of doing, to prove he was still alive. He heard Astra sigh with relief as he tugged the suit, with some difficulty, down over his trainers. It was a good thing to hear. It made him feel honoured—and more optimistic about getting her over the gap.

He held out the skeleton outfit, crumpled, and still warm, from his body. *'Feel it,'* he said. *'Pass it round.'*

The Gorilla Woman took the outfit between both hands, sniffed it suspiciously, licked a glowing rib or two, then thrust it, with a nod of approval, at Malachi Twist.

'Oh my!' Twist shook the suit out and held it up by the sleeves. 'Oh my, oh my.' And he began to dance, whirling the outfit around so fast that the legs flew out horizontally, skimming the pates of Lummox and Bantam as they lumbered around, mimicking the Bendy Man's delight.

'Enough!' commanded Astra. 'It ain't funny. Leastways, not to me it ain't.'

The dwarfs stopped moving, like clockwork. Malachi Twist dropped the limp suit on the ground and tiptoed backwards, towards the furthest wall. Of course. The Fairy Child would be a skeleton herself soon—a boiled-down skeleton hanging in Dr Flint's drawing room. It was her fate. Lots of people would pay good money to see her then. Ladies as well as gentlemen. She was right. Dancing bones were no laughing matter. Not tonight.

161

'I'm sorry,' he murmured. 'I beg your pardon. I do. Most humbly, I do.'

'Right,' sniffed Astra. 'So ye should.' She stomped across the floor, and surveyed the bin liner.

'Wait a sec.' Tom was still struggling back into the skeleton suit, hopping around on one leg as he pulled it up. Astra, however, was in no mood to wait. Grasping the neck of the bag in her two tiny fists she opened it up and peered in. 'Blimey,' she said, reaching in for the devil mask. 'This'll do it. This'll do the trick all right, an' no mistake.'

Tom hurried to take the mask from her, before she found the switch that set it glowering. *'That's for Malachi,'* he said. *'He can put it on later, once we're there. There's horns and a pitchfork too. I'll show you how they work in a minute.'*

Twist edged forward; craning his neck and waggling his ears.

'You won't mind being our devil, Malachi, will you?' Tom asked. His fingers fumbled around for the tiny switch.

Twist shook his head. 'Nay, friend,' he began. ''Tis all in a good cause, and besides . . . whoooaaaaah!!' He leapt back as tongues of red-orange flame began to flicker up the surface of the devil mask.

'Oh no . . . no, no, no . . . ' he protested. 'Not that I'm a coward, friend, but a burnt Bendy Man is a useless Bendy Man. There are those, I believe, who swallow fire with ease, then breathe it back out with no harm done. I am not of that breed, friend. I would go up in a pillar of smoke, like any Smithfield martyr, and then where would we be?'

''E's right,' agreed Astra. 'You're mad to even think of it. Snuff it out for gawd's sake afore ye set me bed alight.'

Give me strength! thought Tom. *Give me patience!*

Explaining the small miracle of electrical charges took time.

'*Torches,*' he announced, swinging beams of lemony light up and around the basement walls. '*These are torches.*'

'Ooooer!' and 'Whoaaah!' cried the monsters, ducking towards the floor.

Exasperated, Tom switched one of the torches off, unscrewed it, and tipped out its innards.

'*Batteries,*' he said, holding two of them out on the palm of his right hand. '*They light things up. That's their job. Useful things, batteries. And safe. Totally safe.*'

The Gorilla Woman leaned forward, sniffing the air above Tom's outstretched hand.

Harummph, she grunted. The grunt said: No danger here. They're only little scuts. First sign of trouble, and I'll bite 'em in half.

The others shuffled forward, feeling less afraid.

'*That's better,*' said Tom. '*That's more like it.*' He switched on the pitchfork and jabbed the air with it a few times. Then he wore the devil mask, to prove to Malachi Twist that it wouldn't roast his brain.

Astra, meanwhile, had picked up a torch and was holding it, reverently, on her lap. 'I would've liked one o' these,' she said, gawping at the bright circle it threw upon the basement wall. 'It would've saved all me glimsticks from meltin' down to nuffink.'

'*You can have one,*' Tom told her. '*Later. After you've crossed the gap with me.*'

No reply.

Satisfied, finally, that Tom's stuff was safe, that it even had extraordinary powers, the monsters turned to examine the black box on the floor.

'*OK,*' said Tom. '*This is the best. This is what's really going to give Spune the fright of his life.*' His finger hovered, for a second, over the buttons of his mother's CD player. '*Are you ready?*'

163

The monsters gathered round him, as trusting as small children waiting for the first words of a story.

'We're ready, friend,' said Malachi Twist, solemnly.

It's music,' added Tom. *'Battery-operated music. And it's loud. Really loud. So, stand back a bit and don't have hysterics when you hear it.'*

'Stop pissin' around,' snapped Astra. 'Tell the bloomin' box to start. An' it 'ad better be good. And scary. If it ain't, we'll get Angel t' menace 'em instead. Right, Angel?'

The Gorilla Woman blinked and nodded. Her eyes were fixed, sceptically, on the box as she wondered how batteries breathed, and what they ate.

'OK,' said Tom. *'Here we go . . . '* And he hit 'play'.

* * *

11p.m.: It is warm, tonight, in Dr Flint's room. Warm, but not too smelly. Not now that Johnny Moffat has tossed the day's human remains into the Fleet, and the air in the room has been freshened by sprigs of bruised lavender, scattered on the floor.

'Tonight's the night!' shrieks the macaw, fluttering from its chair-back to perch, for a minute, on the rim of a bucket.

'Indeed it is, my feathered friend,' murmurs Dr Flint. 'Indeed it is . . . '

He slips the bird a slice of apricot and returns to his journal.

August 25, 1717: Today is my birthday. Took a bath in honour of the occasion, even though I had one as recently as 12th May. Lunched at Dolly's Chophouse before removing the left hand from a seamstress, she having run a needle into the base of her forefinger some three weeks back, and the whole hand having festered most horribly.

He dips his pen in the inkwell and continues:

All is arranged for dissection of Specimens 1 and 2. I await

164

their delivery, in a state of some restlessness, and pray God they will arrive in good condition.

There is nothing more to be written. Not yet. All Dr Flint can do, for the time being, is pace the confines of this room, feed slices of fruit to his bird, and wait upon Rafferty Spune's pleasure. It is the hardest part of the whole business, this waiting. In a way, he would prefer to be out there, collecting the first specimen himself—hacking at grave-soil with a wooden shovel . . . heaving the Giant out by his great big feet . . .

Stroking his chin with the quill of his pen, Dr Flint muses on the phenomenon that was the Giant. Time was, the less he knew about his specimens the better. Making that first, deep, incision was always easier if their lost lives, their very names remained obscure. Not any more. Years of anatomizing have hardened Dr Flint. He could cut up his own mother without flinching.

Yes—Dr Flint would like to have seen the Giant, while he lived; to have studied the way the big man moved, the way his body worked as he sat down, stood up, or shook hands. Rumour has it that the touch of the Giant's hand had been strangely healing, that even the sight of him had made the sick feel better, and the sad smile. All rubbish, of course, like believing that coughs can be cured by a broth made from two puppies and a stewed owl. Or that supping tortoise blood will prevent a fatal convulsion.

Drawn to the window, by a loud cheer, Dr Flint observes, with disdain, the way the rabble below mills around a battered sedan chair, as if the king himself were in it.

'Have care, friend . . .'; 'By your leave, sir . . .' Flint recognizes one of the bearers of the chair as the idiot with the twisted limbs. A pitiful sight. Truly pitiful. What cruel dislocations, he wonders, were inflicted upon this person shortly after birth, while his bones were still soft and malleable? And yet the Bendy Man, Flint knows, is much doted on, in Smithfield. Even his owner loves him enough to give him free rein during the Fair, trusting him to earn his keep, and to return, each night, with every coin thrown.

It would be too risky to bag the Bendy Man for dissection. One day, though . . . one day . . .

The person running behind the chair is wrapped in a black cloak, with the hood up. Dr Flint cannot see his face. The sedan's windows have the curtains pulled. No doubt, thinks Flint, it contains the Bendy Man's keeper, on his way to some den of vice, yet too mean to pay a shilling an hour for someone other than his own monster to carry him there.

Flint licks his thin lips. He quite fancies nipping out to a den of vice himself, but must stay exactly where he is. In this room. Waiting. Behind him, the macaw begins to squawk. It has eaten too many apricots, and will shortly make a terrible mess of the green chair.

'Blister and Purge!' it calls, lifting its tail feathers, purposefully. 'You Go Girl!'

Not for the first time this week, Dr Flint wonders: Who is this 'girl' his bird screeches about? And where is she supposed to be going?

21

On a clear day, in 1717, the view from St Andrew's boneyard would have been lovely. Comforting, even. On a clear day, it would have been most pleasant to stand and watch the grey-green ribbon of the Fleet meander north towards the wooded slopes of Highgate.

Tom, however, knows nothing of this as he crouches behind a massive tombstone, fumbling for a torch. He can feel the Gorilla Woman's breath, hot against his neck. He can hear Twist wringing his hands. The smell of moss, and dry, crumbling stone is strong in his nostrils—but he cannot see a thing.

It is Dark Night all right. Dark as tar and almost as sticky.

''Urry yerself up, will yer?' hisses Astra, somewhere to his right. 'Get them battery things workin' on yer bones. We ain't got long.' Her voice is shaking, along with every bone in her own tiny frame. Even wrapped in a shawl and snuggled against the Gorilla Woman's pelt, even on this sultry, August night, she is as cold as a cricket in an ice house. Cold, and almost catatonic, from the shock of being outside.

Tom finds a torch and switches it on, being careful to direct the beam on to his chest and to contain it, as far as possible, within the folds of his cloak. Before long, his painted ribcage is glowing brighter than the struts of a burning building. Satisfied, he moves the beam lower, to light up his pelvic girdle.

Behind him, Lummox clambers onto Bantam's shoulders, the better to fix the Devil's horns on to Malachi Twist's head.

'Have a care, friends,' whispers Twist. 'And be sure to position 'em right. 'Tis the arch-rival of our Lord I'm impersonating, not a billy-goat.'

Suddenly, from way over by the cemetery gates: a short, shrill cry. *Someone, something* . . .

Tom snaps the torch off. The dwarfs become instantly still—a squat totem pole, with terrified faces.

Seconds pass. Tom's heart is pounding so hard he can see the fluorescent breastbone of his suit palpitating in the dark. He pulls his cloak round himself, to block the glow, and waits.

Silence.

''Twas a rodent, I believe,' whispers Twist, after a while. 'Or some other small beastie.'

'I think you're right,' Tom whispers back. *'It wasn't Chang, anyway. It was nothing like an owl.'*

He waits a few seconds more, then peers round the edge of the great tomb.

Nothing. No muffled footfalls. No thud of tools being dropped at a graveside. No sign of Rafferty Spune. Just Dark Night, pressing in, on, and all around the dark, ivy-draped railings of St Andrew's, and the dark, solid shapes of slabs and crosses.

'It's all right,' Tom decides. *'They're not here. I'm going to finish lighting my legs up.'*

The monsters sigh, collectively. Their thoughts are with Chang the Exotic, all by himself in a patch of nettles, guarding the sedan chair and waiting to hoot like an owl the second Spune and his cronies appear.

Satisfied, at last, that all the bones on his suit are fully charged, Tom switches off the torch and passes it to the Gorilla Woman.

'*Here, Angel,*' he whispers. '*Here's your torch. Don't forget—do exactly as I told you.*'

The Gorilla Woman grunts, and thrusts the torch under her armpit.

'What . . . what . . . about me?' shivers Astra. 'You ain't . . . said nuffink . . . about what I'm . . . to do.'

'*You're to stay right here,*' Tom tells her. '*Right here, understand? Spune mustn't see you.*'

She doesn't argue. She is relieved.

There is nothing to do now, except wait.

Instinctively, as the silence and the darkness intensify, the monsters huddle together. Tom, hunkered down in his own bit of space, feels very small, and very much alone. He tips back his head, to look for stars, but there aren't any. He wonders how his mother is.

Someone pats his cloak. He turns in surprise, taking care not to scrape his invisible face against stone.

'Courage, friend.'

Tom smiles.

'*Twist,*' he whispers into the darkness. '*Hey, Twist. What are we going to do with the Giant? Afterwards, I mean? Nobody's said.*'

Twist clears his throat. 'The river,' he whispers back. 'We must take him to the river.' His voice, behind the devil's mask, sounds muffled and far away.

'*How?*' says Tom. '*We can't just lob up to the Thames with a sedan chair and chuck a dead body out . . .*'

Lummox and Bantam begin to snigger, until a cuff from the Gorilla Woman reminds them to be quiet.

Malachi Twist sighs, gently, behind his mask. 'There are others, friend, who will help us, with that final task,' he adds. ''Tis all arranged. We will not need to trouble you again, after tonight.'

'Oh,' says Tom. 'Oh . . . OK . . . Only . . .'

'Shhh . . . Sh . . . sh . . . shut yer faces. It's . . . it's time . . . Listen . . .'

169

Tom listens.

Nothing. Nothing except a faint rustling, over towards the cemetery gates, the kind of sound a small animal might make as it moves through grass, following a scent.

But then . . . Yes. *Yes*. There it is. Unmistakable this time. A low but insistent hooting; the kind of sound an owl might make—or a human being, as he spies, coming straight at him, the hulking shape of Rafferty Spune.

No one speaks. It isn't allowed. Spune has been known to knock a fellow clean out, just for breathing too heavily while filling in a grave. Mattie Ladd, in particular, is being careful. Last dark night, in this very boneyard, he tripped over a tree root and went sprawling into a patch of nettles. A lesser man, he tells himself, would have screamed blue murder. For a tree root feels mighty like the clutch of a skeletal hand when you're tippy-toeing around folks' graves, at dead of night, without so much as a glow-worm lighting the way. And nettles hurt. They had hurt him a lot. It is a matter of some pride to Mattie Ladd that he had picked himself up, without so much as a squeak, and done it so quick and quiet that Spune hadn't even noticed.

Aha. They are approaching the exact same spot. He can tell. A few more steps and they'll be on it. Mattie Ladd hops a bit to the right, neatly avoiding the tree root. A little smirk lifts the scabby line of his mouth. He is learning. He is getting good. Very soon, he will be able to let go of the rope attached to the ginger man's belt—his only means, up to now, of tagging along, of keeping up with the others as they slink through inky darkness, avoiding the jut of crosses, the bruising points of angels' wings, by instinct.

Soon, concludes Mattie Ladd . . . very soon, he will be striding through this grim, dark, place as dauntless as Spune himself.

He hears an owl hoot, close by. That's fine. He likes owls. It was rats you didn't want to come across in a boneyard. Them and ghosts . . .

Hang on. They have stopped. Why have they stopped? Is this the place? By the nettles? He doesn't think so. Rubbing his nose—for he has collided unexpectedly with the ginger man's back—Mattie Ladd waits in the dark to see what will happen.

It isn't a long wait.

In a trice, he finds himself face down, once again, in the nettles. It happens so swiftly that for a second he thinks the owl has pounced; a great big owl, with talons big enough and leathery enough for one to grip a poor lad by the shoulder, and the other to cover his mouth.

Next thing he knows, though, he is back up on his feet, his head reeling; his face stinging ten times worse than before. And it was Spune, he realizes, who threw him to the ground. It is Spune's leather-gloved hand clamping his lower jaw, while the other moves from his shoulder to his throat. And it is Spune's voice cooing in his ear, so low that only he can hear it . . .

'Tripped again, Mattie Ladd? How clumsy ye are. No better on your feet than a newborn lamb, or a rum-fuddled sailor who cannot walk the land . . . '

The hand circling Mattie's throat tightens. Just a little. Just enough to make him remember his prayers. The voice in his ear grows sweeter still.

'I see everything, Mattie Ladd,' it purrs. 'Everything. Even on dark night. Remember that, next time ye choose to believe that a sprawl in the dirt goes unnoticed. Now *walk* . . . '

On legs that tremble so much they barely shift, Mattie Ladd totters a few steps. Silently, the ginger man prods him into line. Mattie Ladd clutches for his frayed bit of rope, takes a deep, but mercifully soundless, breath, and walks.

And now they are at the right place.

The Giant's grave is marked by granite boulders, one at his head, one at his feet. It will be shallow enough, they know, for the big man was a pauper, for all his fine talk, and got buried on the cheap. The coffin will be of such poor quality that one swift wrench of a crowbar will crack it open easy as pie.

It is the ginger man's job to dig the hole, and Mattie Ladd's to fill it in. Spune does the tricky bits; the bits requiring brains as well as brawn. First, he removes the flowers—noting, by touch alone, the exact position of every item, from a wreath of lilies the size of a cart-wheel, to a bunch of buttercups. They will be put back, afterwards, in exactly the right order. Everything neat and in its proper place. Nothing to arouse suspicion. Nothing to suggest that the earth beneath all those petals and leaves has been tampered with.

He works quickly, Rafferty Spune. Within seconds the grave is bare. The ginger man begins to dig. The ground, baked hard by the sun, does not give easily, but the ginger man is strong, and well used to the job.

Mattie Ladd, hovering nearby, prays that he will do the filling in bit right this time. No clunking the wooden spade against one of them boulders. If he does that again, Spune will take hold of the shovel and bury him alive. He just knows it . . .

The hole is ready now—an almost perfect square, at the head of the grave. Rafferty Spune claps a silent hand against the ginger man's shoulder. It is a job well done, but the next move is his, and his alone.

Taking up his hook and crowbar, he leans over the open grave, as calm and casual as a man checking a furrow for potatoes. Slowly, carefully, as if he has all the time in the world, he lets down first the crowbar, then the hook. Both find their mark straight off, slipping unerringly under the rim of the coffin lid.

Now comes the moment when skill counts. Skill and patience. Go at it wrong and the job will be botched—aye, and the specimen damaged so bad that the good doctor will refuse to pay for it.

Slowly, gently, Spune applies an exact amount of pressure to the crowbar. The earth at the foot of the grave acts as a counterweight. He can feel the thrill of its force running up through the palms of his hands and all along his arms as he responds with an imperceptible, but precise, depression of the bar.

Any second now . . . any second . . .

Get ready, Tom tells himself. *Get ready with the laser.*

He hears the dull crack of splitting wood. His eyes, grown a little more used to the dark, can just about make out the shapes of Rafferty Spune and the others as they bend, purposefully, over the terrible thing they are doing.

Behind him, the monsters hold hands. And these are the thoughts running through their minds:

I'm cold. So cold . . . and frightened out me wits. I should never 'ave come out. I ain't used to it. No. Think of the Giant. He's the important one. Not me. I ain't . . .

Batteries. Humph. Hello, batteries. Are ye too hot under there? Are ye asleep? Got to get to work soon.

Oh, friend . . . friend . . . What they are doing to you this minute is more than a Bendy Man can stand . . . I cannot endure it, friend. It is too sad . . . too wicked . . .

Oh-oh. Up he comes.

Oh-oh. Up he comes.

Tom gropes for the laser torch. His fingers jitter inside their plastic gloves. His hand bumps against the beaker of pink drink, but he manages to field it before it falls and spills.

Clematis, Star of Bethlehem, Rock Rose, and Cherry Plum . . .

That white shape, over there on the ground; that incredibly *big* white shape. That's Him. That's the Giant. Those grave-robbers have tugged him up in no time and plonked him to one side while they tidy up after themselves.

A bitter taste, a horrible taste, rises in Tom's throat. He gulps it back and tightens his grip on the laser torch. It has been all right, up until now. The Giant, stashed away in a coffin, hadn't seemed real. He had been an object—something that needed taking from place A to place B, like a parcel. It is a whole different ball game, now that he is visible.

Tom has never seen a dead body before. Nor does he want to. He particularly doesn't want to set eyes on one that has been dead and buried a few days and then dug up. He is thinking worms. He is thinking stench. He is thinking: That shroud thing had better be well stitched together. That shroud had better be so durable that nothing's poking through or oozing out. That shroud had better be at least fifty layers thick . . .

The touch of the Gorilla Woman's hand almost makes him holler. She is offering something—her torch—and nudging him to get a move on; to use her batteries if his own are too stupid, or too tired, to earn their keep.

It is now or never, Tom realizes. He has never been so terrified. But he can't chicken out. He just can't. Astra would never forgive him.

Silently, insistently, he motions the Gorilla Woman and her torch away. He can hear the dull thud of soil falling back onto the Giant's empty coffin as he feels along the laser torch, thin as a bone between his gloved fingers, and presses the switch. The small, piercingly bright image of skull and crossbones dances, for a second or two, on his own black-cloaked thigh.

Brilliant, he thinks to himself. *Absolutely brilliant*.

174

Slowly, so as not to make the slightest sound, he kneels forward, holding the torch at an angle. Then, leaning out as far as he dares; as far as he needs to, beyond the edge of the tombstone, he brings the torch up, level with his chest, and swings the image of the skull and crossbones out into the darkness.

Away it goes, the image, slipping and sliding across tussocks of grass, over the faces of stone angels and through flowers in wreaths, and flowers in jars, until Tom brings it to a dead stop. And there it hovers, like a warped firefly, on the boulder marking the head of what should have been the Giant's final resting place. And there it shines—two fluorescent bones, and a perfect little skull, etched out of light and grinning, nastily.

Mattie Ladd is the first to see it.

At first, he thinks it is a jewel; some trinket what must've dropped off the specimen, as they slung the rope under its armpits and hauled it up. A big ring, perhaps, or a stone fallen from the setting of a thumping great locket. He looks sideways at the image, taking care not to break the rhythm of his shovelling, for fear of a kick in the pants. No . . . no, this wasn't no trinket off of no specimen. It wasn't nothing like that. It wasn't nothing like anything at all. It was . . . it was . . .

Mattie Ladd could not have said what it was if his miserable life depended on it. Still, he knows it isn't right. He knows it is bad news for someone, and reckons it a fair bet that this someone is going to be him.

The image begins to move. It moves without a sound, slipping up, down, and around the boulder, rapidly at first, then very ve-ry slowly . . .

Open-mouthed now, his wooden shovel held motionless above the partially-filled grave, Mattie Ladd stifles a whimper. No talking. It isn't allowed. Not under any circumstances. No, not even if Judgement Day has

175

come early, and the dead are about to rise up around him, like they was leaping from their beds. No talking. No . . .

He tries to keep digging, but his arms won't work. No man's would, he reckons, not with that . . . that thing next to him, slip-slidin' about in the dark, like a gob of enchanted spittle. He waits for the inevitable—a clout, or a smack from Spune for being an idle sot and a useless filler-in of graves. It doesn't come.

Spune is standing a foot or so away. He is watching the image the way a snake watches a mouse. Nothing that lives could match him for stillness at this moment, as he stares, through narrowed eyes, at the skull and bones, leering up at him from the granite. An ill omen? He grits his teeth, keeping down curses. A pox on ill omens. Trickery, that's what it will prove to be, a piece of low cunning, done with mirrors and such, by the self-same mongrel that ran off with his hat.

Nobody makes a fool out of Rafferty Spune twice running. Nobody. To have jested with him in the Fortune of War was one thing. To do it here, at his place of work, is quite another. Some muckworm is going to pay for this. With his life.

The ginger man, being as slow on the uptake as he is good with a shovel, has yet to notice the skull and bones. All he knows is, the Ladd has stopped doing his job. A good kicking will set him right. Tentatively, he gives Rafferty Spune a little nudge.

'I AM THE GOD OF HELLFIRE!!!!!'

Blasting out of nowhere it comes, a great wall of sound crashing through the dark; erupting into the night as if the earth has split open and the Devil and all his army are popping out to say hello. It is loud enough to burst ear drums, strange and ghastly enough to make the dead and still-safely-buried turn in their graves.

The ginger man is the first to break the no talking rule.

'AAAAARGH!' he bellows. 'AAAAAAAAAARGH!!!'

And he is off, blundering and stumbling towards the gates, leaping over headstones and trampling wreaths in his haste to put several English counties between himself and the hounds of Hell.

'**FIRE!!**' shrieks the awful voice, behind him, to the accompaniment of some clamorous instrument only the underworld could contain. '**TO DESTROY ALL YOU'VE DONE! FIRE!! TO END ALL YOU'VE BECOME . . .**'

Mattie Ladd would have hit the ground running, too. Just as fast as the ginger man. Faster. Only, he has leapt too high, at the first shock of sound—leapt, twisted, and landed, right up to his ankles, in splinters of coffin-wood and clods of earth. Stuck fast, he is, in the Giant's grave, with loose soil raining down on his head, and the breath knocked clean out of him, while the Devil's orchestra plays on, and on, and the Devil himself begins to wheedle and croon . . .

It is all too much for the Ladd. As deep in shock as he is deep in grave soil he is in no danger, for the moment, of breaking the no talking rule.

As for Rafferty Spune. As for the Man Himself. He is listening. Listening to the Devil calling him. Listening with his eyes still narrowed, and his boots as firmly planted at the graveside as they have been all along.

'**NOW'S YOUR TIME**
TO BURN YOUR MIND
YOU'VE FALLEN FAR TOO FAR BEHIND
WOOOOOHOOOOO'

In broad daylight, a close observer might have seen a pulse throbbing at the base of Spune's neck—a sign of what? Fear? Fury? In the dark, it goes unnoticed. In the dark,

177

Spune and the Giant are as similar as they are different: one standing, the other prone; one clothed in black, the other shrouded in white—but both as silent as the passing of time, and neither of them going anywhere in a hurry.

It's not working. Oh, cack and double cack. Oh, Clematis, Star of Bethlehem, Rock Rose, and Cherry Plum. He's still there. Please let him only still be there because he's petrified. Please, please may he run like the wind, any second now—or, at the very least, as soon as he sees Twist. It'll have to be Twist that goes. I can't move. Daren't. Twist must do it alone. Where is he? There. Good. Go, Twist. Move! Someone . . . Angel . . . switch his mask on for him, will you? That's it. Go on, Twist. It's up to you. Go on, Bendy Man, before 'Fire' fades out and we get some crud by Andy Williams. Go, Twist. GO!!!

'FIRE! I'LL TAKE YOU TO BURN!!!!'

The Crazy World of Arthur Brown is moving towards a manic crescendo, as Malachi Twist launches himself from behind the great tombstone.

'FIRE! I'LL TAKE YOU TO LEARN!!!'

Please, prays Tom. *Please, please . . .*

'YOU'RE GONNA BURN . . . YOU'RE GONNA BURN'

The bass line thuds. The electric organ pumps out layer after layer of trembly, menacing sound. The singer's voice grates like a madman's while, out in the darkness, the Devil's mask bobs and flickers, the Devil's pitchfork jabs at the air, and the Devil's horns glow red as stop lights as Twist advances on Rafferty Spune.

In long, loping strides he goes, giving the occasional theatrical leap and muffled 'yee-ha!'

Steady, thinks Tom. *Steady on. Don't overdo it.*

Spune takes one step backwards. Then another. Then another.

Yes!!! thinks Tom. *Yes! Yes! Yes!*

Then whooomph . . . The mask and horns disappear, vanishing so suddenly, and completely, it is as if they have been swallowed. Tom watches the pitchfork go sailing through the air . . . hears it land with a dull clatter against the curls of a stone angel.

Twist has fallen into the grave.

A single, terrified squawk, followed by shouts of 'Help! Help! Get me outer here!' shows that Mattie Ladd considers sharing an open coffin with Satan a reasonable excuse for, finally, breaking the no talking rule.

The words 'Upsy-daisy', and 'Sorry, friend', cannot compete, luckily, with the hullabaloo still being raised by The Crazy World of Arthur Brown. Still, this is nothing short of a disaster. Tom hides his face in his gloved hands. Spune will show no mercy to any of them, he knows that. They are all going to cop it now, every last one of them. It has to be Dr Flint's lucky night. Yep—the doctor is going to be spoilt for choice tomorrow, over who to dissect first.

He doesn't hear the Gorilla Woman heave herself upright. Nor does he notice when she gives her torch a little tap, to let the batteries know they are needed. It doesn't even register when she goes lumbering away into the darkness, holding the torch under her chin, like he'd showed her, so that it shines directly up on to her face.

'*Angel* . . . ' whispers Astra . . . '*My Angel* . . . '

Tom doesn't catch that, either.

'YOU'RE GONNA BURN . . . BURN . . . BURN . . . BURN'

With his eyes tight closed, and his forehead pressed against the fading knee joints of his suit, Tom listens to the clarion call of trumpets, the rising note of madness in Arthur Brown's voice, and waits to cop it. He is surprised at how calm he feels, all things considered. He thinks about his mother. She had been calm. When she thought she might die, she had been the calmest person on earth. It was only later, after they'd chopped the cancer out; after the doctor had told her it hadn't spread, that she had begun to talk, and live, and love as if there was no tomorrow.

'BURN . . . BURN . . . **BURN** . . . '

The Gorilla Woman's face, trapped in the yellow beam of the torch, is terrible to behold. Ugly as sin—no, even uglier than sin—it bears down on Rafferty Spune with its top lip curled, its teeth bared, and its bloodshot eyes fixed on his neck.

'BURN, BURN. BURN, BURN, **BUUUUUURN** . . . '

The growl rising up from the Gorilla Woman's chest is every bit as fearsome as the sounds blasting from the CD player. She can see the Giant's shroud, out of the corner of her eye. It glimmers softly in the dark. It contains a good person. That scut, dithering in the dirt, isn't to have him. Nor will he get his hands on the precious Fairy Child neither. Not if she and the battery-monsters have anything to do with it.

Rafferty Spune stops wondering why the Devil chose Mattie Ladd first, and reaches for his knife. It is either that, or run. Running is looking more like the better option with every blink of those ghastly eyes; with every rise in the pitch and tone of the Devil's song. Yet, even now; even as he stares damnation in the face, Rafferty Spune intends to tough it out.

His brain-to-hand co-ordination, however, is all out of kilter. He is still scrabbling for his knife, in the folds of his coat, when the Gorilla Woman lunges.

Up into the air Spune rises, whisked off his feet by the great, hairy hand clamped around his throat. He cannot breathe. He cannot yell. His Adam's apple is being crushed like a walnut. He treads the air, searching for solid ground. Nothing. The Devil is laughing now—a truly terrible sound. The Devil is laughing . . . the Devil's imps are making music no human ear can stand . . . and this . . . this Devil Ape, not content with squeezing the breath out of his dangling body, is blinding him, into the bargain, with some infernal, searing light.

'FIRE!! I'LL TAKE YOU TO BURN . . . '

'No, Angel. Don't kill 'im.'

Dazzled by torchlight, deafened by rock music and midway to being throttled, Spune only half-hears this sweet, piercing voice coming from somewhere . . . somewhere . . .

'I know 'e's a bad 'un, Angel, but ye mustn't kill 'im. Think of yer mortal soul.'

'FIRE!! I'LL TAKE YOU TO LEARN'

And he's down. Dropped from a great height, it seems, and dropped hard.

'FIRE!!'

And now he is running, like a bat out of Hell; hot-footing it from his place of work while he still has the chance. His curses are terrible, despite the rawness in his throat, but he keeps on running. Even after The Crazy World of Arthur Brown has faded out, in a whoosh of sound very like the whistling of the wind through a boneyard, Rafferty Spune keeps going. He glances back just the once; glances back so quickly, that he is never absolutely certain, afterwards, about what he really saw.

There was a circle of them, he will tell his cronies, at the Fortune of War. A circle of demons, spat up from Hell, and dancing wilder than wedding guests.

'Did you see the Devil?' the lovely Molly will ask, her eyes wide and scared.

'Aye,' Spune will declare, thumping down his tankard. 'Him and his Ape. The one calling out ''Yee-ha!'' as he threw himself around, the Ape shining some fearsome light on the proceedings.'

'And did ye see anything else,' Molly will whisper, 'in the glow of this fearsome light?'

'I see everything, Molly,' Spune will reply, with a faint and dangerous smile. 'Everything. Even on Dark Night. Even without the Devil's light. Remember that.'

And so saying, he will lean forward, beckoning his audience closer. ''Twas an imp,' he will tell them, resting his arms, lightly, on the shoulders of those closest to him. 'An imp with no face, only his bones glowing pale green, like the moon. And a sprite there with him. A slip of a thing. An evil thing . . . '

'And what did it say? What did it say, this sprite?'

Spune will close his eyes, as if the memory causes him untold pain.

'It said: "Oi! You lot! Stop pissin' around!"' he will murmur, pausing a while after, for dramatic effect. 'And then . . . it said: "Come away, come away. *Let's get the Giant.*"'

His audience will recoil, shuddering with the horror of it.

'Poor Giant,' Molly will sigh, wiping a tear from her eye with the corner of her apron. 'Poor monster. Just imagine—carted off by Satan and them others, to eternal torment.'

'Aye.' Spune will wipe ale-froth from his mouth with a swipe of his hand, and shake his head in troubled sympathy. 'A terrible fate for anyone, that. A terrible, terrible fate . . . '

22

It was a miracle, Tom thought, afterwards, that they ever got out of the boneyard. For a start, Twist, once they had hauled him up, hadn't wanted to leave that miserable wretch, Mattie Ladd, behind.

'Peace, friend,' he had called, leaning over the graveside, with his horns and his Devil mask still flashing and flickering. 'Thy master has fled, and we mean thee no harm. Come. Give me thy hand.'

The Ladd's response had been to tuck both trembling hands under his armpits, retract his skinny neck, like a tortoise, and scrunch himself lower into the Giant's broken coffin.

'You're right,' Twist had sighed. 'My grasp has no more clinch than a herring's membrane. Wait ye there, while I fetch us a rope. Oh, and two strong dwarfs and a Gorilla Woman to pull it.'

The Ladd had begun to whimper.

'Twist!' Tom had hissed. 'Hey, Twist. Get away from there. He's a witness. He'll go straight to Spune and drop us in it. Leave him where he is.'

Reluctantly, Twist had shambled across to where Angel and Chang the Exotic stood waiting to lift the sedan chair and get going. Minutes earlier, Tom had averted his eyes as Angel picked up the Giant and deposited him in the sedan's boxy carriage. She had done it so calmly—like a mother sliding an infant into its pram—that Tom had been amazed. Without a word, Astra had nipped in beside the corpse and settled herself down, for the ride.

'Are . . . are you OK in there?' Tom had asked her, from a distance.

'Fine and dandy,' she'd snapped. 'Let's go.'

And now they were running, running fast along a cobbled back street, the sedan chair swaying so violently from side to side that its curtains twitched and its frame creaked alarmingly. Twist, having almost dropped his end of the chair, at least twice, on the outward journey, was running on ahead this time. He had taken off the Devil's disguise, but continued to leap, and to prod the air with an imaginary pitchfork. 'Fire!' he warbled, as they veered down an alleyway. 'I'll take ye to burn . . . '

'Ssshhhh,' begged Tom, his sides aching with laughter. 'Ssh, you idiot.' Behind him, Lummox and Bantam were having trouble keeping up. Angel and Chang were a good team. They were running in tandem now, holding the chair and its precious cargo steady as a small cottage between them.

These were dingy, nasty streets they were hurrying through; well away from the site of Bartholomew Fair. The few stragglers they passed gave way without a murmur or a backward glance—too drunk, or too ill, to do anything more than shuffle to one side. Tom thought he could smell the river. He was wrong.

Left they went, then left again, then right into wider, more familiar, territory.

'Oh!' Tom skidded to a halt. Lummox overtook him on one side. Bantam overtook him on the other. Up ahead: the sign of the raven; as clearly recognizable, in what was left of Dark Night, as the face of a mortal enemy.

'What . . . are you . . . playing at?' demanded Tom. His breath thudded against his ribs. 'Why . . . here? We're supposed . . . to be . . . at the . . . river.'

Chang and Angel stopped beside the railings of his gran's house. His gran's future house. His future gran's house. Stooping, carefully, they deposited the sedan chair on the ground, then straightened up.

'We have problem,' said Chang. 'Honourable chair owner, he need chair back. He have living to earn, before dawn. He say: this chair not right here, this spot, this hour, we in big big trouble.'

Malachi Twist had gone capering up to the tavern door and was calling for everyone inside to come out:

'All within! Come see the show! Come see the Bendy Man's amazing new act! An extraordinary act, ladies and gentlemen, featuring monsters never yet beheld. Not at this Fair. Not in this City. Nor yet in the whole of this fair land. Come, all within! Follow me down! Follow the Bendy Man down to Cow Lane. Be astonished, there, by his cunning tricks. Marvellous tricks, ladies and gentlemen. And each one illuminated, without use of taper or candle, by that tiniest and most extraordinary of monsters— the Batt-Ery.'

Open-mouthed, Tom watched as the Black Raven's patrons came streaming out, to follow Twist down an alleyway like rats after the Pied Piper.

'Now what?' he demanded angrily, after they had all disappeared. *'Now flaming what?'*

Chang's face remained as bland as butter. 'We take Giant and Fairy Child back into cellar,' he replied. 'Then, they go with you. You keep them safe for a bit of time, in your world. You do that, for them.'

Tom felt his invisible face grow tight. *'You've set me up,'* he shouted. *'Haven't you? You planned this all along, didn't you? All of you?'*

'Not me,' piped Astra from inside the chair. 'Not me, I didn't. For I ain't leavin'.'

'Shut up!' yelled Tom. *'Just shut up, and let me think.'*

It was hard to think. The way he saw it, he had two problems on his hands. Two people—one living, one dead—needed to be rescued. One was refusing to cross the gap even though he would willingly take her; the other didn't care one way or the other, while he, Tom, would sooner be boiled in oil than take him.

'Come,' said Chang. 'We go in now. Day coming.'

He was right. The sky above was shading from black to grey; would soon be streaked with light. As angry and exploited as he felt, Tom had no wish to be caught out for a second time by the breaking of the dawn. Not with this lot for company.

The dwarfs, however, had blundered away, back to a keeper who would be so relieved to discover that they had not, after all, run away to sea, that they would get breakfast, instead of a thrashing. It was just Tom, then, and the Changeling Child, who followed on, as Angel and Chang hoisted the Giant's body out of the sedan chair and carried it between them, into the Black Raven.

Astra tottered weakly at Angel's heels. Her legs were too frail, too wasted from lack of exercise and nourishment, to move very far or very fast. It would be easy, Tom realized, to make her stay outside with him until dawn. He only had to grab her, and hang on to her, then they would both end up in his time—but without a dead body to worry about. He almost reached out, as she passed him, but, when it came down to it, he couldn't. She might have fought like a cat, if he'd tried, or she might have given in. She might, perhaps, have been secretly relieved. But he couldn't force her. He would never do that.

Angel was holding the door open for him, using her big left foot, in its buckled velvet shoe, as a wedge. The shoe was filthy; covered in grave soil. Astra, too exhausted to walk much further, lolled beside her, clinging to the soft folds of her skirt.

Tom hesitated. Angel grunted. The grunt said: Move it, monster, or I'll tear your throat out.

Tom moved.

Through the tavern they went, this strange procession of Exotic, corpse, Gorilla Woman, Changeling Child, and boy . . . through the tavern and into the back room. There was nobody about. Not a soul. All had followed Malachi Twist, leaving tankards of ale un-supped and wreaths of tobacco smoke drifting in the air. It was like stepping aboard the *Mary Celeste*, thought Tom. Everybody's gone but, somehow, it doesn't feel like it.

The thick wooden door leading down into the cellar swung open at the touch of Chang's toe.

'*Careful,*' warned Tom. '*The steps are slippery.*' Going down, he sniffed the air. Cautiously. Politely. They were in a seriously confined space now and one of them—the dead one—ought, surely, to be smelling a little ripe.

He sniffed again, a bit harder this time. Nothing terrible—only damp-stone smells, beery-smells, and a musty aroma that was probably just mice. Or rats.

Chang and Angel had to put the Giant down, while they pushed bricks out of the wall, clearing the way through to next door. Tom kept his distance, the bin liner full of stuff clutched, protectively, against his chest; his mother's CD player at his feet.

Astra settled herself at the Giant's side and placed one tiny hand on the hem of his shroud.

Tom frowned. He had to ask. '*Doesn't he . . . you know . . . doesn't he stink a bit? Up close, I mean?*'

'Who?' said Astra. 'Ye mean our dear friend the Giant?'

'*Of course I mean the Giant. Who else would I mean?*'

In the gloom of the cellar, Astra looked exactly like one of the stone figures in the boneyard. Small and still.

'The Giant weren't no ordinary mortal,' she said, quietly. ''E was a blessed saint. And blessed saints ain't stinky. Any more stupid questions?'

'Yes,' said Tom. *'Are you going to cross the gap?'*

Her reply—if there was one—was lost against the sudden crash of falling rubble. 'We through,' declared Chang. 'We go now. Hurry please.'

Tom watched as, moving swiftly and neatly, the Exotic hopped through into Gran's basement, turned, and held his arms out to receive the Giant. Angel, having dragged the corpse with as much respect as she could muster across the cellar floor, lifted it with ease and levered it, head first, through the jagged hole in the wall.

Blimey, she's strong, thought Tom. *Strong and gentle, all at once. How does she do that?*

Astra went next, scrambling and trembling over the rim of broken brickwork, heading for the safety and comfort of her strawstack. Tom moved to follow her.

'One minute, please.' Chang was coming back through.

'What?' said Tom. *'Aren't you staying?'*

Chang straightened up and bowed from the waist. His hands were together in a prayer-shape. 'We leave you now,' he said. 'You bring Giant back tomorrow night, to grant final wish and take to river. Bring torches again. The Child, she stay with you, in your time. Is best.'

'But . . . '

'We go.'

So that was that, then. He had been snookered. Cornered. Left in the lurch with a small, stroppy female and a dead saint to look after.

Chang went, trotting smartly up the slippery steps. Angel stayed put, beside the hole in the wall. She seemed reluctant to leave. After a while, the silence in the cellar grew uncomfortable and strangely sad.

'You were fantastic,' Tom said, when the tension became unbearable. His voice was too loud, too jolly, but he pressed on: *'Back there, in the boneyard. You were brilliant.'*

188

Angel made no sign of having heard or understood. She had her back to Tom and was bending down, her shoulders heaving beneath the richly-embroidered bodice she wore. She was peering through the dust and the rubble, saying a silent goodbye to the Fairy Child.

'Oh . . . ' Picking up, at last, on the Gorilla Woman's distress, Tom racked his brain for some words of comfort. They didn't come easily. They didn't exactly trip off his tongue. How could they, when Astra's fate was so uncertain; when Astra herself was so casual about what was to become of her?

'Don't worry,' he said, at last. 'I'll look after her. At least, I'll try.'

Angel turned, then, and lumbered away up the steps. Her soiled shoes dragged and clattered against the stone, protesting each step that took her further away from the Child. The hand that had shaken Rafferty Spune by the throat was clenched almost as hard, now, against the front of her bodice. To keep her heart from breaking.

Left alone, Tom stood for a moment or two in the strange, sad, silence, gathering his thoughts. He was tired. Tired and cold. Knowing he still had to persuade Astra to cross the gap was a big weight on his mind. Wondering what he would do with her, if and when she did, was beyond him.

It was quiet next door. Too quiet. With a weary sigh, Tom dumped his bin liner full of stuff through the hole in the wall, set the CD player down beside it, and began easing himself after them, arms and head first.

There was still a lot of dust swirling around, from the displaced bricks. A single candle—the one in the sconce, above Astra's strawstack—guttered weakly. There wasn't much light, but Tom's eyes were getting used to making out shapes in the dark. He could see Astra quite clearly, slumped on her tatty nest. He could see the gap as well, glimmering in a faint line across the floor.

189

He could not, however, see any trace of the Giant.

'*Where's he gone?*' he said, standing up and dusting himself down with his gloved hands. '*Where's the Giant?*'

Astra didn't move. 'Chang sent 'im on afore ye,' she replied. Her voice was muffled against the crook of her arm. ''E'll be waitin' over yonder. In your world.'

Tom set aside, for the moment, some major concerns of his, re: having a dead body at his gran's. Any minute now, he reckoned, the sun would rise and that would be it—all hope of saving Astra gone. He walked, purposefully, over to the door and positioned himself right next to the gap.

Across the room, Astra lay curled on her side, with her eyes shut. She had burrowed herself deeper into the straw, like a mouse, and was clutching something tight in her arms. Her biscuit tin. Her picture.

'*Come on, Astra,*' pleaded Tom. '*Come on. You can bring your picture.*'

No reply.

The candle spluttered. Outside, beyond the planked-up window, a single bird began to sing.

Four minutes until dawn.

Then Tom saw the foot. A man's foot. A big, heavy foot in a scruffy boot, sticking out from behind the mirror. He saw it, and it took every ounce of self-control he possessed not to cry out. Instead, he opened the bin liner and began groping around, with shaking fingers, for the beaker of pink drink.

'*Astra,*' he said, just loud enough to be heard. '*Come over here. Come and look at this. It's not a trick, I promise. It's . . . it's something magical. Something even better than the picture. Come and look. Please.*'

For several long-seeming seconds she appeared to be ignoring him.

Then she raised her head.

Pointing, frantically, with his free hand, Tom willed her to look towards the mirror; to see the foot.

She blinked, puzzled. The invisible monster had a flask in his hand. There was something in it. Food, maybe, or a drink. She was hungry. She was half-starved. She had been hungry and half-starved all her life. That doctor. Flint. He would have her bones, if not tonight then tomorrow, or the day after that. It was her fate. No point fighting it. But all condemned prisoners were allowed a final slurp of something, weren't they? So . . . she would eat or drink, yes she would, of whatever was in that flask. It was her right.

Three minutes until dawn.

Sliding to the ground, Astra began to totter towards the door, her starfish-hands held out towards the pink drink. Her mouth watered. Her eyes were fixed, greedily, on the flask. She didn't see the foot move, nor hear the shifting of something high up against the wall.

'*Look out!!!!*' yelled Tom.

And 'Oh!' was all she could reply as her world caved in . . . as a rush of air went whistling past the fluff on her head . . . as the heavy gilt-framed mirror struck the floor behind her and smashed into shards, as jagged and lethal as blades.

'I've gotcher! I've gotcher! Don't ye move now. Don't ye move!'

'Is Nibs: bearing down on his creature with a sack and a noose. 'Is Nibs: trampling broken glass, like thin ice, underfoot. 'Is Nibs: cramped and cranky after coming down to bag the creature for dissection . . . coming down to do the job himself, because that smooth-talking trickster Spune hadn't shown . . . coming all the way down here, to find his wretched creature gone, and then . . . CRASH . . . having to dive behind the blasted mirror as a load of bricks came tumbling out of the wall.

'Stay where y'are now. Don't move. And you—you, creature, by the door. Get back to the Fair. Get back to yer own keeper, quick sharp, or I'll break yer neck.'

Two minutes until dawn.

Astra couldn't move. She was rigid with shock. 'Is Nibs inched closer, the sack held open between his hands. His eyes were mesmeric; sparking with cruelty and greed.

Astra thought, fleetingly, of her picture. Angel would have liked it. She wished she had thought, earlier, about giving her picture to Angel. The sack was directly above her. She could smell its rotting fibres; feel its loose threads tickling her face.

Then the magic happened. It sailed over her head, in an arc of shimmering pink—so pretty, like a liquid ribbon; so slowly, it was as if time itself had stopped to watch it. Over her head it went, in a perfect, perfect curve. She couldn't compare it to a rainbow, or a fountain's splash, for she had never seen these things. But she knew it was something quite extraordinary.

'Is Nibs watched the magic happen too. Only, he saw it as witchcraft. As Satan's spew. As yet another wave of fire and brimstone, coming straight at him. Instinctively, to protect his eyes this time, he ducked.

Clematis, Star of Bethlehem, Rock Rose, and Cherry Plum . . . Clematis, Star of Bethlehem . . .

The sack and the noose hit the floor as the best part of a pint of pink drink splattered the top of 'Is Nibs's head and trickled down his neck.

Clematis, Star of Bethlehem . . .

Stunned, but not quite senseless, his scalp the colour and consistency of boiling ham, 'Is Nibs cowered among bits of mirror, and whined for his life.

'Take 'er! Take 'er! Only, don't douse me again . . . Don't . . . I'm beggin' yer.'

192

Tom ignored him. Striding across the basement floor, taking care to avoid the broken glass, he felt along Astra's strawstack until his hands closed on the biscuit tin. There was a blob of candle wax on the lid. He prised it off as he walked back.

Astra was waiting for him. Beside the gap.

'Come on,' she whispered. 'Let's go if we're goin'.'

'I ain't a bad 'un,' grizzled 'Is Nibs. His scalp was cooling, but slowly. Drops of pink drink flew in all directions, as he shook his beleaguered head, like a dog. *'I looked after 'er. I did. I loved that creature like she was me own flesh and blood . . .'*

There was no one there to hear him. Nor could he hear anything much, himself, through the soya milk clogging his ears. Not the trilling of the dawn chorus beyond the planked-up window. Not the burbling of the gap, as it began to recede. Not the heavy tread of footsteps on the basement stairs.

'I ain't a bad 'un,' he repeated to himself, as the door swung open and a shadow—black-hatted, broad-shouldered, and as steady as an executioner's aim—fell across the gap.

For a second or two the shadow remained deathly still. 'Is Nibs shuffled forward a little, on his haunches, and peered through the dripping strands of his hair. Who was this? Who was here?

The shadow loomed larger; along the floor and up the wall, until it seemed, to 'Is Nibs, to fill the entire room.

'Get up, man,' ordered Rafferty Spune. His voice was low. Dangerously low. One-specimen-down-and-approximately-three-hours-behind-schedule low. 'Get up THIS INSTANT, you snivelling oaf, and take me to the Fairy Child.'

193

23

'Astra?'

'What?'

'Are you all right?'

''Course I am.'

'OK. It's just that I can't see you. You realize that, don't you? Now that you're here, in my time, I can't see you at all.'

'What, none of me?'

'Well, only your clothes. I can see them.'

'So, I'm missing now then, am I? Like you?'

'But I'm not . . . Hang on. Wait a minute. Have you got your eyes closed?'

'I might 'ave.'

'Well then, open them. Don't be scared. You'll have to open them some time . . . Well . . . ? Can you see me now, or not?'

'Yes . . . only . . . only . . . '

'What is it? What's wrong?'

'Nuffink. Nuffink. Go away. Where's me picture?'

'Astra! Calm down. What's the matter with you?'

'Ye never said . . . Ye should've said . . . '

'Said what? WHAT?'

'That yer eyes are the same . . . just the same . . . exactly the same . . . '

' . . . as my grandad's. I've got my grandad's eyes. Blue as birds' eggs, my mum says.'

'No! No! Go away! Go on! I don't want to see yer no more. I wish I'd never seen yer. YE'VE GOT THE SAME BLESSED PEEPERS AS 'IS NIBS!'

There was no consoling her. Tom offered her food; torches; another picture—pictures galore—but she huddled down in the exact spot where her strawstack would have been and refused to budge. At a loss for words, Tom looked around for a thing or a subject to distract her. The Giant's body was under the window. Its shroud, though not clean, was at least visible, and had remained intact. If you didn't know, thought Tom, you'd think it was a roll of bedding. It was no trouble at all, really. And it still didn't smell. Odd, that.

Astra sneezed. Tom studied the tattered dress and shawl, which were all she currently was. They were lying in a heap, like baby clothes waiting to be put away. He didn't know what to say. It upset him that she found him so repellent. He had secretly hoped she would think he was cute. No, not cute. Handsome. How could she liken him to 'Is Nibs, just because they both had blue eyes? *How could she?*

'You can't sleep like that,' he said, eventually. 'I'll bring you down a duvet from the airing cupboard. It'll be like an eiderdown. Much softer than straw.'

He had a sudden thought. 'Doesn't it bother you?' he said. 'Touching the floor like that? Doesn't it burn your arms? Or the side of your face? Doesn't it *hurt?*'

'*No.*'

This amazed him. 'Well, it would hurt *me*,' he said. 'In your time. It would sting or itch me, like crazy.'

Her dress shrugged its tiny shoulders. The shawl twitched tighter.

'Well, maybe I ain't a wimp after all,' she said. *'Or a coward. Or a chicken. Maybe I'm brave—and you ain't. Now, piss off.*

It was hardly worth going to bed; hardly worth closing his eyes for all the sleep he was likely to get before his mum or his gran woke him up. For what seemed like hours he lay on top of his sleeping bag, exhausted but wide awake. This must be what jet lag feels like, he thought to himself. If I ever go to Australia, to visit my dad, this is how I will feel.

He worried, for a while, about Astra. What was he going to do about her? She couldn't stay in the basement for the rest of her life. He and his mother would be going back to Dorset eventually, and then what?

Of course, it was just possible that he might be able to smuggle her home. She could hide on the back seat of the car, invisible among the clothes, and the coat-hangers and the rest of his mother's clobber. He could keep her in his tree house until the weather turned. She would like it up there, with real branches and leaves to look at, and no gentlemen waiting to touch her. He would buy her a jumper, and visit her every day, before and after school. At weekends he would take her out. They could go to the beach. To the cinema, even. She would be safe with him. Safe and happy. She might even grow.

10.15: He had slept after all. Not for long, but enough to make him feel better. He dressed quickly, wondering who to check on first, Astra or his mother. They were both just as likely to give him a hard time.

His mother's bedroom door was open. She was lying on her back, with the sheet pulled taut, to her chin, and staring up at the ceiling.

'Hi, Mum. I've brought your CD player back.'

No answer.

'Mum? How are you feeling? Have you had your green drink?'

No answer.

196

There was a cup of tea cooling on the bedside table. His gran must have brought it up.

'You haven't drunk your tea. Don't you want it?'

'No.'

Tom felt his heartbeat quicken. 'What's up?' he said. 'Do you need the doctor again?'

His mother sighed and closed her eyes. 'No, it's all right,' she murmured. 'I'm just sad. Sad and worn out. We'll go home soon.'

Tom took a little sip of the cooling tea while he wondered what to do. The tea had sugar in it, and a lot of fatty milk. His mother didn't take sugar any more, or drink cow's milk. What was Gran trying to do? Make her puke?

He banged the cup down, turned and left the room. His gran was a selfish, thoughtless old bag. She needed telling. She needed tearing off a strip. She needed to wake up to the fact that her daughter had given up on this visit. Had given up on everything now, by the look of her.

'Gran? Where are you? GRAN?'

She was in the kitchen. He could hear her washing up. He took the stairs two at a time, his trainers, and his heart, thumping.

'I'm in here, darling. What's the matter?'

At the foot of the stairs, he hesitated. He wasn't used to giving grown-ups a piece of his mind. Not grown-ups like his gran, anyway. Having an occasional go at his mother, for embarrassing him, was one thing. Telling his gran she was a lousy parent, and ought to be ashamed, was something else. He almost changed his mind, but the thought of his mother lying upstairs, all weighed down, still, by emotional baggage, spurred him on.

I'm 'ungry. I'm 'alf starved down 'ere.

Glancing towards the basement steps Tom's face softened. Scrambled egg. He would take Astra some scrambled egg, in a minute.

Don't want no eggs. Don't want that thin meat again, neither. I fancies larks' tongues and apricot tart. Or a leg of mutton. Or a herring . . .

Tom shut the kitchen door behind him. His gran was swirling something in the sink. She wore yellow rubber gloves and a thin smile. There was a strong smell of bleach.

'Breakfast, darling?'

Tom scowled. 'No,' he said. 'And it's not me you should be doing things for, it's my mum.'

His gran turned her back on him and began to prod whatever it was she was soaking. Look-at-me-when-I'm-talking-to-you, Tom's mother would have said. Tom, however, found it easier to talk to his gran's back.

'If my mum gets worse,' he continued, 'if . . . *if she dies*, you'll be sorry you didn't get on with her, while you had the chance. You'll be sorry you didn't talk, or go to Bosom Buddies, or . . . or . . . do anything while we were here except . . . except . . . go *out* all the time.'

He paused for breath. His gran was wringing a dishcloth out, wringing it hard, like the neck of a swan. Tom gulped. 'I'm glad you're not my mother,' he said. 'You must have been very wicked. When Mum was little. You must have been a real cow.'

She turned then, wheeling round so fast that Tom backed, instinctively, against the kitchen door. Then she snapped her rubber gloves off and threw them onto the draining board.

The telephone rang.

For a second they both looked at it, startled by the interruption.

'Are you going to get that?' said Tom.

His gran continued to stare at the telephone as if it might leap off the wall and bite her. It didn't ring very often, Tom realized. Hardly ever, in fact. He watched her

198

move—slowly, reluctantly—across the room. It was clear she wanted him to go away, so he stayed put.

She picked up the receiver.

'Hello?' she said. Then: 'I see . . . Yes . . . Thank you for letting me know. I'll come straightaway.'

Her face, when she turned, was as white as the tiles behind her.

Something's happened, Tom told himself. *Something shocking*.

'What is it?' he said, stepping forward. 'What's the matter?'

His gran looked at him; a strange, distracted look, as if she had forgotten he was there. Then she reached across to the breakfast bar and picked up her handbag. Her hand was shaking.

'I have to go out for a while,' she said. 'It's important. But I won't be long and . . . and it will be for the last time. All right?'

Tom nodded. There seemed little point in arguing. Not now. He moved aside, to let her pass. Whatever was going on was clearly none of his business. Maybe Oxfam was having a crisis.

Breakfast. He would get on with making some breakfast. Heading for the fridge, he noticed something beside the sink. Gran really is in a flap, he thought. She never goes anywhere without these.

'Gran!' he called, hurrying after her, down the hall. No sign. He opened the front door and scanned the street. Another hot day. The chalk board outside the Black Raven said *'Karaoke Night'* and *'Lunchtime Special: Eel fritters'*.

Not a soul about.

Oh well . . .

Tom went back to the kitchen. There was green drink in the fridge—his mum could finish that off. Astra would have scrambled egg and like it. He cracked eggs into a jug, stirred in a splash of milk, and put the jug in the microwave. Three minutes. That would do it.

Then he took his gran's dark glasses out of his jeans pocket and put them back beside the sink, where she would be sure to find them later. She wore them so much it was as if she had left part of her face behind.

The microwave pinged. The eggs were done.

24

T he basement floor had a patch of sunlight on it, the shape and size of a sandpit. Astra's clothes lay on the edge. When Tom saw them—the dress spread flat, the shawl a crumpled heap—he almost dropped the big wooden tray he was carrying.

Where was she? Had . . . had something happened?

The sound of her laughter, pealing in the square of light, was so reassuring he found it hard to be cross with her for scaring him half to death.

'OK,' he said. 'I get the joke. I've brought you some breakfast. You can have a bath afterwards, if you like.'

He put the tray on the floor. The packing crates were all too tall to act as tables and the only other raised surface in the room—the Giant's corpse—was hardly suitable for eating off.

'Come on,' he coaxed. 'What are you doing?'

The scrambled egg began to wobble, then to disappear, in surprisingly large chunks. The glass of milk was lifted up and tipped. Tom watched its contents vanish, to the accompaniment of loud glugs.

'It's not that warm, down here,' he said. 'Don't you want to put your clothes back on?'

'*No. I don't. Could ye see me bones back then? In the sunshine?*'

Tom wondered what she meant. Then remembered:

. . . *You may see the whole Anatomy of its Body by setting it against the Sun* . . .

'I didn't see anything,' he told her, gently. 'You're

201

invisible now. And, even if you weren't, I wouldn't *want* to see your bones. You're safe here, from all of that.'

He watched the empty glass return to the tray.

'Fancy a look around upstairs?' he said.

There was quiet, for a moment. It was hard work, Tom realized, dealing with someone you couldn't see. You found yourself straining your ears . . . relying on words, or the quality of a silence, to reveal what would normally be read in someone's face. Astra, for all he knew, could have been thrilled at the prospect of leaving the basement—or absolutely terrified. She could have been gazing up at him in gratitude, or as if he had just wormed his way out of the Giant's shroud.

'I'll borrow my gran's dark glasses,' he said. 'If my eyes are still upsetting you.'

'Nah. 'Twas a shock at first, but I ain't much bothered now. Ye've the same peepers as 'Is Nibs all right, an' no mistake. But yours are . . . I dunno . . . softer.'

Tom was pleased. 'That's all right then,' he said. 'Now—do you think you can manage the stairs?' It was a silly question. Of course she couldn't manage the stairs. Not without help. She was too frail. Last night, Angel had carried her up from the basement, and back down again. He couldn't do that. It was out of the question. Even if she were to put her clothes back on, he wouldn't dream of touching her. It was good that she no longer thought he was a scumbag, because of his eyes, but that didn't mean she would let him pick her up. Too many men had touched her in a bad way. It would be awful if she thought that he, Tom, was going to do that too.

Then the glass was lifted from the tray, and placed on the floor, followed by the empty plate and the unused pieces of cutlery. Then Astra's shawl rose up in the air, where it billowed for a second before landing to cover the empty tray, like a magician's cloth.

'There. I don't want no crumbs stickin' to me arse now, do I?'

'What? Oh—I get it. That's a good idea. Are you . . . are you ready then? Are you all right like that?'

'Fine and dandy. Let's go. Let's go an' see upstairs.'

Tom braced himself and lifted the tray. It was so light, that he thought she might be playing another joke. But 'You drop me an' I'll bite yer ankles . . . ' she hissed, and he knew she was there, perched on the tray, with her head held high and her eyes fixed, greedily, on the way out.

I bin 'ere before. 'Tis the same, only different. That room with the closet . . . the cold closet wiv all the food in it . . . that ain't the same. Bright. So bright it 'urts me peepers . . . And the way the room gets brighter, when you touch the wall. Just touch the wall an' this pole fixed along the ceiling shines harder than the sun, the moon, an' all the stars put together. No flies neither. We 'ad blue flowers in pots, we did, to keep the flies away. Don't need 'em, says the monster. Don't need 'em any more.

Up the stairs we go, me on me plank, the monster treadin' careful like I told 'im to . . . 'Shhh,' 'e says. 'My mother's asleep. She's not well.' Funny to think of 'im wiv a mother. I ain't never 'ad one. None of us 'ave, except Angel, an' hers sold 'er off double quick as soon as 'er beard started growin' . . .

Into the 'barth room'. 'I'll run you a barth,' says the monster. 'And this here's the Toy Let.'

'Speak the King's English,' I tells 'im.

'Is face goes as red as a radish while 'e shows off the privy.

'I ain't pissin' in no noisy well,' I tells 'im. 'I'll 'ave a chamber pot, if ye please. The white one wiv roses painted all over. There's one around 'ere somewhere. From before. I knows it. I remember . . . '

203

'E says there ain't. 'E says: 'ow do I know? I says I just do . . . I just do, that's all . . .

The barth's no better than the privy. Big and white and noisy, wiv two lots of water crashin' into it from some ugly spouts at the end. Very clever. But: 'I ain't no mermaid,' I says. 'I'll 'ave me barth water in a bucket, and that's an end to it.'

Out we goes, into another room. Dark, like the cellar, until the monster touches the wall. I likes this room. It smells nice, although there ain't no flowers around. I sits in a chair, all comfortable wiv a cushion just so. 'I'm 'ungry,' I says. 'I'm 'alf-starved. Let's go back to that closet—the cold one, downstairs—an' steal a hunk o' cheese.'

I'm thinkin' I might like to go outside later, to take the air; to buy cherries, maybe, from the girl in the sky-blue cloak; or some tasty morsel from the oil and pickle shop. I'm thinkin' how it's odd I can picture these things so clear—the girl in her cloak; the sign above the oil an' pickle shop, swayin' in the breeze . . . I'm thinkin', I must've dreamt 'em, one night . . . Must've dreamt 'em up, down in the cellar, along wiv the pots of blue flowers an' a chamber pot wiv roses painted on . . . Must've wanted stuff like that so bad, down there in the dark, that I made 'em up, in me head . . .

Then the monster gives a little jump, like 'e's bin caught stealin' birds' eggs. 'Oh,' 'e says, 'I didn't hear you come in.'

So I turns around in me chair, to see what's what. And there she is, standin' in the doorway. Pale as curds an' whey. No wig. No hair even. Older, too, but still the same. Still the one. I'd recognize 'er anywhere, I would. It was Jane, standin' there. 'Is Nibs's daughter, Jane.

It gave Tom quite a start, to see his mother in the room. Had she heard Astra going on about cheese? Or had she heard him, earlier, in the bathroom, flushing the toilet about six times while he explained the wonders of modern plumbing?

'Oh,' he said. 'I didn't hear you come in.'

His mother trod, slowly, across the carpet.

'Don't sit there!' Tom grabbed her arm and steered her away from Astra's chair. 'Here. Sit here.' She followed him obediently, like a sleepwalker.

'Thought I'd see what's on the box,' she said, sinking onto the settee. 'I'm going loopy up in that bedroom, by myself.'

Tom found the remote, switched on the television, and began flicking from channel to channel. There was a kids' programme on . . . A cookery demonstration . . . a chat show . . . an old black and white film . . . the weather forecast . . . back to the kids' programme.

'You've just missed the news,' he said. 'Do you want the weather?'

His mother hauled herself back on to her feet. 'Not bothered,' she said, heading for the door. 'I'm going back to bed.'

Tom waited for a minute, until he was sure she was out of earshot.

'That was close,' he said. 'I thought she was going to squash you.'

No reply. Behind him, on the TV screen, actors in masks and padded suits were lumbering, merrily, around the grassy slopes of Teletubbyland.

Tom pointed the remote, and switched them off.

'Ye . . . Ye've killed 'em . . . ' Astra's voice was hushed. Appalled.

'No, I haven't. They're not real. They're just pictures, on a screen. That's a television. It's . . . it's like a magic box. There aren't real people in it.'

'Fiddle faddle. I ain't blind. Them rabbits on the grass was real. That purple monster nearly trod on one an' it hopped away. Them rabbits was real all right . . . '

Tom switched the television back on. Then off. Then

on again. No good talking about satellites, aerials, or even cameras. She wouldn't grasp any of it.

'There,' he said. 'See? A magic box.'

He switched the set off and put the remote down on the coffee table. 'That was my mum,' he said. 'In here, just now. She's usually a laugh, but she's been through a rough time.' He hesitated. *Did they know about breast cancer in the eighteenth century?* he wondered. *Did women die of it, back then, or was it all plague, and smallpox, and wasting away after childbirth?* 'I think you'll like my mum,' he added. 'Once you get to know her.'

No reply. Perhaps he hadn't made himself clear.

'What I mean is, I think you ought to stay here. In my time, where you're safe. Mum needn't know you're around, if you don't want her to. I mean, it's not like she can see you, is it? What do you think?'

The silence was hard to read, but went on long enough for him to assume she wasn't keen.

'Astra?'

'I dunno . . . I ain't sure . . . I ain't sure about things. What's 'er name? Your "mum"?'

'Catherine. Although her friends at home call her Cat. Why?'

'I dunno . . . it's just . . . I dunno . . . I'm tired now.'

'And hungry?'

'Yes.'

'OK. I'll make you a cheese sandwich. After that, I thought I'd take you out. There's a park near here with flowers and trees. You'll like it. You won't have to walk. You can stand up in my backpack and look around while I carry you.'

'Cherries,' she said, softly. *'Can we buy cherries?'*

'We might be able to,' he said. 'If the mini-mart's got some. Don't ask for larks' tongues or a leg of mutton though. Mutton's not all that popular round here. And there's probably some law against selling larks' tongues . . . '

'Tis warm in the monster's 'backpack', but I feels safe enough in it, wedged in wiv me shawl, and wiv me head pokin' out the top so I can see what's what. The monster says there are things I need to know about, before we take the air. Things wot might scare me if I ain't prepared.

So 'e tells me about 'cars' and 'buses' and about buildings blockin' the sky. 'E tells me about 'petrol fumes' wot stink, and about people walkin' about talkin' into little boxes called 'mow bile fones'.

'E says the Fair ain't on. I says it must be. The Fair is always on in Smithfield, this time o' year.

The monster shrugs an' sticks 'is 'backpack', wiv me in it, up on 'is shoulders. I can smell them 'petrol fumes' as soon as we opens the door to step out. 'Tis enough to make me retch. 'Tis so bad I 'ave to close me peepers, and go somewhere else in me mind, the way I used to, when entertainin' gentlemen.

We goes down the steps and along a bit. I still feels like pukin', but I opens me peepers anyway, to see what's what, an' who do I spy walkin' past, dressed like a lunatic escaped from Bedlam, but the keeper of the Black Raven.

'Hello, Deck Lan,' says the monster.

Deck Lan? I thinks to meself. But 'is name's not Deck Lan. 'Tis Sam.

'Hello, Tom,' says Deck Lan/Sam. 'It's Carry Oaky tonight. Will your mother be up for a bit of a song?'

I closes me peepers again, and stops listenin'. 'Tis all trouble and confusion. There's a noise up ahead wot I don't like the sound of. A roarin', like some big animal, only this animal don't stop for breath.

'Them's "cars",' says the monster as we go joggin' along. 'And "buses".'

207

I think of the cherry-seller, and of wot I might fancy when we gets to the oil an' pickle shop. I think of Jane who 'as lost all 'er 'air an' become this monster's mother. I wonder, again, how it is I know about these things . . . how they can seem so real . . .

Then the monster stops walkin'.

I opens me peepers.

I am in Hell.

25

'Astra? Come on, now. It's all right. You're safe now. It's all right . . .'

Tom felt bad. He should have realized how terrifying modern-day Smithfield would be to a girl who had spent the best part of her life on a strawstack, in a cellar, during the early seventeen-hundreds. He was a knuckle-head. He had cack for brains. He would be more careful, next time.

'Are you hungry?' he said. 'Shall I get you some cake?'

'*No. I don't want nuffink.*'

She had put her clothes back on and was sitting beneath the basement window, next to the Giant. Tom was glad he could see where she was. He could tell, from the way the folds of her dress fell, and from the tautness of her shawl, that she was sitting bolt upright. She had her biscuit tin on her lap, like a little piece of luggage.

'*I wants to go back,*' she sniffed. '*I want Angel.*'

It was cooler in the basement, now that the sun had moved round. I'll bring her down a duvet later, thought Tom. And a pillow. If she insists on straw, because that's what she's used to, I'll go out and find a pet shop.

'Don't be silly,' he said. 'You saw what 'Is Nibs tried to do to you. You wouldn't last five minutes back in your own time. It's going to be hard enough getting the Giant across. Anyone might be waiting. 'Is Nibs. Spune too, maybe. They won't see me, and the Giant won't care. But

209

you . . . they'll be after you. You'll be dead, and in that sack, before you can say two words.'

The shawl flapped, like the wings of an angry blackbird.

'I . . . don't . . . care. I ain't stoppin'. I don't like it.'

Tom looked at his watch. 3.45. 'Look. I've got to go upstairs for a bit,' he said. 'I want to make sure my mum's all right, and see if my gran's back. Will you be OK down here by yourself?'

The shawl tightened as she folded her arms. *'I ain't by meself,'* she snapped. *'The Giant's 'ere. And anyway, I ain't settin' foot up there again. Not for any reason I ain't.'*

Tom sighed. 'I'm really sorry,' he said. 'About earlier. Taxis don't usually hoot like that. And I'd forgotten to tell you they were demolishing buildings. I'd forgotten to mention cranes.'

He picked up his empty backpack and moved towards the basement door.

'You'll be all right,' he said. 'When you get more used to everything.'

At the door, he paused. 'Do you need a . . . you know . . . a chamber pot,' he said. 'Because if you do, I can find you a bucket, for now, or a bowl, or something . . . '

'I don't need nuffink,' she snapped. *'But I'll have some more o' that cheese later. Before I go.'*

It was quiet upstairs. So quiet that Tom could tell, at once, that his mother was still asleep and his gran hadn't come home yet.

For something to do, he went into the bathroom and began rummaging around in the airing cupboard, looking for bedding for Astra. There were sheets and pillow cases, but no duvet. His own sleeping bag wasn't thick enough to act as a mattress, as well as a cover, or he would have given Astra that. No. He needed to find a duvet. But where?

Then he remembered the little room. The one overlooking the back yard. His mother's old bedroom— the one she wouldn't let him sleep in. Maybe he would find some bedding in there.

Quietly, he crept to the second floor. *Silly to tiptoe*, he thought. *I'm not doing anything wrong*. Still, he tiptoed anyway, right up to the door of the little room where he hesitated before touching the handle.

Locked.

Ridiculous.

So what was in there, then? Why couldn't he go in? He gave the door a petulant shove. It opened—not locked, after all; only stiff from being kept shut all the time.

It was the wallpaper he noticed first. Red roses, only a little faded, clambering, on twisted stems, from floor to ceiling. And cornflowers, lots of cornflowers, dotted blue, here and there. There was no bedding to be seen. No bed, even. Just boxes, and binliners, crammed full of stuff. A junk room. That's all it was now. A room full of junk.

Tom was about to shut the door when he noticed the fold of a blanket overlapping the top of a box. That would do. He would take that, for Astra.

There was a pile of clothes on top of the blanket. Men's shirts—mostly blue, all grubby—and a pair of trousers. Tom moved them and pulled out the blanket. It, too, looked in need of a good wash. Would Astra mind? Tom supposed not.

He looked, again, at the clothes. Someone must have donated them, for Gran's Oxfam shop, and she had put them in here, out of the way.

Was it just men's clothes in the bin liners? he wondered. Maybe there were some kids' things as well. Little shoes, T-shirts, or dresses. Something Astra could wear.

211

He began to rummage. More shirts . . . some horrible ties . . . a couple of towels, rough as sandpaper from years of use . . . He didn't like touching these things. There was something miserable about them. It was all men's stuff after all, he realized. No point searching any— His fingers closed on something slim and flat. A book? No. A passport. Somebody's passport, tucked in among the clothes.

Mildly curious, he opened it. COTTERILL, he read. JAMES ARTHUR. He looked at the date. Five years old. This passport was only five years old.

Then he looked at the photograph.

The man in the photograph had grey, thinning, hair and stubble all round his chin. He wore a horrible tie and a shifty expression, as if the camera had caught him doing something wrong. The man in the photograph had eyes as blue as sparrows' eggs.

Tom slapped the passport shut, threw it into a box and wiped his hands on the knees of his jeans. Then he edged himself out of the room, and closed the door. Firmly. He didn't take the blanket. The blanket seemed, suddenly, far too dirty, so he left it in a heap on the floor, looking like a tramp's cover, or a shroud.

26

T om was sitting at the breakfast bar when his gran came home. He had drunk three Seven Ups and watched the clock notch up an hour.

'I know about my grandad,' he said, the second she walked in. 'I know he's still alive. I found his passport. Upstairs, with all his clothes. Where is he?'

His gran put her handbag down beside the sink and came to sit opposite him. She was still as white as the tiles, and she moved like someone in a dream.

'Well?' Tom said. 'You'd better tell me.'

She took both his hands in hers, and held them, carefully.

'This is going to be hard for you to take in, Tom,' she said, 'I know it is. But your grandfather died today. In hospital. He had a stroke ten days ago, and now he's dead.'

Tom thought of the shirts upstairs, with their grubby blue collars, and of the almost-new passport. 'I don't understand,' he said. 'I thought he died years ago. When Mum was eleven. Just before you moved here.'

His gran shook her head and took a deep, jagged breath. 'No,' she said. 'He left us. That's what happened. For another woman.'

Tom took his hands away. 'He *left* you?' he said. 'So, he didn't have some blood thing after all. He just *left*?'

He didn't know what else to say. It was too much . . . too much to get his head round. In the space of a few hours, this grandfather of his had gone from being dead, to being alive, to being dead again. *What was he supposed to think?* It was crazy . . .

'Does my mum know?' he said, after a while. 'That he's alive—was alive.'

'Yes, of course, darling. She's always known. I'm so sorry. This must be a terrible—'

'And has she seen him? Did they keep in touch?'

'No, darling. She didn't want to see him. Neither of us did, once he'd gone. After a while, it was as if he really had died. When some charity worker came calling, to tell me he'd collapsed in some horrible hostel, right here in London, and would I visit him . . . look after his things . . . it was as if he had come back to haunt me!'

She bent over the breakfast bar, pressing her fingertips against the sides of her head. She wants a drink, Tom thought. She wants to put her dark glasses back on. She wants to live her life all over again, only differently.

He couldn't feel sorry. Why should he, after all? She had lived a lie, and expected his mother to live one too.

'The thing is, Tom,' his gran was saying, 'your grandfather wasn't a particularly nice man. Not really. He gave a good impression, but, underneath, he was a bit of a bully.'

Tom frowned. He already knew that much. 'So why pretend anything?' he said. 'If you were glad to see the back of him, why didn't you just say so?'

His gran got down from her stool and went over to the fridge. 'I'm going to make Catherine her drink,' she said. 'The pink one.'

She took strawberries, raspberries, and milk across to the blender. 'Things were different in my day, Tom,' she said, shaking red fruits into a colander and turning the cold tap on, to rinse them. 'When your grandfather went it was . . . difficult. Not financially—I had money of my own, thank God—but in other ways. I didn't want people to know about it. About him. I just wanted to move here, with Catherine, and start again. You see, being a single parent wasn't something you boasted about back then. It was—well—shameful.'

Tom watched her tumble the berries into the blender. 'My mum doesn't boast,' he said. 'She just gets on with it.'

'I know,' said his gran. 'I know she does. And I'm very proud of her. She's done a splendid job.' She added milk to the blender, then went back to the fridge for the bottle of Rescue Remedy.

'Four drops,' said Tom. 'That's all you need.'

'I know,' his gran replied.

'*She* could have died,' Tom added. 'My mum. She could have died of cancer. And you and she hadn't spoken for ages. Not even on the phone.'

'I know that too,' said his gran. 'And I'm truly sorry.' Her hand trembled over the jug. 'Oops,' she said. 'I think that was six drops, not four. Shall I throw it out and start again?'

'No,' said Tom. 'It'll be fine.'

His gran poured the drink.

'Are you sad?' said Tom. 'About my grandfather?'

'Not really,' his gran replied. 'I'm relieved. And your mum will be too. I must go and tell her. Do you want to come with me?'

Tom slid from his stool. 'Yes,' he said. 'All right. I . . . I think I'd better.'

His gran reached for her handbag. 'Just a minute,' she said. 'I have something here . . . ' She opened the bag and took out a small shape, wrapped in tissue paper.

'A present,' she said, unwrapping the paper so that he could see. 'For your mother. Do you think she'll like it?'

Tom looked at the comb. It was silver, with a blue diamanté butterfly set into it . . . a single butterfly, catching the light. 'Yes,' he said. 'I think she will.' All of a sudden, he had a plan—not much of a plan, but something to be going on with.

'It's karaoke at the Black Raven tonight,' he said. 'I think you and Mum ought to go.'

'Oh, I don't know about that, darling. It hardly seems appropriate, under the circumstances.'

Tom smiled. It felt all right to smile, in spite of everything. It even felt necessary.

'My mum doesn't believe in doing what's appropriate, under the circumstances,' he said. 'When she's old she's going to wear a T-shirt with "You Go Girl!" written on it. Did you know that?'

'No, darling,' said his gran. 'I didn't know that. But I'm glad you told me. I'm glad I know it now.'

27

*C*an't sleep. Too quiet around 'ere. An' I ain't feelin' right.
Not bad, exactly, just not . . . right. Funny 'ow I could
sleep like a dead 'un in me own time, for all the yellin'
and carousin' goin' on in the street. I misses them sounds. I
misses my Angel.

I bin talkin' to the Giant, for the want of some livin' breathin'
company. 'Giant,' I says, 'me and thee, we're goin' to be all
right. We're goin' 'ome this night. You to the place Twist knows
of—the place under the water where ye'll be safe from them body
snatchers . . . Me to . . . I dunno . . . I dunno where I'm goin',
but it ain't back to 'Is Nibs, I got a feelin' about that. I got a
notion I won't never clap eyes on that devil again. No, nor none
of them poxy gentlemen neither.

'And, Giant,' I says. 'you know what? I'm that blessed 'appy,
sittin' 'ere wiv you, all peaceful, wiv no one to entertain, that I
don't rightly care wot 'appens next. Even if I snuffs it . . . Well,
maybe snuffin' it ain't the worst thing can 'appen to a person.
To a monster, anyways. Cos you've snuffed it, ain't yer? An'
you're all right, ain't yer? Ain't yer?'

I gets no answer, of course.

I'm tired now. Too tired to ponder what's what any more.
Me peepers are feelin' all heavy. An' me 'ead—me 'ead's
spinnin' round, inside, like a blessed top. If I closes me peepers
and drifts off, for a bit, 'tis likely I'll feel right as rain
later . . . 'tis likely I'll be just fine . . . and . . . dandy . . .

8.30p.m.: No one could have accused the Black Raven of

cramming too many people into the bar for karaoke night. No one was going to complain that the numbers contravened health and safety regulations.

Declan's face lit up when he saw who was sitting at the corner table.

'We've one or two eel fritters left from lunch,' he called over. 'Can I tempt you, ladies?'

'Oh, go on then,' said Tom's mother. 'I don't mind fish. Only, make sure they're heated right through. I don't want to end up back in bed, with a gippy tummy.'

Tom said he'd have a plate of chips, thanks. His gran stuck to gin and tonic.

At the far end of the room, the barmaid, Madeleine, was up on a makeshift stage, crooning into a microphone and flicking back her curls.

'She's crap,' said Tom's mother. 'I can sing better than that.'

Tom smiled. He felt relaxed—content, even—sitting here with his mum and his gran, waiting for his chips. They were all right, the three of them. Shell-shocked, but all right.

It had been heavy, for a while, back at the house—so much crying, and talking, and needing of hugs; so much emotional baggage getting unpacked and sorted out. He had been glad when his mother had finally blown her nose and said: 'Enough! That's enough sharing and caring for one day,' and they had laughed.

His gran had left the bedroom then, to go and watch some telly.

'Are you all right, Tom?' his mum had said. 'You must be furious that I didn't tell you the truth?'

Tom had shrugged. 'It doesn't matter. It doesn't sound as if I'd've liked him much anyway.'

'No,' his mum had said. 'Nobody liked him much.

That's why he ended up alone, in some grotty bedsit, with no one giving a monkey's whether he lived or died.'

'Do we have to go to the funeral?' Not that he cared, one way or another. The death of a cat, or some actor, would have moved him more than this.

It had been his mother's turn to shrug. 'We don't have to do anything. But if your gran wants to go she might welcome a bit of moral support. I mean, it's bound to be a pretty dismal send off—there'll be no one else there, for a start.'

'OK,' Tom had said. 'Whatever . . . '

'Good,' his mum had replied. 'That's that then. Now, pass me my boob will you? I'm getting up.'

There had been no time to check on Astra before going to the pub. Actually, there had been. He could have popped down to the basement while his mum was getting up, and his gran was watching the soaps. Only, he had needed time to himself. Time to think. To adjust.

Now, tucking into his chips, he felt guilty.

'If you don't mind,' he said to his mum and his gran, 'I'm going to leave you to it, when I've finished these. I'm zonked.'

They didn't appear to mind. There was a man with a quiff the size of a tidal wave up on stage singing 'Heartbreak Hotel' very badly, and they were laughing at him behind their hands.

'We could *both* do better than that,' Tom's gran declared, splashing more tonic water into her glass and tapping her feet to the beat. 'What do you think, darling?'

'Definitely,' said Tom's mum. 'Give us a little swig of that gin, will you? Those fritters were disgusting . . . '

They seemed happy enough to be left alone, just the

two of them. Here in the pub, with other people around, and plenty to criticize, they would probably be fine. It would take a long time, Tom knew, before their relationship really began to heal. But sharing a gin was a start. And getting up on stage to belt out 'I Will Survive', or something equally naff would, he supposed, be good therapy.

'I'm off,' he said. 'Before you two make a right show of yourselves.'

His mum and his gran both smiled. 'I thank my lucky stars for you, Tom,' said his mum. 'You're the best. See you in the morning.'

His gran gave him a look that said she, too, thought he was the best. They were going to talk, as well as sing. Tom could tell. Really talk, woman to woman, until very late. His mum would probably get plastered, but that was OK. It wouldn't kill her.

He said goodnight to Declan.

'No ice cream tonight, Tom?' said Declan. 'No mint choc-chip?'

'No, thank you,' Tom replied. And he went out, into the street.

It was still warm outside, but dark already. There was something about the air which, even in London, hinted at the arrival of autumn—a kind of heaviness; as if the night was as ripe as it could get without splitting, or falling, or changing in some way.

Tom was thinking, rapidly. It was as though there were two switches in his mind; one labelled 'Mum' and the other 'Astra'. He had to switch 'Mum' off for a while now, to focus on Astra.

He was loping along the pavement, wondering what else, besides cheese, might suit the Changeling Child for supper . . . hoping she had seen sense, and decided to stay. Then he saw the ribbon.

Look for the sign. A red ribbon on the railing, so ye'll know the deed is done.

No.

It couldn't be. It mustn't be. It was a little girl's hair ribbon, that was all. A little girl had lost her hair ribbon and someone had picked it up and tied it to one of the railings outside Gran's house. The little girl, or one of her parents, would walk back this way tomorrow and find it. Lost things were often stuck on railings, weren't they? Mittens. Ribbons. The heads of traitors . . .

No.

The ends of the ribbon fluttered a little, and Tom knew it was a sign. The sign. He knew it meant that 'the deed' had been done. That Rafferty Spune had been and gone. That down there . . . down in the basement, on his side of the gap, or the other, lay . . . lay . . .

'ASTRA!'

He could never remember, afterwards, actually getting from the pavement, into the house, and down the steps to the basement. It seemed to take seconds. It seemed to take forever.

'ASTRA! WAKE UP!'

She was lying on her side, next to the Giant's shroud; lying small and neat with her shawl folded beneath her invisible head and the arms of her dress scrunched close to her chest, as if she had been trying to warm both hands under her chin.

'Astra . . . Oh no, Astra . . .'

Tom flung himself down on his knees. His hands hovered. A sound like no other rose up in his throat.

The dress moved.

'What?' murmured Astra, stifling a yawn. *'Are we goin'? Is it time?'*

She sat herself up and shook out her shawl.

'Where's me cheese?' she grumbled. *'I'm 'alf starved.'*

Tom felt something unravel in his chest. 'I thought . . . I thought something had happened to you,' he cried. 'When I saw the ribbon . . . and when I saw you, lying there.'

'I was dozin',' she said. *'No need to piss yerself. I weren't feelin' right after smellin' them fumes, but I'm fine an' dandy now. I wants me supper. An' then I'm goin' back. To me own place. Wiv the Giant.'*

'But what if . . . ?' No. He couldn't say it . . . Not out loud. He couldn't scare her, not without knowing for sure. Only, he was thinking . . . what if time was all twisted up, somehow? So that even though she was here, safe in the twenty-first century, her life was still going on—or had still gone on—in her time? What if she went back over the gap only to find herself—gone. What then? Would she melt away before his eyes like something in a horror film? Or would there be two of her: one on Dr Flint's slab, the other still living and breathing.

Playing for time, Tom went back upstairs, for the cheese. While he was at it, he fetched his plastic gloves and the torches, and sorted out some new bags and elastic bands for his feet. Then he poured what was left of his mother's pink drink into two containers—the beaker that he planned to take, once again, across the gap, and a tall, clean glass, for Astra.

Doing practical, necessary things helped to calm him down. His mind was clearer, his heart less skittery, by the time he returned to the basement.

'Light up one o' them things will yer?' said Astra. *'One o' them torchies.'*

He almost said no, it will waste the batteries. But then he remembered—he had promised her a torch if she crossed the gap with him. If he gave her all of them—the laser one as well—would she stay? He knew, now, that she would not. He could promise her the

222

moon, in her own two hands, and, still, she would want to leave.

In the criss-cross beams of torchlight, Tom watched a cheese sandwich disappear. The glass of pink drink seemed to glow, like a rose-coloured lantern, on the floor. For a long while, Astra didn't touch it.

'Aren't you thirsty?' Tom said. 'Don't you want your drink?'

'I'm lookin' at it,' Astra told him. *'It's pretty.'*

'It's *healthy,'* Tom said. 'Good for teeth and bones.'

She laughed at that, so shrilly, and for such a long time that he thought she might choke on a crumb. It was good to hear her laugh.

'I don't want you to go,' he said. 'I'm scared of what might happen to you, if you go.'

'Well, don't be,' came the reply. *'Cos it don't matter. I ain't scared of nuffink no more.'*

The glass of pink drink rose an inch or so off the floor, then stopped.

'It's . . . it's like the magic,' whispered Astra. *'Like the magic what doused 'Is Nibs.'*

'It's the same stuff,' Tom told her. 'But it won't do you any harm. It will do you good.'

'What's it taste of?'

'Oh . . . fruit and things. I don't know really. I've never tried it.'

Slowly, the glass rose higher. More slowly still it tipped a little as the Changeling Child took a sip . . . then another . . . then another.

Clematis, Star of Bethlehem, Rock Rose, and Cherry Plum . . .

'Oh . . . ' she sighed, lowering the glass back to the floor. *'That was so tasty it was like . . . like . . . I dunno. I dunno what it was like. I ain't never tasted nuffink like that before.'*

223

She had a milk moustache, pearly-pink above the space of her mouth.

' 'Ave a swig,' she said to Tom. *'Go on, there's a bit left.'*

To humour her, Tom picked up the glass and took a sip of what was left.

'Wow,' he said, quietly.

The sandwich was all gone.

'That's me supper finished,' said Astra. *'Come on. Let's go. You'll 'ave to roll the Giant. Only, do it careful—no joltin' 'im around.'*

Tom stood up.

'Are you sure?' he said. 'Are you sure this is what you want?'

He felt something touch his fingertips. It rested there a moment, as lightly as a moth, without burning, itching, or causing him anything but mild surprise.

'I'm sure,' said Astra, before moving her hand away.

28

The gap was humming as it carved its usual path across the basement floor. It was the kind of sound a railway line makes, seconds before a train zips past—not dangerous, or worrying, in itself, but a definite sign. A warning.

''Ello! 'Ello!' crowed Astra, kneeling down beside it. *'Anybody in there?'*

Tom was standing over the Giant's body, steeling himself to touch it. Should he grasp the shroud in both hands and try rolling the body over? He didn't want to rip holes in the cloth, or—worse—accidentally pull it off. It would be far easier, he knew, to get hold of the big man's feet and tug. But yeuch, yeuch, yeuch . . . What if the feet had gone all squelchy? What if he pulled *them* off?

He bent a little closer and sniffed.

Nothing.

The worm of doubt, lodged in his mind since yesterday, began to wriggle. *What if there wasn't a corpse in there at all?* He only had other people's word for it. Dead bodies stank. It was a fact of nature. And if this man was a saint, how come he needed help getting saved? Why hadn't he saved himself?

There could be *anything* hidden away in there, Tom realized. A load of treasure. A load of nothing. What if the Giant's corpse had disappeared *before* Spune and his cronies got to him? What if it had been dug up by rival grave-robbers—the kind who would get a real kick out of filling this shroud with rubble, or sand, just to make Spune mad? What if . . . ?

Behind him, Astra's shawl fluttered and settled as she got ready to jump. *'Oi!'* she snapped. *'Stop ditherin' around, or ye'll miss the moment.'*

'I'm there . . . ' said Tom. 'I'm right there . . . '

There was nothing else for it. Positioning himself at what he could only assume were the Giant's feet, Tom took a very deep breath, stooped down, and made a grab. He connected with something. Ankles. Were they ankles? Or were they a couple of tree roots? Or oddly-shaped stones? Ankles. For Astra's sake he would believe that they were ankles.

'Mind out!' he yelled. 'Mind out! We're coming through.'

'Not yet!' squealed Astra. *'It ain't time!'*

But Tom was on a roll. To his utter astonishment, the dead weight he had braced himself for was as light as feathers. He was moving fast—too fast—taken off balance by the speed at which he was able to drag the Giant across the floor.

'This is too easy,' he exclaimed, as he went careering towards the gap. 'Why is this so easy?' Then, 'Oh!' he added. 'I get it. I've just realized something . . . '

'Look out! Look out, for pity's sake!'

But there was nothing Tom could do, no brakes he could apply to stop himself reeling backwards—right up to, and then into, the gap.

With a terrified yell, he let go of the Giant, leaving him, at least, on safe and solid ground as first one foot, then the other went plunging through ice, and he felt himself being sucked down . . .

Surprise. That was his first reaction. Surprise so sudden, and complete, that it left no room for fear. It had

226

all happened so quickly. In seconds. *Why . . . ?* he thought, as he felt himself sinking, and shrivelling, beneath water so cold that it hurt. *Why me? Why now? Why?*

There were weeds curling round his ankles. Thin weeds, like stringy fingers, intent on holding him fast in the freezing water.

No, he thought. *Not me. Not now. Not like this.* And he began to fight.

I'm getting out. I am. I am. Mum. Astra. I am.

Three frantic kicks and he was free of the weeds. With busting lungs, he paddled, and swam, and fought his way to the surface of whatever sea, or lake, or bottomless pit he had landed in. The top of his head struck something solid. Ice.

No . . .

He was sinking. He was going. It was over . . .

Something clawed at his shoulder. It was rough, and it hurt, but it clung fast to his clothing and hauled him up, streaming. He heard a man's voice, muffled through the ringing in his ears.

'Out you come, sonny. I've got you. You're all right. Out you come.' And when he opened his mouth it was a lungful of cold air that he swallowed, not the rush of pond water that would have killed him.

Where am I? What happened?

He was retching and gasping, and breathing all at once. His chest felt as if the Giant had just sat on it.

'Grab the umbrella, sonny. Just grab it, and hold on tight.'

And in a blur of impressions, before he clutched the end of Astra's shawl, and she hauled him out of the gap, Tom saw snowflakes whirling from a leaden, January sky . . . heard the cracking of ice across Highgate Ponds . . . touched the sodden, glacial, shoulder of Thomas Simpson's coat before it disappeared.

Thomas Simpson. Forgotten Londoner. A good man. A hero.

'Blessed 'Enry. I thought ye'd 'ad it for a moment there. I thought ye was a goner . . . ': Astra's voice, shrill with relief, seemed far away at first. Tom, flat on his back on the basement floor, kept his eyes tight shut and let the sound of it wash over him.

'Good job everyone's a little 'un, down there in the gap. Good job ye were no bigger than a blessed herring, a flippin' and a floppin' around, otherwise I'd never've hoiked y'out.'

Tom opened his eyes. Safe. He was safe. He felt his clothes. They were dry. He wasn't shivering; didn't even feel cold.

'Right,' he said, getting shakily to his feet. 'You'd better hang on to my hand, when we jump. It's no fun landing in there.'

Still dazed, but otherwise fine, he eyed the gap, uneasily. It had stopped humming. Its surface was calm. Malachi Twist was reclining upon it, a broad grin slung, like a hammock, across his face.

'Upsy-daisy, friends,' he said. 'Over ye come.'

'Is it safe, your side?' Tom wanted to know. 'For Astra? Is it all right for her to come back?'

Twist wasn't listening. He had been bumped into by Admiral Lord Nelson and was discussing with him the best kind of knots to use for anchoring lobster pots.

'Twist! Hey, Twist!' Tom yelled.

Lord Nelson was nodding, sagely, as Twist, using both arms and legs, demonstrated the loops of a particularly tricky hitch knot.

'Leave 'im,' said Astra. *'Let's jus' go.'*

Reluctantly, Tom manoeuvred the Giant so that he lay alongside, and parallel to, the gap.

'Problem,' he said. 'I can't lift him over. He's light,

because he's invisible at the moment. But he's still big. I daren't even try lifting him, in case I drop him in.'

He pondered for a moment. 'Actually,' he said, 'why don't I drop him in? What does it matter where he ends up, so long as Spune can't get to him?'

'We ain't droppin' 'im nowhere,' snapped Astra, *' 'Cept in the river, like 'e wanted. An' near enough to the day, month, and year 'e snuffed it as we can get 'im. It's important.'*

'Fair enough,' said Tom. 'But, I still can't lift him.'

Lord Nelson had bobbed away, but Malachi Twist was hanging on. 'Hurry, friends,' he called. 'For the current is strong, and my grip has no clinch to it . . . '

'The magic!' cried Astra. *'Try the magic again!'*

The beaker of pink drink was still under the window, next to the empty supper plate. Tom ran across the room and grabbed it.

'Mind out, Twist!' he called, tugging the lid off the beaker as he hurried back. 'Mind out, I'm just going to try something.'

But: *' 'E's gone! 'E's disappeared!'* The ends of Astra's shawl trailed dangerously close to the bubbles in the gap as she peered in, searching for the Bendy Man's face. *'We're too late. We've missed the moment!'*

Skirting the Giant, Tom held the beaker high over the place where Twist had been. He had nothing to lose—except a precious amount of 'magic' liquid which, he supposed, couldn't be helped. Tipping the beaker, he allowed a small amount of drink to trickle over the rim.

Clematis, Star of Bethlehem, Rock Rose, and Cherry Plum . . . Clematis, Star of Bethlehem, Rock Rose, and Cherry Plum . . .

'Aaaah,' breathed Astra as a spill of pink went streaming into the gap, filling it with iridescence and the heady scent of roses.

And *'Yes!'* exclaimed Tom as the gap parted in the middle; parted easily and smoothly, to leave a strip of solid floor at its centre.

Across the divide, thickets of tapers lit up the basement like a church. The broken shards of mirror had all been swept away and someone had covered Astra's strawstack with a blanket.

The place looked almost welcoming.

Twist was there, licking his hands and doing his best, with them, to smarm down the strands of his hair. The Gorilla Woman was there, dressed in white, like King Kong's bride. Chang the Exotic was there, his face impassive in the flickering light.

'Angel!' shrieked Astra. 'My Angel!' And through the gap she ran, invisible one second, visible the next.

Right . . . Tom thought to himself. Here we go. And he rolled the Giant home.

Aieee. The monster has a face. He has hair and two eyes, a nose and a mouth. He has both ears, a neck, and all of his teeth. He is a man. No, he is a boy. He is a boy, but he is almost a man.

Hurumph. Don't like his eyes. Want to rip 'em out. That scut Nibs has eyes like that. Don't trust those eyes. But the Child is here. He brought the Child back to me. The Child is safe . . .

Oh, friend! Friend and fellow monster—it does a Bendy Man's heart good to see thy face. Indeed it does . . .

'What?' Tom straightened up; uncomfortably aware of the silence, and the stares. 'What are you all gawping at?'

Astra raised her head from the Gorilla Woman's hug.

'You ain't missin' no more,' she chortled. 'They can see yer. All of yer.'

'Oh . . .' Startled, Tom raised a hand to his face. He felt shy, all of a sudden; so shy he could feel himself blushing.

230

Awkward, too. Shy, and awkward, like the back end of a pantomime horse whose costume has just slipped off, in full view of an audience.

'I . . . I don't understand,' he said. He looked towards Astra's mirror, forgetting, for a moment, that it was no longer there. 'Why aren't I . . . "missing"? I usually am.'

'Mebbe it was that drink,' Astra answered, snuggling into her friend's lap. 'Mebbe the magic did it.'

Tom pushed his fringe off his forehead. He didn't know what to do with his hands, after that, so shoved them into the pockets of his jeans. The Gorilla Woman's eyes were on him like binoculars. He smiled, weakly, back. At least I'm fully dressed, he thought to himself. At least she's not checking me out while I'm starkers.

Looking off to one side, he noticed something odd.

'Why is the door open?' he said.

Malachi Twist plodded across the room and extended his neck around the doorframe. 'We don't know, friend,' he said, popping his head back into place. 'But the coast is clear. There is no one up there who wishes us harm.'

He pivoted on his toes, pointed a finger, quite steadily, at the Giant, and said, ''Tis a good omen. It means our dear departed friend can leave this cellar with dignity. Not hauled through the hole in the wall like we planned. Not dragged, upright, through the tavern, with a cloak o'er his head, like some rum-fuddled princeling about to puke in the street.'

Chang nodded, sagely. 'Yes,' he said. 'It is a better way. More honourable.'

The Gorilla Woman rose up and placed the Changeling Child, gently, down on her own two feet. With no need for further discussion, both she and Chang the Exotic took up their places, at opposite ends of the Giant, and bent to pick him up.

'Hang on,' said Tom. 'Let's think about this. It might be a trap. 'Is Nibs might be up there, waiting to grab Astra. Spune might be up there. *How can you be so sure the house is empty?'*

The candle flames wavered. The Gorilla Woman grunted as she hauled up her end of the Giant.

Twist was twitching and twirling beside the steps. 'Have faith, friend,' he told Tom. 'You have a noble face and all of thy teeth, but not one ounce of faith in that which ye cannot see and comprehend.'

'But . . .'

A sudden commotion upstairs. Someone banging on the front door. Banging loudly, insistently, and calling out a name.

'Chang! Chang the Exotic?'

Tom looked, questioningly, over at Chang. But the Exotic merely inclined his head, motioning the Gorilla Woman to start shuffling, carefully, backwards with their precious cargo.

Bang, bang, bang.

'Chang! Oi! Anyone within?'

'We go now, please,' said Chang. 'Honourable chair owner, he full of agitation. He not wait forever.'

Reluctantly, Tom fell into line. Astra, wrapped tight in her shawl, appeared beside him. 'Well, I ain't stayin' 'ere by meself,' she snapped, as he looked down at her, with a worried frown.

'OK,' he replied. 'Your choice.'

And they followed the Giant out of the basement.

'CHANG! D'ye want the chair this night, or not?'

Then a new sound, the sound of footsteps hurrying overhead, stopped Tom in his tracks.

'There *is* someone up there,' he hissed. 'There is. Wait a minute, you lot. Listen!'

Without thinking, he grabbed the drooping hem of

Chang's jacket, to hold him back. The material felt soft in his hand, soft and silky, the way the best Chinese brocade ought to feel. *I can touch things,* he realized. *I've forgotten the gloves . . . but . . . I can touch things . . . It doesn't hurt any more!*

He heard the heavy scrape of the front door being opened, then the rise and fall of a female voice, scolding the chair owner for making such a din.

'A woman,' he said, in surprise. 'There's a woman up there.'

Chang had pulled free and was halfway up the steps, his back stooped over the weight he was carrying. Astra was scrambling after him, scaling each step with surprising ease. Twist, meanwhile, had disappeared out of sight, round the bend and into the hall. 'Madam,' he was saying. 'You are a good woman and a true Christian. The Giant would bless you, for this.'

'Fiddle-faddle,' came the reply. 'Just get him out of here.'

That voice. There was something familiar about the woman's voice.

'And your husband?' Twist continued. 'What news of Mr Nibs?'

'Pah! None. Good riddance, I say . . . '

Tom and the others were at the top of the steps now. One by one, they edged their way into the hall. The Giant's shroud sagged between Angel and Chang, like a bolster. Tom looked around, half expecting to see white-tiled walls and a breakfast bar through a part-opened door. But the hallway was dark; so dark he could see no rooms leading off it at all.

'Come on, Chang! I got a livin' to earn. I ain't got more than 'alf an hour to spare for this . . . this motley crew of monkeys an' such.'

The owner of the sedan chair was regretting his

involvement in all of this. The Giant had been an extraordinary man. The Giant had cured the chair owner's daughter of the fever, just by looking into her eyes and brushing the sweat from her brow. The Giant deserved to rest in peace and it had been a privilege, so far, to be of service. But time was money. He needed to get back sharpish.

'Gaaurumph!' snarled the Gorilla Woman, none too pleased at having been called a monkey.

''S all right, Angel,' soothed Astra. 'Don't 'urt the man. We needs 'is chair.'

'Forward, please,' said Chang.

Tom kept out of sight, dodging around behind Chang's back, bringing up the rear. He couldn't help wishing he was still invisible. He had felt safer that way, despite the risk of pain.

He cast a quick glance over Chang's shoulder, curious to see the woman who had the misfortune of being Mrs Nibs. She was standing beside the open door, holding a candle set into a dish. He couldn't see her face. The light from the candle cast her shadow on the wall, but the shadow wore a bonnet, or some kind of nightcap, obscuring the hair and the outline of the features.

All of a sudden, the woman knelt down and flung out an arm, barring the way out. The Gorilla Woman stopped short, with a grunt of surprise. Astra stopped too, her tiny face illuminated in the candle's glow, her thistledown hair as bright and wild as a slipped halo.

'Poor little mite,' the woman sighed. She let her fingers rest a second on Astra's cheek. 'Shut away down there . . . I never realized . . . And look at you. Just look at you.'

Astra squirmed away. Surprised and embarrassed, she huddled against the Gorilla Woman's skirt, trying to hide herself in its embroidered folds. But Angel prodded her in the back, making her stay put. The prod said: smile. Be nice. Let this woman help you. Let her care.

234

Astra smiled.

'There,' said the woman, moving her arm away from the door. 'There now. That's better . . .'

And she let them go.

Tom kept his head bent as he scurried out of the house and down into the street. The sedan chair stood waiting; its curtains drawn; its owner stamping up and down beside it.

'Madam,' said Twist, bowing and scraping his way down the front steps, 'we monsters are obliged, indeed we are . . .'

'Get on with you,' scolded the woman. 'Go lay that Giant to rest, before every anatomist in London makes a beeline for my cellar. And if ye want to show me thanks, a drop or two of gin, brought round in a jug, will suit me very nicely . . .'

Astra, poised to leap into the chair, next to the Giant, turned and gave the woman another wide, toothless, smile.

'You bring that little mite back here, when you're done,' the woman said, her shadow sweeping across the door as she raised her candle to light up the steps. 'She'll be safe here now, with me and my Jane.'

Twist did a little dance on the cobbles. 'Yee-ha!' he whooped. 'D'ye hear that, Child?' Then he skidded to a halt, his face all of a scrunch. 'But what of 'Is Nibs?' he asked. 'What, madam, will your husband have to say when he returns to find his creature living upstairs, like a proper being?'

The shadow threw back its head. From where he stood, half-hidden behind the bulk of the sedan chair, Tom heard the woman laugh. It was a harsh sound, but oddly triumphant.

'I don't think we need to worry about that,' she said, before shutting the door and dropping the latch. 'I don't think we need worry about that at all.'

29

We're goin' now. We're on our way. And if it weren't downright impossible, I'd swear this Giant knew what was what. 'E's propped up inside this chair like a blessed lord, fallin' over a bit, when we goes round corners, but not so's it matters, or squashes me shawl.

'Giant,' I says to 'im as we trundles along, all snug in the dark, 'it's turnin' out all right, for me an' thee, ain't it? In a while, ye'll be in that special place beneath the river. Don't know where, exactly, but it's under the bridge, some place; way down deep where the tide don't flow an' the fishies don't swim. It's like a cave, or summat. Twist knows it. Twist'll get yer there. 'E can swim like a blessed eel, Twist can. And 'e's strong, too, for all 'is grip ain't got no clinch. 'E'll wrap 'is legs around yer in a great big knot, more than likely, and carry thee down easy.

'And, Giant,' I says, 'I know I ain't never met yer, not face t' face, like, but I reckon it must be true what folk are sayin' about ye being a blessed saint. 'Tain't fiddle-faddle, is it? I know it ain't, cos ye did me a miracle back there, didn't yer? Ye've fixed it, ain't yer, so's I don't 'ave to live in that cellar no more? 'Is Nibs ain't comin' back, is 'e? And there'll be no more gentlemen callin' neither. I'm goin' to live wiv that lady, I am, and 'er daughter, Jane. And there'll be blue flowers, won't there, Giant, to keep the flies away, and a chamber pot wiv roses painted on it . . . ?'

Oi!! . . . Somefink bumped against the chair, just then, givin' me a proper fright. 'Twas somefink soft, like a little bird, flyin' smack into the side. Only, little birds don't fly at night; I knows that much. Then I 'ears the Bendy Man callin': 'Rejoice, friends! He is saved! The Giant is saved!' and I reckons there's no need to piss meself, whatever's goin' on.

'So, Giant,' I continues, 'will ye do me one thing more? Another one of them miracles, just to make everyfink fine and dandy?'

The chair goes lurchin' off to one side, and I 'ears a commotion goin' on out there—a load of folk cheerin' and laughin' at some antic or other.

'It ain't too big a miracle, I'm askin' ye for,' I tells the Giant. 'It shouldn't weary thee too much, gettin' it done. Only, it's Angel. I wants my Angel to live upstairs too, please.'

Tom had expected the journey to the river to be a hush-hush operation, conducted along back streets, with much diving out of sight into alleyways. He was right about the route. The streets they took grew darker and narrower as he scampered along at Twist's heels. But there was no diving anywhere, once they were away from Smithfield. No attempt at secrecy at all, which surprised him.

The sedan chair was moving fast. Too fast.

'Ease up!' the chair owner yelled to the Gorilla Woman who, much against his better judgement, had been allowed to pick up the two rear poles, and act as second carrier. 'Slow down NOW, if ye please.'

But Angel was enjoying herself. No one called her a monkey and lived. She ran a bit faster, the heels of her velvet shoes pounding the cobbles like hammers. The chair owner, resigned to running until his muscles seized up, puffed, groaned, and cursed his co-carrier for a hairy lunatic. Angel ran faster . . .

When the first people appeared, throwing flowers, Tom ducked. He, and Twist and Angel and the chair owner, were going at such a cracking pace they couldn't stop. It was hard to tell if these people were malicious— their faces passed in a blur. Nor could he guess what they were throwing, until the head of a marigold got caught in his hair.

They lurched left, into a street of houses so ramshackle they appeared to be leaning on each other, to keep from falling down. And here, suddenly, were more people . . . women scattering petals from casement windows . . . little children huddled on doorsteps, waving dirty hands and handkerchiefs . . . whole families spilling out of their homes, murmuring and pointing as the sedan chair went careering past.

'Rejoice, friends!' cried Malachi Twist, leaping and lolloping over a pile of refuse. 'He is saved! The Giant is saved!'

A great cheer went up then. And Tom felt swept through with pride and gladness as he ran to the end of the mean little street, with buttercups raining down on his shoulders and applause ringing in his ears.

Eventually, the only people they passed were slight shadowy beings . . . dark entities who went sidling away, down passages so narrow that only shadows could have entered them. The stones beneath Tom's running feet became slippery, as if part of the river had oozed up over the wharves, then retreated, leaving layers of slime behind.

'Ease up!' yelled the chair owner. 'Ease up, for pity's sake, woman, or ye'll have us all tipped off the Bridewell dock, and swimmin' for our lives!'

Reluctantly, the Gorilla Woman slowed to a trot. That cheeky scut deserved a good dunking; but the chair mightn't float, and the Child couldn't swim.

Tom slowed down too; shivering a little as a chill from the river fanned the sweat on his bare face and arms. Twist skidded to a halt. 'This way,' he beckoned, waggling his fingers towards a flight of steps leading down, between vast, leaning warehouses, towards the sound of running water.

The chair owner opened his mouth, as the chair overshot the turning to the steps. 'Halt at count of four!' he gasped. 'Slow down for count of three ... One ... two ...'

The Gorilla Woman halted at the count of two, jerking the chair owner back so abruptly, between the front poles, that his shoulders almost popped from their sockets.

'A thousand curses on ye, woman!' he roared, rubbing his arms and stamping his feet in front of his now-stationary chair. 'And where's that wretched Chinaman when he's needed? There ain't no way this chair'll go down steps. Dead 'uns get carried from here.'

Twist came cartwheeling along, halted neatly, upside down, and beamed politely. 'A thousand apologies, friend, but Chang has other business now. Will ye not help Angel carry our dear departed Giant to the water?'

'Not in this life. And stand up, man. I've 'ad enough of these shenanigans.'

Twist's legs became a lover's knot and he joined his feet in prayer.

'Not a chance,' growled the chair owner. 'My eldest boy'll be 'ere any minute. Then we're pickin' up this here chair and then we're off.'

He felt a tugging on the sleeve of his jacket; heard a high-pitched little voice near his elbow.

'Oh, please, sir,' piped the voice. 'Angel won't 'urt yer, goin' down them steps. She won't, I promise.'

The night was a dirty colour, here by the river, and the moon nowhere near ripe enough to shine on the Changeling Child as she stood, small and trembling, beneath the chair owner's forearm, begging for this favour.

'What?' The chair owner peered down. 'Did someone say something?'

Astra could smell the man's sweat and sense his antagonism, but she stood her ground, meeting what she could of his gaze.

'Please?' she said, again. 'For the Giant's sake?'

The chair owner hesitated, confused by what little he could see. Who was this creature? It looked too small to speak. It looked too small to *live*. Its face, no bigger than the palm of his hand, glimmered in the dark like something glimpsed underwater. Its fingers, still resting on the sleeve of his jacket, had the heart-stopping innocence of a single star.

'All right,' he mumbled. 'All right, then. I'll do it. Only—the monkey ain't to rush me. And if some muckworm runs off wiv me chair while I'm gone, there'll be hell to pay . . . '

The steps were uneven, and perilous with muck and slime.

'All right, friends?' said Twist, capering on ahead. 'All right, Angel?'

'Harumph!' The Gorilla Woman tightened her grip on the Giant's ankles. The temptation to butt the dead man's skull against the chair owner's back was hard to resist. The stupid scut couldn't keep in step, anyway. Serve him right if he went sprawling. It was only for the Child's sake that she held back from pushing him over. The Child had said not to hurt him on the steps. Well, then, she wouldn't. Sniffing the air, she swung her head from side to side, anxious in case the Child lost her own footing on these infernal stones.

'I'm all right, Angel,' trilled Astra, from close by. 'Keep goin'. I'm all right.'

The blue-eyed monster was looking after her, it seemed. Hurumph.

Tom moved slowly, flattered that Astra wanted him near while she made her own careful way down. She could, of course, have held his hand but he hadn't told her, yet, that it no longer hurt him to be touched.

He could hear the river quite clearly now; the rushing, gargling sound of it echoing against walls that loomed and dripped on either side of the steps. 'Yeuch,' he muttered, holding his nose as the stench of dung and sprats, of mud and rot, of drowned puppies and the sweepings from butchers' stalls rose up to meet him.

They had reached the mouth of the Fleet Canal, where it spewed into the Thames. They had reached the place where a waterman waited, his elbows resting, easily, on a long pair of oars, his boat loosely tethered to a rusty iron ring and bobbing, like a log, in a swirl of foam. The waterman's face was inscrutable as he watched the dock. At first sight of the Giant, he raised a lantern.

'Chang!' exclaimed Tom. 'It's you! Is this your boat? Can you row it?'

The Exotic bowed over his oars, but made no reply.

Tom could have kicked himself. Of course Chang could row a boat. Why wouldn't he be able to? Because he had a pigtail? Because his eyes were slanted and he said 'tomollow' instead of 'tomorrow'? Tom had convinced himself—mistakenly, it seemed—that Chang was just another freak, in town for Bartholomew Fair. He had assumed he had a keeper, like Lummox and Bantam and all the other monsters. But, no, Chang was his own keeper . . . an independent person . . . a waterman on the Thames.

'Right,' said the chair owner. 'Heave-ho, then away I go.' And he swung his end of the Giant into the front of the boat, fully expecting the monkey-woman to follow through with a heave-and-a-ho of her own.

'Watch out!' Tom grabbed the chair owner by the collar and flung him backwards, just in time to stop him losing his balance and toppling headlong into the unsavoury, mingling waters of the Fleet and the Thames.

The boat rocked, perilously. For several awful seconds it looked as if the Giant, thrown one way by the chair owner, pulled the other by Angel, was destined for a much shallower and muckier final resting place than he had been promised.

Somehow, Chang managed to grab the shroud with one hand and steady the boat with the other. He didn't even lose the oars. And with a feeble but well-intended shove or two from Malachi Twist, enough of the Giant's body slid into the boat for it to remain there, wedged head-down in the prow.

The chair owner staggered to his feet and stood, swaying, on the dock. What the devil had happened? One thing he knew for sure: the sooner he got back to earning his living, the happier he would be.

'I'm off,' he announced, wavering towards the steps. 'I've had enough of this . . . this madness.'

The Gorilla Woman, thwarted in her attempt to dunk the scut once he was off the steps, gave him a swift cuff on the head as he passed.

'Oi!' bellowed the chair owner. 'What's that all about? What've I done to deserve that?'

Tom looked up from levering the Giant into a safer, and more dignified, position in the bottom of the boat. 'That's not nice, Angel,' he said. 'Don't do it again.'

Grrrrumph! The Gorilla Woman lifted her petticoats and stepped, heavily, into the dipping, bobbing tub that was to take the Giant to safety. Blue-eyed scut. What would he know?

'Cast off!' crowed Malachi Twist. 'Cast off, Angel, if ye please. The knot on this rope defeats me, for my fingers have no more grasp than a herring's . . .'

'Astra!' interrupted Tom. 'Where's Astra?'

He reached out both hands to grope among coils of wet rope; then, more frantically, along the splintered plank he was sitting on. 'I can't find Astra. Where is she?'

'I'm 'ere,' came the reply from the very tip of the prow. 'No need to piss yerself.'

The boat spun in a whirl of scum as the Gorilla Woman loosened the rope from the iron ring.

'Yeee-ha!' whooped Twist, and the vessel rolled even more wildly as he did his little dance between the seats.

'Please to sit down, everyone,' said Chang, leaning hard on one of the oars. 'We go now.'

'You crazy crew!' scoffed the chair owner, cupping his hands round his mouth, the better to shout from the dock. 'You bunch of raving bedlamites!' And he shook his head in mock despair as the boat righted itself and was carried away downstream.

Gradually, the splash of oars and the glow from the lantern grow fainter. Eventually, all the chair owner can make out is a diamond of light, dipping up and down in the dark, as the Chinaman's boat, chock-full of monsters, cuts a course for London Bridge.

The tide is flowing fast, tonight. They will be there before they know it.

The chair owner scratches his chin and sighs. It is cold and damp, down here on the steps of Bridewell Dock. His leg muscles ache, like the very Devil, and there is a bump on his head that will be the size of a duck egg by morning.

243

At the top of the steps, the chair owner's eldest boy paces the cobbles. He is growing more uneasy by the second. Time is money, yet the sedan chair stands empty between its poles, and the nearest paying passenger is nowhere near this Godforsaken end of town.

'Father!' the boy calls. His voice quavers down the steps. 'Are ye there? Are ye hurt at all?'

The chair owner stirs himself. He must go. He has a living to earn.

He casts a final glance downstream, but there is nothing, now, to see or hear. He has done his bit. The Giant is on his way.

'God speed,' he murmurs, before turning away. 'God speed, ye valiant bunch of lunatics.'

30

London Bridge is falling down, falling down, falling down,
London Bridge is falling down, my fair lady . . .

Tom cannot get this old nursery tune out of his head. It keeps on and on repeating itself as Chang's boat dips and ploughs towards the great arches spanning the Thames. They are getting close; so close that the din of rushing water drowns every other sound.

Chang has to shout to be heard: 'Current strong tonight. Not good.'

As if to underline his point, the boat gets caught on the rim of some undertow and starts to spin.

'I don't like this.' Astra buries her face in Angel's shoulder, and prays for one more miracle. (*Just a small miracle, Giant, if ye please. Don't let this boat turn upside down. Don't let me snuff it in the river, or get eaten by a blessed whale.*)

Malachi Twist is perched, cross-legged, on the plank in front of Tom. He has both arms wrapped round his neck, like a muffler, and is humming a little tune. Tom taps him on the shoulder, to get him to listen to what Chang has to say about the current.

'Yikes, friend! Don't hurt thy fingers on my account.' Twist twizzles around, on his plank, full of concern. 'Where are thy mittens? Where is thy protection?'

'I don't need it any more,' Tom shouts back. He clutches the edge of the boat as Chang strains against the oars, still fighting the tide. 'I'm all right now. I can touch things. I haven't had the gloves on all evening. I don't need them.'

The Bendy Man's eyes soften. Tentatively, he reaches out, across the dark, bobbing space between the planks, and touches Tom's fingers.

'See?' says Tom. 'Doesn't hurt at all.'

Gurning with delight, Twist flings both arms wide and wraps Tom in a bear-hug so rubbery that it squeaks.

'Oi!' shrills Astra, as the river splashes her knees. 'You're rockin' the blessed boat. Sit down.'

'Listen.' Tom is pink with embarrassment and lack of breath. 'Listen, Twist. Chang says the current's strong. How are we going to get the Giant to this place of yours? Where is it?'

They are so close to London Bridge that Tom feels threatened by the houses that jut out over the water. It is too black, still, for him to pick out a row of tall iron spikes up there. Nor does he register the bony rattling of traitors' heads through the noise of the river as it crashes through the arches.

'‘Tis just over yonder,' Twist replies. 'Beneath the seventh arch.'

The seventh arch looks much like all the others. Dangerous.

Chang has rowed as close to the bridge as he dares. Any nearer, and the rip of the tide will smash them against a parapet, or suck them under an arch, into a six-foot waterfall that will swamp the boat and send its passengers tumbling. Chang's face remains unreadable, but his mind churns as he uses every bit of skill and strength he possesses to keep his boat from being drawn any further downstream. This is wrong. This is unexpected. He has never known a current so treacherous. It is a bad omen— the work of an evil spirit.

Tom eyes the Giant—a big, pale, shape in the gloom.

'What do we have to do?' he asks Twist. 'Weigh him down with something, and drop him in?'

Twist stands up. His bare feet squelch. The boat rocks like a cradle as he removes his jacket. His face is unusually still. 'Nay, friend,' he says, at last. 'That is not the sum of it. That is not what we have to do.'

Chang raises the lantern. The movement is so swift and sure that you wouldn't know his hands had left the oars. He has manoeuvred the boat out of immediate danger, but must continue rowing, hard, just to keep in roughly the same place.

'Current strong,' he repeats.

Twist spits on his palms and slicks back the anchovy-strands of his hair. He is ridiculously skinny, standing there, in his singlet and tattered trousers. If he hears Chang, he does not let on. He tips back his head, as if searching the sky for something. Then he gives himself a hug.

'Angel,' he says, still staring up into the impenetrable night, 'ye must act alone. Chang cannot leave his place. Can ye do it?'

The Gorilla Woman is guarding the Child, holding her close, as the river sucks on the boat and Chang the Exotic drags on the oars, like a man spooning concrete. She growls, low in her throat. I can do it, says the growl. I can do this thing. She lumbers to her feet and, in one swift movement, places the Changeling Child next to Tom— right next to him, on the plank, so that he can hang on to her and keep her safe. This swirling, leaking tub that the Chinaman has seen fit to cast them adrift in is no place for the Child. It is no place for anyone with half a mind and a beating heart.

Astra clings to Tom like a limpet. It is a mercy, she thinks, that he no longer jabbers and yelps at the slightest touch. It is a miracle and a mercy, for she would surely die of fright, or go overboard by accident, without someone to hold.

Tom hardly notices she is there. He is watching Angel lifting the Giant; lifting him so carefully that the movement makes little difference to the spinning, tipping motion of the boat. He is watching Twist prepare to enter the water.

'No!' he shouts. 'Tell him, Chang! Tell him it's too dangerous.'

Twist kneels down in front of Tom's plank. His face, in the swing and sway of the lantern's light, twitches so earnestly that Tom knows there is nothing he can say that will stop this happening. Not one single thing. Still, he tries:

'Let's do this another night,' he cries. 'When the current's not so strong. Let's take the Giant back to the basement. Your time or mine, I don't care. He's all right in the basement. He doesn't smell. He's no trouble. Let's . . . let's go home.'

Malachi Twist shakes his head.

'I made a promise,' he says. 'And I must keep it. Haven't ye risked life and limb, thyself, to help thy fellow-monsters? Yes. It is so. Ye have a noble heart, sir, and thy soul, I now firmly believe, is as untarnished as thy teeth.'

He waggles his ears and straightens up. 'Have faith, friend,' he says, 'and watch for my return. I would shake thee by the hand, only . . . '

'I know,' says Tom, through the ache in his throat. 'I know . . . '

Angel grunts. The grunt says: Get a move on; this Giant's no feather.

And now the boat is rocking. And Twist is in the river. His hammocky smile is as broad as ever as he grips the edge of the boat with his toes, and prepares to receive the Giant.

''E can swim like a blessed eel, the Bendy Man can,' Astra whispers in Tom's ear. ''E'll be fine an' dandy, you'll see . . . '

The boat rocks even more and Tom cannot bear to look as Angel eases the Giant's body into the dark, swirling water and the Bendy Man, with a flick of his rubbery heels, and a final, triumphant, 'Yee-ha', takes him down.

We saw 'im just the once, after that. Leastways, Chang did. I never saw nuffink, cos the boat was rollin' around worse than ever, and I 'ad me peepers closed.

Chang says 'e reached the seventh arch all right. 'E says 'e saw 'im bob up, just for a second, punchin' the air wiv' 'is right arm. 'Tis what 'e used to do, the Bendy Man, when 'e was full of joy—leap up and punch the air. Chang says it was a good omen; a sign that the Giant 'ad bin properly laid to rest.

Well, it weren't no good omen for the Bendy Man.

At first, I thought to meself: 'E's takin' 'is time, that's all. 'E's makin' sure the Giant's fine and dandy down there in that cave, settlin' 'im in just so, wiv a rock at 'is 'ead, mebbe, an' another at his feet. 'E'll be sayin' a prayer, or doin' a dance . . . biddin' the Giant farewell, in 'is own fashion. But I knew in me 'eart that the Bendy Man would never put 'is friends and fellow monsters through such a torment of waitin'. It weren't in 'is nature.

I don't know 'ow long we stayed there in the boat, but it were a long, long while. Angel took the oars, for a bit, so's Chang could rest 'is arms. But the blue-eyed monster just sat beside me on the plank, starin' out, towards the bridge, and sayin' not one word.

'E loved Malachi Twist. We all did.

Then it seemed to me that the sky was growin' lighter, and the boat weren't pitchin' around like a blessed animal quite so much. And I knew the night were nearly over and that we would wait no more.

'No!' shrieked the blue-eyed monster when Chang said the thing we 'ad all been thinkin' an' fearin'. 'No! We can't leave him. He might be all right. He might be waiting for the tide to turn, before swimming back to us. We can't go yet.'

But Chang shook 'is 'ead. 'Day coming,' he said. 'River soon get busy. Our friend, he make big sacrifice to save that Giant. Current strong. He gone now, for certain.'

That made it real, Chang talkin' like that. I ain't never cried proper tears in me life, not for nuffink or no one, but I felt bad, then, thinkin' about leavin' the Bendy Man behind for the fishes to nibble and some blessed mudlark to find. And I thought: What if 'e's driftin' along for any old rogue to 'appen across? What if someone sells 'is body to an 'ospital, and a doctor cuts it up?

Angel was thinkin' the same. I could tell. She cries for all humanity, does Angel, but was weepin' an extra river for Twist.

'Don't fret, Angel,' I said, as Chang turned the boat around. 'The Giant'll look after Malachi Twist. The Giant won't let nuffink stop that Bendy Man's soul from goin' straight up to Heaven.'

The blue-eyed monster was cryin' too—so 'ard that 'is nose was all bubbly. 'E was in need of some comfort, I could tell. And I was just thinkin' about strokin' 'is arm, and about 'ow I wouldn't mind touchin' 'im like that, for all 'e was almost a grow'd man . . . I was just thinkin' it when Angel went staggerin' over to where 'e sat, and gathered 'im up like 'e was a great big monster-baby. I was sorry, then, that I 'adn't moved quicker. But at least 'e got comfort from someone.

And so, we went away from them arches. And we was almost back at the dock when it seemed to me like the sky were suddenly full of glimsticks, lightin' up the spaces between the grey. I'd never seen nuffink like it before. It were that beautiful, wiv all them soft colours gettin' brighter an' more splendid, that I found meself thinkin': This must be Heaven, this must, openin' its doors for the Giant.

'Look!' I said. 'Look up at the sky!'

So they all looked up, only none of 'em seemed surprised, or as overjoyed as I was, to see Paradise spreadin' out up there in all its blessed glory. Indeed, the blue-eyed monster looked fair terrified. 'Oh, no,' 'e said. 'It can't be. Not now. Not yet.'

''S all right,' I said. 'The Giant'll 'ave a word or two about yer. 'E'll make sure ye get a place up there when the time comes. No need to piss yerself.'

I was that excited. I thought: Any second now we'll 'ear beautiful singin' voices and there'll be golden steps comin' down through that light for the Giant to go walkin' up. And maybe Twist'll be right there behind 'im, whirlin' 'is arms around, to dry 'imself off, and yellin', 'Make way, saints and angels, if ye please! Make way for the Bendy Man.'

I was that much of a ninny, back then—fresh out of the cellar and knowin' nuffink whatsoever about the workings of Mother Nature.

It was Chang put me right.

'E was bone-weary, Chang was. I ain't never seen 'im like that, not before nor since. 'Is pigtail was all undone and 'is face weren't smooth like normal. There was wet on 'is face as 'e lifted it—tears or river water . . . I dunno which . . . 'E 'ad rowed us to safety, by then, and we were close enough to the dock for 'im to rest on 'is oars, while 'e looked up, at the beauty of that sky.

'Dawn breaking,' 'e said.

And I wished, then, that I could cry.

* * *

251

Tom was both afraid of, and resigned to, the coming of the day. He knew, full well, that the chances were he would find himself treading water, alone, as first light fast-forwarded him into the twenty-first century. Yet, after a few seconds' panic, he simply closed his eyes, leaned back against the Gorilla Woman's warmth and waited to see what would happen.

If I end up having to swim for it, he told himself, I will do it. I will struggle and fight in the Thames, the way I struggled and fought in the gap. To live. To get home.

And so he waited, on his plank, knowing there was little point in doing anything else. *Hang in there*, his mother would have said. *Hang in there. Wait and see. It's all you can do.*

He wondered what Malachi Twist had thought before plunging, voluntarily, into the river. It hurt him to wonder. *Don't go there*, he told himself. *Don't think about it.* But he had to. 'Have faith, friend,' Twist had said. But faith in what? In fate? In Twist's own judgement? In his ability to swim like an eel? Or in something greater? Something divine?

At his feet, rolling around, was the plastic beaker. It was empty. Tom had flung the last of the pink drink over the side; flung it quickly and clumsily, when the pain of waiting for Twist to reappear had become too much to bear.

There had been no flash of iridescence as the drink hit the river. No turning of the tide. No miracles. Only a small slopping sound as the milk blended with the murk of the water, and simply disappeared.

Clematis, Star of Bethlehem, Rock Rose, and Cherry Plum . . . Even the words had lost their power. They would stay in Tom's memory for as long as he lived, but he would never again say them in sequence, or aloud.

It was done. The Giant was saved. The magic wasn't needed any more. Tom shuddered as the light quickened. The Gorilla Woman tightened her grip around his shoulders and gave him a gentle squeeze.

'Dawn breaking,' said Chang.

And Tom's last, conscious, thought, before darkness swept in, was that for the Gorilla Woman to touch any living male, in a manner that didn't involve shaking, pushing, or throttling, was so unusual that it was, in its way, a kind of magic. A miracle, even.

31

'**O** i! Wake up! Wake up!'
Cold stone under his spine. Something rough, and prickly, pillowing his head. A woman's voice, faraway, singing a song about merry green woods . . .

'Mu . . . Mum . . . ' Tom's throat was so dry he could barely speak. His eyelids felt as if they had been glued. Waking felt like swimming up from a dark place. Not through water though. That was good. That was something, at least.

He opened his eyes. The singing had stopped.

Astra's face hovered above his own. It was cleaner than he ever remembered seeing it, except for traces of jam around the mouth.

'Hello,' he croaked. 'What happened?'

'Dunno.' Astra sat back on her heels. She was wearing a proper dress—blue, with a white collar—and her hair had been washed and brushed to an aura of fine, golden fluff. 'Ye just closed yer peepers and went all floppy. Chang and me, we thought ye'd snuffed it. We thought we 'ad another blessed body on our 'ands. But Angel, she could 'ear yer heart thumpin' through yer garments. She stopped us throwin' yer to the fishies.'

'Oh,' said Tom. 'Good. I'm glad someone bothered to check for a pulse.'

Struggling into a sitting position, he found himself on the basement floor, beside the remnants of Astra's strawstack. A plank had been prised from the window, to let some daylight in, and the door had been left open.

There was no sign of the gap.

''Ere,' said Astra. 'Take this.' She pushed a cup of water towards him, and a hunk of dark bread.

Tom gulped the water and nibbled the bread. There were so many things he needed to ask . . . so many answers he dreaded having to hear.

'Twist,' he began. 'Did he . . . have you . . . ?'

'No,' said Astra. ''E's gone. 'E snuffed it. Definitely.'

Tom waited for the pain of that to pass, knowing that it never really would. 'And what about 'Is Nibs? Is he back?'

'No, 'e ain't. And if 'e shows 'is poxy face anywhere near, the ladies of the 'ouse will bash it in wiv a stovepipe, I reckon. They're glad to see the back of 'im. They told me so.'

Upstairs, the singing began again.

'That sounds like my mum,' said Tom.

'That's Jane.' Astra beamed, gummily. Already, she adored 'Is Nibs's daughter. They had a lot in common. 'Jane's nice,' she said. 'She knows you're down 'ere. She said she'd like to meet yer. To say thank you.'

'What for? What does she want to thank me for?'

'Dunno. For savin' the Giant, I expect.'

Through the cleared space at the window, Tom could see that the sun was high. It must be lunchtime, or even later. Mum and his gran would be having twenty fits.

He made himself stand up. His legs felt odd, as if he hadn't walked for years.

Astra was still prattling: 'That Giant, 'e was a blessed saint all right, an' no mistake. 'E's done me another miracle, 'e 'as. Cos Sam—that's Angel's keeper—'e's Jane's sweetheart; leastways, that's wot I reckon seein' as 'ow she went all pink when I said 'is name . . . So . . . '

'Sorry? What? Who's Sam?' Tom was pacing the basement floor, looking for cracks, flaws . . . anything that might stop the panic rising up in his stomach.

'I told yer. 'E's Angel's keeper, in the Black Raven. 'E ain't a bad 'un. Not really. And wiv 'Is Nibs out the way, 'e an' Jane'll be fine and dandy, I can tell. So, then, if Jane says please an' thank ye to 'im, all dainty like, 'e'll let Angel live upstairs. I know 'e will! I knows it!'

She clapped her hands, shivering with glee. And her tiny face looked so alive . . . so *young* . . . that Tom paused, and smiled at her.

'That's great,' he said. 'I hope it works out.'

He turned back to the floor. *Please*, he whispered to it, in his head. *Don't do this to me*.

Astra had trotted away from him, and was rummaging in her strawstack. 'I'm takin' me picture upstairs,' she announced. 'And one o' them torchies, if ye please. For Angel.'

Tom thought he saw a flicker of movement, over by the door. But it was a trick of the light, nothing more. The panic was turning his innards now. He would be sick, in a minute, if he didn't sit down.

His mother . . . what must she be thinking? He had left nothing behind that would give her the faintest clue about where he had gone. She must have been so relieved, all those years ago, when he had toddled back from being missing—just toddled over the gap, with straw in his hair, and his thumb in his mouth. She must have felt like crying with relief. He hadn't understood then about loving people, about the fear of loss that goes with it, like a flipside to joy. He hadn't known, then, how scary it would be to feel that way about someone. Or how amazing.

'Oi? What's up wiv yer? Are ye all right?'

Tom raised his head from between his knees. 'No,' he said. 'I'm not all right. I'm almost pissing myself, actually.'

Astra came and stood before him, her picture pressed against the front of her new dress. 'Come an' see Jane,' she said. 'She'll look after yer.'

Tom dropped his head in his hands and groaned.

'You want to go, don't yer? Back to yer own time? Back to them "cars" an' "buses" an' "mow bile fones"?'

Tom could hardly even bring himself to nod. What was the point? The Giant was saved. The magic wasn't needed any more. The *gap* wasn't needed any more.

'Go on, then.'

'What?' His head jerked back, so abruptly that his neck cricked. 'What was that you said?'

'I said, "Go on then". Are ye deaf?'

'But . . . ' His gaze swept the floor.

There! Yes! There it was! Over by the door. That spot where the light had been playing tricks, just now. It was shifting. Yes, it was! It really, really was! Shifting and splitting and inching its way along.

Relief, so strong it almost hurt, had him back up on his feet, and across the room in a trice.

'Oi! Monster!'

He half turned. The gap was travelling in fits and starts, like something old and tired. He felt the need to watch it; to will it to keep going.

Astra had put her picture down and was holding out her arms. He blinked and opened his mouth to speak. Everything was happening so fast . . . There hadn't been time to think . . . to talk . . .

Then she snapped her fingers. 'Where's me torch? Me torch, for Angel?'

'Oh . . . ' The gap was halfway across the floor now, and struggling. He threw it a message: *Don't stop*, and ran to where he had left the carrier bag with his stuff in it.

'There,' he said, tipping all three torches at Astra's feet. 'Tell Angel . . . tell her they won't always work.'

'Why not?'

'Because . . . because batteries die. Eventually.'

'Oh.' She looked up at him, her face solemn, for a

257

moment, beneath the floss of her hair. 'Poor little monsters,' she said. 'But we'll look after 'em. Me and Angel and Jane. We won't let them doctors cut 'em up, after they snuffs it. I promise.'

The gap gave a final lurch.

'Astra . . . '

'Quick!' She pointed, urgently. 'The gap! It ain't stoppin'.'

He wheeled round. She was right. The gap, having touched the far wall, was starting to congeal. He had just seconds before it withered away completely.

'Go, monster! Quickly! Quickly! Go!'

And he ran.

'Go, monster . . . Jump! . . . Go on . . . '

And he leapt.

'Go . . . monster . . . '

The gap snuffed it, very fast, after that. Astra watched it happen, then turned stiffly away. She hadn't heard anyone coming down the steps, but her face brightened when she realized who was there.

'Have I missed him? Your friend. Has he gone?'

Astra looked back at the place where the gap had been. 'Yes,' she said. ''E's gone now.'

'That's a pity. Will he return, do you think? Before the Fair ends?'

'No,' Astra said. ''E won't appear no more.'

She stooped to pick up her picture. She would come back for the torchies later. The little battery monsters would be safe enough down here, for now. No one would touch them. They wouldn't be hurt.

'I'm 'ungry,' she declared. 'I'm 'alf-starved.'

'Come along, then.' Jane reached out her hand. 'We have some bread left, and some jam. And, later, I will walk as far as the oil and pickle shop to buy us something tasty for our supper. Does that sound like a good plan?'

'Yes,' Astra told her. 'Fine and dandy.'

They left the cellar together, shutting the door behind them.

* * *

And not far away, as the crow flies, Dr Jeremiah Flint stands beside his dissection block and glares at his students. The students shuffle their feet. The doctor is clearly out of sorts today. They will have to stay alert. Be sharp.

'Take it or leave it!' shrieks the macaw. 'Blister and Purge! You Go Girl!'

'Shut up!' roars Flint. 'Shut up or I'll wring your scabby neck!'

Oo-er. The students exchange meaningful glances.

The tools of Flint's trade lie ready and waiting, the hooks and knives in order of size; the sharp-toothed saw he uses, for hacking through bones, placed within easy reach. The cutting edges of these instruments reflect a lot of light. Dr Flint can hardly bear to look at them. They are winking at him. Mocking him, as he broods on his miserable luck.

The students turn to the dissection block—a vast wooden slab, channelled to allow blood to drip into buckets of sawdust. They are perplexed, and who can blame them? They had been told to expect a miracle—two miracles, to be precise, two perfect miracles of nature. And instead?

Dr Flint could have cheerfully thrown Rafferty Spune into his kettle, yesterday morning, and boiled him alive. He could have hurled the man's entrails into the Fleet, and hung his vertebral column from a chandelier, without the slightest pang of conscience.

Take it or leave it, indeed.

It is time, Flint thinks, to branch out . . . to explore areas of medical science which do not depend, at any stage, upon the assistance of low-life grave-robbers. For a long time now, he has dreamed of preserving bodies instead of chopping them up. Last summer he heard tell of freshwater fish which, though frozen solid during the winter, revived after the spring thaw. Since then, he has frozen and thawed enough fish to fill a cart. None lived. What he wants—indeed, yearns—to

259

do is experiment on something larger. Something warm-blooded. Something . . . human.

None of Dr Flint's associates have given him more than a cat in hell's chance of persuading a sane man to be frozen alive. 'Bag a lunatic,' they tell him. 'Or freeze a beggar. Do someone who won't be missed.'

But Flint wants a willing subject . . . a man with enough wit to understand the process . . . a man with so little to live for that the thought of being an ice block for a year or two has a certain appeal.

Yesterday, Flint got wind of just such a man. Matthew Ladd. Apprentice grave-robber. A simple cove, according to Spune, but not so moonstruck that he won't comprehend the task, nor so dense that he will under-estimate the honour of being chosen, by science, to find out if men, by freezing themselves as solid as a pig trough in winter, might keep themselves alive and thus avoid the grave.

This Ladd, according to Spune, is keen to avoid the grave for as long as possible, by any means going. So, Flint will talk to him tomorrow. It is something to think about. Some small recompense for the fiasco that has deprived him of two prime specimens.

The students grow impatient. They have paid good money to learn the basic structures of anatomy in this room. Dr Flint cannot disappoint them. Not totally. One of them is hoping that today's lecture will focus, at some point, on the web of glands and nodes beneath the armpit. For he has studied everything ever written about the disease that has taken his mother and her sisters and has a hunch that, although the Flemish anatomist, Vesalius, was right to recommend removal of the breast, there is more . . . much more, to be learned.

'Take it or leave it,' Spune had said, flinging down his sack. He had known, of course, that no doctor worth his salt will say no to a fresh corpse. Any corpse. Even one so clearly inferior to a grossly over-sized male and a grossly under-sized female that it makes Dr Flint almost weep to compare them. Still, a corpse is a corpse when all is said and done. This one is better than nothing, so Flint will simply make the best of it.

'Gentlemen,' he announces, 'we have here a male specimen of average height and proportions.'

His left hand hovers over a piece of the sacking that hides the body from view. The students shuffle closer.

'Tonight's the night,' chips in the macaw. 'Bring me the head of John the Baptist. Yes indeedy. Crazy little tyke. I'll give him green birds.'

Dr Flint's fingers close on a corner of sacking. 'A very average specimen,' he repeats. 'However, there is something . . .' His free hand reaches for a knife—the small one with the curved blade, designed for scooping. ' . . . there is something here which, I think you will agree, is highly unusual and worthy, therefore, of our closest attention.'

He flips the sack away from the specimen's eyes.

'There we have it, gentlemen,' he says. 'Did any of you ever see such an astonishing shade of blue?'

32

Tom's mother had a hangover, but was refusing to take anything for it.

'I know, I know,' she laughed. 'If I'm going to poison my system with gin, then I might as well go the whole hog and do aspirin. Tell you what, I'll have two green drinks in a minute. How about that?'

Tom leaned against the sitting room doorway and tutted.

'Shall I put the blinds up?' he said.

'No. Aaargh. No light. I feel like the bride of Dracula this morning.'

'This afternoon, actually.'

'Is it? Oops.'

The room was in a right mess—cushions and empty glasses on the floor; the *Radio Times* face down on the footstool with its pages all askew; his mother's duvet in a lump on the settee. Tom turned the dimmer switch, making the apricot lights glow a little brighter.

'Did you sleep down here then, last night, or what?' he asked.

'Must've done. Do I look like death?'

Tom went over to the footstool, moved the *Radio Times*, and sat down.

'You've looked worse,' he said. 'It probably did you good, getting blotto with Gran.'

'It did.' She sat up, slowly. 'Uuuurgh. Never again though. Not in this life.'

She opened one eye and focused, blearily, on her son. 'You need some new clothes,' she said. 'Look at you. That

262

T-shirt looks like it's shrunk and your knees are practically through those jeans. We'll have a shopping spree, shall we, before we go home?'

'OK,' said Tom.

He could hear the radio playing, downstairs, and the clatter of pans. The Giant was saved. His mum was smiling and his gran was cooking breakfast. Astra was free. He ought to be happy.

His mother had both eyes open now and was reading his face.

'What is it, Tom?' she said.

How could he tell her? What could he possibly say? There were no words to describe how he was feeling about Astra, Twist, and Angel. No words. Not in this life.

She was waiting for an answer, her face clouding. He would have to say something.

'My grandfather,' he said. 'I hope I don't end up like him.'

'Of course you won't!' declared his mother. 'Never in a million years. You're nothing like your grandfather, Tom. You're going to be a wonderful man. Sensitive, caring . . .'

'Mu-um.'

'No, it's true.'

He was pleased, despite himself.

'Was my dad like that?' he wondered. 'Sensitive and caring, I mean?'

His mother's eyes took on a faraway look. Not pained, exactly. Just faraway.

'He tried to be,' she said. 'He wanted to be. He did his best, Tom, particularly after you were born, but he—well—he just wasn't very good at commitment. He was never going to change, and I couldn't stand it, so he had to go. You understand that, don't you?'

Tom nodded.

'He hated leaving you,' she said. 'He used to come at weekends, to take you to the beach and spoil you rotten with ice cream and sweets. Do you remember? You must have been about three.'

Tom nodded again, although he could barely remember any of it.

'Maybe you'll get to go to Australia one day,' she added. 'He's still your dad, after all.'

In his mind's eye, Tom saw himself surfing a wave. He saw koala bears up gum trees and galleries full of Aboriginal art. Try as he might, he could not see the man who was still his dad.

'I think I'd rather do India,' he said. 'With you.'

Downstairs, his gran was calling: 'Yoo-hoo, darlings. Breakfast!'

'That'll be your green-drink-hangover-cure, madam,' said Tom. 'Or did you say two green drinks? On second thoughts, better make that a whole jugful.'

She grabbed a cushion from the sofa and swung it at him.

'Ouch!' he giggled. 'Watch out!'

Her elbow had caught the edge of a photo frame, sending it clattering, face forward, on the coffee table. Tom set it right. 'Not broken,' he said. And then, 'Oh . . . ' For he was looking at a picture of himself. The one his gran had kept hidden away at the back of her bureau—on display now, in this beautiful silver frame.

'Your gran did that, last night,' his mum said. 'We'll have to send her a more recent one.'

'So we're a proper family now, are we? You, me, and Gran?'

His mother had the grace to look ashamed.

'We are,' she said. 'Yes. Your gran and I—we're just a couple of silly women, Tom, who let a stupid rift go on for far too long.'

'Was Gran really mad when she heard you'd thrown my dad out?'

'Furious. I think it got to her that I could be strong, like that, while she put up with all kinds from your grandfather, before he finally left. It was all a bit too close to home.'

Tom considered the photograph. 'Did you send her this?' he asked.

'Of course. And copies of your reports. Your gran's very proud of you, Tom. And she's kicking herself over having missed so much—of you growing up, I mean. She'll probably spoil you rotten from now on. She'll probably leave you this house!'

Tom laughed, then looked, once more, at his picture.

'Was I really that cute?' he wondered.

'Yes. You really were.'

'I hate my eyes though. I've always hated them.'

'Well don't.' His mother stood up and stretched, like a cat. 'You have beautiful eyes. Eyes to die for. Be glad.'

He blinked twice. Smiled.

'Really?' he said.

'Really,' she replied.

It is pleasant, here in the park. I come here a lot, since my accident. The burns have healed, but the scars are bad. I don't like to be seen, so I put on my straw hat, with the floppy brim, and sit quietly on this bench, with just pigeons for company.

Sometimes I doze. It's the roses, you see . . . such a powerful scent. I had a dress like a rose, once—layers and layers of gauze, shading from crimson to pink. I danced in that dress. I danced like a dream.

It is quiet, here in the park. Not many people come. Children talk to me sometimes. They don't mind the way I look. But their parents stare straight through my face as if it were air, or water.

265

*Oh, the roses. The colours, this summer, have been glorious.
All those reds and yellows and oranges, blurring together in the
heat. Like flames. Like layers and layers of flame.*

*There was a boy here today. He has been twice before. Once
with his mother and once by himself. I hoped he would come over.
I hoped he would notice me today and listen to my story. But he
stayed beside the wall, where the plaques are. He was there so
long that I grew curious. And then he went. Just like that.*

*I keep away from the plaques, as a rule. Too much sadness.
Too much death. I am happier here on this bench, among my
pigeons and the roses. But today, after the boy had gone, I felt
compelled to walk across. My injuries, that night, were terrible.
Because of them, I walk with care.*

*It was a solemn moment for me, approaching the wall. Good
evening, I murmured to the others. Good always and forever. Rest
easy.*

*I noticed straightaway that something was different. The space
above Mary—the one who gave up her lifebelt when the* Stella
*went down in 1899—had been filled. The new tile is smaller than
all the rest, and the inscription not so neat. This is what it says:*

Malachi Twist—Bendy Man.
Disappeared beneath the seventh arch of London Bridge,
while saving a friend.

August 1717

*Sweet boy, I thought, as I returned to my place; my own place
upon the wall. (Sarah . . . Sarah . . . that's the one . . . January
24, 1863 . . . twirling and burning, twirling and burning all
the way off stage . . .) Sweet boy, to put up a plaque for someone
he never knew. Someone forgotten. And although the new tile is
a little out of line—somewhat 'twisted', dare I say—this Malachi
was clearly as much of a hero as any of us ever are and I, for
one, am happy to have him here.*

* * *

It didn't take long to kit Tom out with new clothes. He wasn't fussy. A pair of jeans, the next size up in trainers, a couple of sweatshirts, and it was done. Shopping for his mother was something else.

'I want a whole new look for the autumn,' she said. 'Something smart. Let's go to Harrods.'

The assistants in Harrods looked as if they had just stepped off a catwalk. Tom smiled at one of the younger ones and she smiled back.

'I *was* a size fourteen,' his mother was saying. 'But I've lost a lot of weight. I'm probably nearer a ten now.'

Her assistant's mouth twitched, politely. 'Which diet were you on?' she asked.

'The cancer one,' Tom's mother replied. 'Not that I'd recommend it. Have you got this skirt in anything other than black?'

They went to the pet department, so that Tom could buy something for Goldie.

'I was wondering,' said his mother, as they waited to pay for a bone, 'whether you'd mind if Declan came to stay for a weekend. Towards Christmas, maybe. Not over Christmas itself, because your gran will be with us then, but around that time. What do you think?'

'I think that would be good,' said Tom. 'Yes. I'm happy about that.'

'He's got this dog,' his mother continued. 'She's the ugliest thing you ever saw, so he tells me, but her bark's worse than her bite. She'll be fine with Goldie, I'm sure.'

'What's her name?' Tom asked.

'I don't know. Why?'

'I just wondered. I just thought it might . . . Never mind.'

They bought presents for Gran, and for friends at home. They bought fruit for the pink drink, and stuff for

267

the next day's supper, so they wouldn't have to stop at a supermarket on the way down to Dorset.

'Right!' Tom's mother said at last. 'That's it. We're done.'

Knightsbridge station was crowded. 'We might have to stand,' said Tom's mother. 'I hate having to stand—and it isn't even rush hour.'

She whipped off the hat. The points of her hair shone red-gold and almost even.

'It won't work,' said Tom, as they stepped on to a train.

'What won't?'

'Pretending to be ill, so someone will give you their seat.'

His mother threw him a look. *You're growing up*, it said. *Slow down, will you?* Then she stuffed the hat in the back pocket of her jeans, braced herself, and stood.

The train lurched forward.

'Shall we rent a video for tonight?' she asked as they hurtled through tunnels. 'Something light. A comedy. I think we've all had enough drama for a while.'

'Sounds good,' said Tom. He grabbed the bags as they approached their stop.

'It's been cack for you, this holiday, hasn't it?' said his mother, as they stepped on to the platform.

'Not really,' he told her. 'You'd be surprised.'

Up ahead, in the walkway, a small crowd had gathered round a busker.

'Helen—come and look at this bloke!' they heard someone shout.

'He must be good,' Tom's mother said, as a loud cheer went up. 'People don't usually stop and hang around.'

Tom felt in the back pocket of his jeans for change.

'I can't hear a guitar or anything,' he said. 'I can't hear any singing.'

It was hard to see the busker, through the press of his audience.

Tom found a pound coin. 'What's he doing?' he said, as he and his mother drew closer. 'Is he sketching something? Is he an artist?'

'Who knows?' said his mother. 'He's probably just some poor homeless guy doing whatever he can.'

Then Tom saw the busker's feet. They were up in the air, and they were waggling.

Clutching the pound, clutching it so hard that it felt embedded in his palm, Tom squirmed between backs and arms and shoulders until he reached the spot where the busker stood—on his head, his legs pedalling the air, as he prepared to play a penny whistle through his nostrils.

Have faith . . . And watch for my return.

Tom wasn't sure. He couldn't tell . . . The hair looked thicker; the face a little fuller. And those feet . . . weren't those feet just a bit too clean?

The busker had his eyes closed. Other people were crowding round, pushing Tom sideways. He threw his pound coin, straining to make sure it went into the hat as he was jostled further to one side.

'Thank you, friend,' said the busker.

Was it?

Tom and his mother stepped on to the escalator.

Could it have been?

Tom felt the marvel of it. Of knowing, absolutely and for always, that anything is possible. It filled his whole being. His mother took his arm as they moved slowly up and away. Behind them came the disembodied voice of the tannoy:

'Mind the gap,' it said. 'Mind the gap.'

From *The Merrybegot* by Julie Hearn
ISBN 0 19 279157 5
Publishing February 2005

The Confession of Patience Madden
The Year of Our Lord, 1692

*Good day, brothers. I am ready to talk to you now. Ready to tell
you the truth. Pray forgive the croak in my voice. It has been . . .
it has been . . .*

Water? Yes. Thank you . . .

Are you listening? I can barely see you. It is so dark in here . . .

Are you ready?

Then I will begin.

*I never meant it to end the way it did. Grace might have done,
but not me. Grace was fifteen, as artful as a snake, and already
on the slippery slope to Hell. But I, Patience Madden, could have
stopped any time—uncrossed my eyes; made my arms and legs
be still; and called a halt to the filthy words jumping out of my
mouth like toads. I could have spat the pins from under my
tongue and admitted they came not from the Devil but from the
cherrywood box our mother kept tiny things in.*

*I could have sat up in bed, looked around at the villagers come
to whisper and gawp, and said No. Stop praying for me. Stop
bringing me bay leaves and splashes of holy water. For I don't
deserve your lucky charms, nor any help from the Lord. Neither does
my sister. She deserves them even less. It was her fault. She started
it. And now she's hurting me. Yes, she is. Pinching me black and
blue beneath the coverlet, lest I weaken and tell you the truth.*

*Grace, I whispered, on the third evening, after our neighbours
had drifted away, to feed their hogs, their children, or their own
nosy faces. Grace, I'm scared. I want to get up. Grace, I'm hungry.*

Be silent, she hissed. Or, if you can't be silent, call out some more about imps at the window, and a crow in the corner. That was good. They liked that. We'll do more with the imps and the crow.

She promised me I would not have to behave like this for much longer. In a day or so, she said, we would stage our recovery. Wake up all smiles, ready to put on our itchy bonnets, and do our tiresome chores, like good, obedient girls.

A few days more, she said, and our lives would go back to normal. As dull as scum, but blameless.

It did not happen like that. It went too far.

We went too far.

APRIL
1645

The cunning woman's granddaughter is chasing a pig when she learns there is to be no frolicking in the village on May morning. Minister's orders.

'Bogger . . . that,' she pants. 'And bogger . . . this . . . pig. There's no . . . catching . . . him . . .'

Clutching her sides, she gives up the chase, and collapses, laughing, against the gnarled trunk of a tree. Above her head, pink blossoms shake like fairy fists. Spring has arrived. A beautiful time. A time when it feels absolutely right to think of dancing barefoot in the dew, and absolutely wrong to dwell on the new Minister, with his miserable ways and face like a trodden parsnip.

'That's what they be saying,' the blacksmith's son tells her. 'No pole. No goin' off into the woods. No nothing. It ain't godly, Nell, to frolic so. That's what the Minister reckons.'

Nell picks a blade of new grass and begins to chew it. Her stomach rumbles beneath her pinafore, but she is used to that. Out of the corner of her eye she can see the pig rooting around. It is a bad pig. A bothersome pig. Her granny will sort it out. This is how:

A Spell To Soothe A Truculent Pig

First, catch your pig. Do it on a Monday,
on a waning moon, when the time be right for
healing. Point him to the north, and hang on tight.
Rap his snout three times with a wand of oak, and
call: 'Powers of earth, tame and soothe this
creature that he may become docile and no longer
a bogging nuisance.' Wait seven beats of the
heart, then let him go.
So mote it be.

A light breeze frisks the orchard. There are things Nell ought to be doing, but she stays where she is, squinting up at the blacksmith's son and thinking about May morning.

'And who be you wishing to frolic with anyway, Sam Towser?' she chuckles. 'As if I couldn't guess . . . '

The lad reddens. He is a month short of sixteen and all swept through with the kind of longings that can tie up a boy's tongue and have him tripping over everything, from clods of earth to his own great feet, twenty times a day. He has a mop of corn-coloured hair, and a cleft in his chin so deep it might have been pressed there by his guardian angel. He is too ungainly; too unfledged, as yet, to be truly handsome. But he will be. The promise of it is all about him, like the guarantee of a glorious day once some mist has cleared.

'No one,' he mumbles. 'I got horses to see to. No time for fumblin' around with some daft maid on May mornin', nor any other time.'

'Pah! That's a fib!' Nell flings both arms wide and twists her face to look like a parsnip. 'Beware, sinner!

Beware what you say! Repent! Repent! For Satan loves a fibber, and will carry you off to burn in Hell. In Hell, I tell you, where fibbers go. And frolickers. And women who wear scarlet ribbons, or sweep their hearths on Sundays . . . '

'Hush . . . Hush up, you daft wench . . . '

'Repent! Repent! For I am your Minister. God's representative in this heathen place . . . Repent! For though my nose drips and I do not know a hoe from my . . . '

'NELL, hush!'

' . . . elbow, I know a sinner when I see one. And a fibber. And a frolicker. All rolled into one vile, wretched . . . '

'Right!'

' . . . body . . . and a . . . Yieeek! . . . '

He has pounced and is tickling her—tickling her to what feels like a giggly death, while the sun pours down like honey, and the truculent pig looks on in mild surprise.

'You two! Have a care! Mind that tree, and stop your messing.'

A woman has entered the orchard. She stands some distance away, almost in the nettles. Her face, beneath a bonnet the colour of porridge, is grave.

'What?' Nell scrambles to her feet. 'What is it, Mistress Denby? What's happened?'

The blacksmith's son gets up. There are twigs and fallen petals in his hair. He looks like Puck. He looks drop-dead frolicsome.

'Gotter go,' he mutters. 'I got horses to see to.'

The woman and the girl pay him no mind. They have already jumped the stile and are hurrying away, along the crooked path leading down to the village. Women's stuff, he supposes. Someone getting born. Or dying. Or doing both in the space of a few breaths.

He doesn't want to be seen trotting at the heels of womenfolk, towards whatever, or whoever, needs their attention in some fusty room. The sun is high, now, and he has his own ritual to perform.

The apple tree he chooses is truly ancient; its timber as knotted as a crone's shins; its blossom strangely pale. No one knows how long it has stood here, or why it was planted alone. Much older than the rest, it continues to bear fruit so sweet that to press cider from it, and drink the stuff, is said to send the mind dribbling out of the nostrils and the legs in several directions at once.

It is to this tree the Apple Howlers come, on Twelfth Night, to scare away evil spirits. It is here that they form their circle—a raggle taggle of villagers, young and old, banging pails and pots and howling *'Hats full! Caps full! Bushels, bushels, sacks full!'* loud enough to wake the dead.

It is on these branches, and around this trunk, that the Howlers hang their amulets and leave cider-soaked toast for the piskies. The orchard swarms with piskies. Everyone knows that. Little folk in rags, their skin as rough as bark, their heads sprouting lichens and moss. A few are downright malicious, the rest merely troublesome and high-spirited. All are uglier than dead hedgehogs and as greedy as swine. Over the hills, in a neighbouring county, lies fairy territory—a prettier species, by far, the fairies, but just as pesky, so rumour has it . . . just as demanding of treats, and remembrance.

Be good to the piskies, the old folk say hereabouts, and they will be good to you. Treat them with respect, on Twelfth Night, and they will stay by the trees, watching over the fruit until picking time comes.

The cider-soaked toast has been eaten long ago by robins and other things. But the amulets are still here, swaying gently at the end of their strings, like small, hanged felons.

'May I?' says the blacksmith's son, before pressing the point of a horseshoe nail into the old tree's trunk.

Yep, something replies, the sound of it such a faint rasp that the blacksmith's son assumes the pig has farted.

Slowly, carefully, he begins to cut. Not his full name—Samuel—for he isn't sure of all the letters. A single 'S' is the mark he makes, the down stroke wobbly as a caterpillar against the wood. He can't spell the other name, either. The one that is on his mind day and night. The one he only had to hear, in passing, for a fluttering to start in his belly, as if larks are nesting there.

He knows his alphabet though. Just. And he knows, from the way the girl's name is said, which letter he needs to entwine with his own. It is one of the tricky ones that sound different, depending on the word. As the metal point of the nail forms the letter's curve he finds himself wishing it made a soft sound like the beginning of 'gentle'. He would have liked that. It would have seemed significant.

The girl's name, though, begins with a hard 'G', like 'gallows' or 'god'.

When he has finished, he steps back to inspect what he has done. And then he sees one. At least, he thinks he does. There and gone it is, between knots of blossom, its face as coarse and grey as the tree, its small, bright eyes fixed intently on the 'S' and the 'G'.

'*Oh* . . .'

He looks quickly, all around, and then back again. Nothing. There is nothing there. A trick of the light, perhaps? But no . . . His sight is good, and he isn't given to fancies.

He stays a minute more, half dreading, half hoping to see the thing again. What did it mean? Was it lucky, to see a piskie when you were a month short of sixteen and so desperate to get your hands on a certain someone that you would probably die of frustration if it didn't happen soon?

Did it mean that he would?

Did it?

It takes just seconds for the blacksmith's son to convince himself that he has been sent an auspicious sign. That, come May morning, he will be frolicking away to his heart's content with the girl whose name begins with a hard-sounding 'G'.

She will be all over him like a vine, yes she will, for all she is the minister's daughter and seems as distant, and cool, as a star. He will have her. No doubt about it. For they are joined, already, in his mind, and on the tree. And their union has been blessed. He has the piskie's promise.

The blacksmith's son feels light on his feet as he swings himself over the stile, and he is whistling as he strides away.

'Silly young bogger . . . ' goes the sighing and the rasping among the topmost branches of the trees. *'Silly . . . little . . . whelp.'* And the letters 'S' and 'G' begin slowly turning brown, the way a cut apple will do, or naked flesh beneath hot sun.

Julie Hearn was born in Abingdon, near Oxford, and has been writing all her life. After training as a journalist she went to Australia where she worked on a daily tabloid newspaper. She then lived in Spain for a while before returning to England where she worked as a features editor on a chain of weekly newspapers as well as writing freelance for magazines and the national press. After her daughter was born she went back to her studies and obtained a BA in English and an MSt in women's studies. She is now a full time writer. *Follow Me Down* is her first novel for Oxford University Press.